A GODDESS UNRAVELED

A GODDESS UNRAVELED

Book One in the Olympus Rising series

MORGAN RIDER

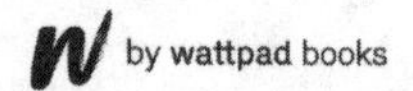

An imprint of Wattpad WEBTOON Book Group

Published in Canada by Wattpad WEBTOON Book Group, a division of Wattpad WEBTOON Studios, Inc.

36 Wellington Street E., Suite 200, Toronto, ON M5E 1C7 Canada

www.wattpad.com

First W by Wattpad Books edition: May 2025

ISBN 978-1-99885-466-0 (Trade Paper original)
ISBN 978-1-99885-467-7 (eBook edition)

Library and Archives Canada Cataloguing in Publication information is available upon request.

Printed and bound in Canada

1 3 5 7 9 10 8 6 4 2

Cover design by Emily Wittig
Images © STILLFX, Sfocato via iStock; © Pine And Lark via Shutterstock; © VademVasenin via Depositphotos; © Vasily Kozorez via Unsplash; © The Everlasting Story via Creative Market
Author Photo © Morgan Rider
Typesetting by Delaney Anderson

To my hubby, who believes I can do anything.

One

He watched her gaze at the screen of her phone, a carry-on bag tucked protectively under her arm, her posture straight but not severe. She smiled to herself as she waited for her chauffeur to load a set of matching luggage into the limousine, absently tucking a twist of hair behind her ear while the rest flowed in radiant waves down her back. It was auburn, her hair. He was partial to auburn.

It's not what you look at that matters, it's what you see.

The quote came to him as he admired her from a distance. Did she appreciate the works of Thoreau? Was the gentle tilt of her lips caused by a literary piece she was reading as she stood beneath the airport awning? He wanted to believe she took pleasure in poetry and prose. Words seduced when conveyed with the proper finesse.

In a nearby spruce tree a pair of songbirds chatted—a cheerful confirmation that they'd heard each other and cared enough to reply. Could she hear their message too? He knew she'd been raised with means and privilege, which had a way of distracting people from their greater purpose.

He'd also heard she lived a sheltered life, much like a bird kept in a gilded cage, providing others with a connection to the world but not experiencing it themselves. It troubled him how well he could relate.

The chauffeur finished his duties and opened the limo door, waving her inside. She'd just received a call and made the man wait as she pressed the phone to her ear. But it seemed the caller had not been the one to delay her. She was turning to investigate the tree, craning her neck as she peered into the upper branches. This caused her hair to cascade farther down her back.

As she spied on the birds, they paused their song, and she lingered there, raised on her toes, the phone in her hand hanging at her side. She *had* heard them, and he considered this as she finally stepped toward the limousine, smiling at the chauffeur before climbing inside.

The hem of her skirt rode up her legs, although he hadn't been staring. They reflected a life of sport and play, tapering gracefully to slender ankles. Perfect for kissing . . . or binding.

The limo door closed, severing those thoughts. But he couldn't help wondering, as the taillights ticked off and the car rolled away, if she was bolder than her protected upbringing suggested. He'd come with no expectations, but perhaps he would need to tread more carefully.

Two

"It wasn't a goldfinch, Mara. They aren't seen this far east." Lexi cradled the phone between her shoulder and ear as she dug in her bag for lip balm. "This bird had brown feathers, and there was a yellow aura around it, like the one I saw around that crow."

"Then it was probably a reflection of the sun, same with the crow. I called to talk about your graduation party, not birds that may or may not have auras. So, who's on the guest list besides your uncle Z?"

Lexi didn't question how Mara knew her uncle Z would be on the list. Her friend had heard the stories and knew that he never missed an opportunity to assert his dominance over a captive audience.

"Lady Twila and Sir Henry are flying in from the Amalfi Coast."

"Oh good. You'll have to tell me who's better dressed. That sequined jacket Sir Henry wore for your last birthday was a riot. Will the twins be there?"

"Yes. They're probably carpooling with Emily so they can argue the whole way. I've never known three more competitive people in my life. And Burt, of course. He's supposed to bring a case of Chardonnay he got on a recent trip to Burgundy."

"Who's your uncle Z bringing as his plus-one? Do you know?"

"Nora."

"Nice. I know you two get along. Is that it?"

"As far as I know, unless someone shows up unexpectedly."

"So, have you made arrangements for Morocco yet?"

Lexi rolled her eyes as she finally unearthed the lip balm from her bag and applied a generous amount. Mara had been her closest friend all through college, and Lexi loved her like a sister. But Mara was the nosiest person she'd ever known, and that was saying something considering Lexi's parents had micromanaged every aspect of her life.

"My dad put a hold on further arrangements until he looks at my itinerary again."

"Well, it *is* pretty full. You've got yourself booked through the end of July. And you'll be all alone. You know how they worry."

"Yes. And I know how *you* worry. Just let me get to the estate. I'll keep you posted on all the graduation merriment."

"Merriment." Mara's tinkling laugh echoed into the back seat. "Finally, after four years, my cool lingo has rubbed off on you."

"Sure, let's call it cool."

"I'm sorry I can't be there for you, sister-friend. But I'll be thinking about you."

"I know you will."

Lexi hung up, and she knew there'd be no returning to her latest romantic read and the fictional couple she'd been taking notes on. Her chauffeur's gaze was unavoidable.

Ham, short for Hamilton Austin Chadwick III, had worked for her family since her father had built their Nova Scotia estate.

And, like one of the family, Ham would want to talk about every insignificant thing that had happened to her since spring break—the same spring break she'd been forced to spend at their monument by the sea instead of in Atlantic City with her lacrosse team.

"So, your mother's Graham Thomas roses are already budding. Imagine that." Ham glanced in the rearview mirror, his silver eyebrows lifting dramatically over his sunglasses like he was announcing the engagement of the pope.

"Graham Thomas roses are known for their early blooms." Lexi met Ham's mirrored gaze with a smile as she tucked her phone away. His banter wasn't so bad, and who knew if this would be the last time she'd see him. If things went her way, life was going to get wild.

"Yes. I expect we'll be enjoying roses into October."

"She *does* obsess over her garden."

At least she used to. Lexi glanced at the landscape passing by at a leisurely pace. Although the window's gray tint subdued the spring colors, she was still cheered by them. Despite the chill that settled over her whenever she visited the estate, she couldn't deny it had been placed on a spot that seemed to have been blessed by the gods. The rocky seaside, thick marshlands, and swaths of wildflowers were enough to make a person want to break into song. It was heaven compared to their cookie-cutter home in Boston, which was more like a tourist attraction with zero lot lines.

Would her brother have her mare saddled and ready for a ride across their property? It was probably too late to go to the gorge. Maybe Dion would take her to the beach for a race. Her parents still didn't like her riding alone, but that would change soon enough.

"Congratulations on the bachelor's degree, by the way," said

Ham. "Are you looking forward to your graduation party? I know your father hosted a party for you and your friends in Boston last week. But this time you'll be surrounded by family."

And by "family" Ham meant the clan of unrelated misfits who had been mooching off the Maxwells since the estate was built.

"Sure. I haven't seen Uncle Z since Christmas. And I always enjoy practicing my Italian with Lady Twila."

Lexi wasn't so much looking forward to the party as what would come after the obligations were over. She was flying solo on an extended vacation, and maybe she wouldn't stick to the itinerary. She'd been following a righteous path her whole life: excellent grades, sporting victories, almost valedictorian. *Damn that Wendy Chapman.*

But Lexi had yet to accomplish so many things, like dancing without a chaperone, partying with her friends and not her parents, or working a part-time job for crying out loud. She hadn't even been kissed properly. At least, not like the characters in the books she'd read, where things progressed past the lips.

Lexi had always considered the consequences of her actions, often without questioning why those actions held such consequences, like her nonexistent dating life. Why was it so important for her to save herself for the right one? Wasn't trial and error part of life's lessons?

Well, she was done blindly following someone else's instructions. Her parents would soon learn that their carefully planned party was just the kickoff to a new chapter for Alexandra Maxwell. She could feel it in her bones. It was time her story got real.

He hadn't been waiting long beneath the canopy of pines when the limousine arrived at the estate. He'd used the respite to admire the mansion's three-story architecture: its scalloped gables, the white marble staircase leading up to fluted columns, the neatly trimmed topiaries placed strategically to hide the family's secrets. It bore a remarkable resemblance to the other gaudy residences that his colleagues preferred.

It made sense that the Maxwells would want to mimic the style that most appealed to the friends they called family. The ones who spent a good deal of time exploiting the sprawling manor. Despite being counted among their circle, he'd never been formally invited to take advantage of the estate, and he looked forward to availing himself of the stable, the ocean with its private beach, and the live-in waitstaff.

He supposed they were uneasy about the requests he might make and the influence he might wield. On the surface, the Maxwells were a family of wealth and power, but there were other powers at work here, and while he wasn't known to use his influence often, this was where he considered it to be the most useful.

The limo door opened and she stepped out, her shapely legs emerging first, taunting him. As she rose to her full height the sun danced off her hair, reflecting the color and sheen of mahogany, the kind kept polished by a loving hand. He'd hoped to catch a glimpse of her eyes. He'd heard they mirrored the sea, but the estate now held her attention.

In fact, after planting her feet on the pebbled drive, she made no move toward the mansion. Had something caught her eye? Perhaps a feature of the home's flamboyant facade? She inhaled but didn't release it, hesitating like a traveler who'd lost their compass. He could only guess what she might be thinking. She was still a mystery to him.

Her chauffeur reached into the back seat and pulled out her carry-on bag. His presence must have startled her, as her chest appeared to deflate. Then, as if nothing unusual had happened, she took the bag, flung it over one shoulder, and strode toward the entrance with confidence and grace.

Lexi didn't know what to think. Why would her parents have painted the estate yellow? It wasn't even a pretty yellow—more like a muted gold—and there were spots that looked unfinished. She stood like a deer about to be hit by a truck until Ham distracted her with her bag. When she looked back up, the estate was white again. Another trick of the sunlight? She was doubting that explanation more and more.

She forced her legs to carry her forward, letting the shadows of the pine trees swallow her. Then she counted each marble step as she ascended the sprawling staircase, the familiarity offering a smidgeon of peace. For a while she'd been fascinated by the swirls in the marble. She would sit and trace them with her fingers, pretending she was alone in the quiet while the waitstaff watched from the windows.

The spell was broken as the front door swung open. "Hey, brat! You want to saddle up the horses and take them for a spin?"

It was Dion, standing like Peter Pan and grinning at her from the door frame. Dressed in a new pair of riding jeans and a stiff collared shirt, he looked like he'd come from a photo shoot for expensive watches. He'd always been a stickler for proper appearances, which carried over into his life as a corporate drone. It probably drove his co-workers crazy, but it didn't bother Lexi. She could be hardcore herself.

"I was thinking the same thing on the way here." She barreled into Dion's arms, getting a whiff of strong aftershave and a face full of overly gelled hair. "Give me a minute to change and greet the parents."

"No problem. I'll see you at the stable in ten."

He took off around the house, and the polished marble followed Lexi inside as she stepped over the threshold and dropped her bag in the foyer. The competing scents of vanilla and melted Parmesan wafted through the house, and she pictured Chef Lorraine's minions whipping up Lexi's favorite treats.

"There's my baby girl!"

Her dad shouted across the cavernous space that served as the estate's formal living room and party central. The sunken floor made it feel like a swimming pool filled with custom upholstered furniture instead of water. He stood at the oak wet bar, a shelf of liquor bottles stretched out behind him, adding ice to a freshly made gimlet. An arm went up from the couch where her mom sat with an empty lowball glass.

"The prodigal daughter returns," she said grimly, smiling at Lexi through burgundy lipstick.

As always, Lilith Maxwell was dressed to impress: designer-label pantsuit with plunging neckline, diamonds sparkling at her ears. She even worn a white apron, giving the impression she still cared about hosting the extravagant parties the Maxwells were known for. These days, it was just for show. "No offense, dear. You know what I mean. How was the flight?"

Actually, Lexi didn't know what her mom meant. "The flight was uneventful. Um, just curious, did you do something to the outside of the estate? It looks different?"

Her parents exchanged their obligatory glance. They rarely offered answers without checking in with each other. They were practically the same person.

"What looks different, sweetheart?" her dad asked.

Lexi hadn't mentioned the strange things that had been happening to her over the past year—the auras, the exploding water fountain, the library book that inexplicably landed on Wendy Chapman's foot. Mara was the only one she'd been confiding in. And the fact that Mara had become somewhat apathetic didn't bode well for Lexi's skeptical parents.

"The color. It's not as white, that's all. Probably just pollen. I think the place needs a good hose down."

Her mom laughed without her usual false soprano. "You took the words right out of my mouth. Let's put a good hose down on the to-do list, Charles." She raised her empty glass and Lexi's dad replaced it with a fresh one.

From her lofty position in the foyer Lexi remained an observer, as she often was, noticing the strong smell of men's cologne mingling with the kitchen scents. It created a cocktail of both fond and crappy memories, accompanied by a familiar wave of nausea. Her dad was wearing his favorite pink silk shirt, but his sixty-year-old stature would soon force him into a larger size.

"Dion and I are heading out with the horses. He's meeting me at the stable. What time will guests be arriving?"

Lexi snatched up her bag and walked toward the stairs, ignoring the look her parents gave each other. They couldn't deny her this. She was twenty-two, for fuck's sake. A college graduate. And Dion would be with her.

As she reached the open-air staircase, a showpiece in itself, bending out toward the living room so that grand entrances could be made, her dad was tugging up his sleeve to check the time on his expensive watch.

"You have two hours," he said. "That'll give you time to take a nice ride on the beach together. How long has it been? Christmas?"

"Yes." *Because Dion was allowed to enjoy spring break with his friends.*

"I'm sure I don't have to give you the speech."

Her dad waited while Lexi recited their family mantra on her way up the stairs. "Keep your eyes on the horizon, your feet in the stirrups, and your head in the game."

What a load of crap.

Three

The seagrass had crept closer to the beach since Lexi's last visit, growing into the path where she and her horse, Jackie O, liked to run. Dion galloped beside her, keeping a close eye on their pace and trying to pretend he wasn't all-in as they raced toward the outcropping. She would never tell him that the only times he won was when she and Jackie O let him. But the abundant seagrass wasn't the only thing she noticed as they raced toward the finish line. The yellow aura haloing her mare's head had not been there the last time they rode together.

Lexi beat Dion by a neck, and he slowed down while she continued toward the next crop of rocks that marked her boundary line. Dion got his horse galloping again when he realized she wasn't ready to turn back.

"Hey, brat! Where are you going?" he yelled.

"I was thinking Halifax. From there, maybe Iceland."

It was hard to talk and gallop at the same time, so Lexi slowed down and let him catch up. He was breathing heavily as he pulled beside her.

"What's gotten into you, Lexi? There's a party starting soon."

"We don't need to be there as soon as it starts."

"I don't, but *you* do. It's your graduation party."

"Woo-hoo. I graduated with a bachelor's degree in poli-sci. Throw me in with the rest of the fish."

When he didn't say anything, she looked over and found him glaring at the horizon like he wanted to pick a fight.

"Something wrong, Dion? Trouble in corporate paradise?"

"No. Although I wouldn't call it paradise. It's a job."

"A job you love. Don't try to deny it."

"Yes, I love my job. It's pretty much the only redeeming quality in my life."

Lexi continued to stare at her brother. Had something happened since the last time they'd talked? "What else could be wrong with your life? You're the eldest son, heir to the Maxwell Sporting Goods throne. Your hair hasn't receded yet. And you pretty much get away with anything."

It took him a minute to answer as their horses carried them farther from home. "Just ignore me. I guess the commitments are weighing a little heavier than usual. Family obligations are a bitch."

"Don't get me started on obligations. I've reached my wit's end. I might do something crazy, I swear."

"What kind of crazy?" Dion pulled his horse to a stop, and Lexi was forced to turn Jackie O around to talk to him.

"I've been a legal adult for over four years. I've earned my college degree. I've pretty much crossed off everything on the Maxwells' to-do list under the name *Alexandra*. They can't stop me from doing whatever I damn well please from this point on."

Dion forced out an exaggerated sigh, like he wanted the universe to hear him. "If you figure out how to do that, let me know. Speaking of things you don't know, I feel obligated to tell you that something's coming. Something I'm not allowed to tell you. And it's going to fuck up your reality. At least, your version of it."

"What is it? Why can't you tell me?"

He glanced around as if he thought someone could be listening. "The only reason I'm saying anything is because I don't want you to hate me when you find out. I'm covering my ass."

He spurred his horse into a canter and started back toward the estate, while Lexi steered Jackie O in circles. What was this thing that would fuck up her reality? She didn't even want to guess. Sure, her life had been paved with gold—two beautiful homes, a high-end education, luxuries so outrageous they often made her feel guilty—but it all came at a cost. Even her parents were showing the signs of wear. What more could they ask of her? It had to be bad if Dion wasn't allowed to say.

Lexi stopped her horse to stare at the horizon, watching the sun take its final bow and appreciating the certainty that it would be there again tomorrow. She could make a run for it. Go back to the airport and take the first flight out. Would they freeze her assets and force her back home? They'd threatened it before, and a few times she'd been angry enough to test them, almost. She knew that money meant freedom, and she really needed her freedom right now. Did her family have that much power over her? Was she truly that fucked?

The first guests to arrive were Lady Twila and her man, Sir Henry. Descendants of Italian royalty, they always looked like runway models. Lady Twila claimed she never wore a speck of makeup, and every time Lexi saw the woman, she appeared younger and more stunning. She probably spent a fortune on skin care.

Today, the Italian beauty was dressed in a silver gown. It was gathered at her slender waist with a braided belt, also spun from silver, the kind you find in a mine, not a fabric store.

"*Buonasera, signora Twila.* Your dress is *bellissima*," Lexi said as she offered an exaggerated curtsy.

Lady Twila lifted the hem of her gown, sweeping it back and forth. "Don't you love how the delicate strands reflect the room's light? And you look like a vision of heavenly beauty this evening, *signorina Lexi*. I love the floral motif."

"*Grazie.*"

Lexi glanced self-consciously at her V-neck sweater. She'd chosen the yellow one with three big dandelions on the front. It had been an impulse buy, far from her norm, but she'd been drawn to things that weren't her norm lately. She'd paired the sweater with jeans, and black suede Prada heels with studded ankle straps to class up the look.

"How are you, Sir Henry?"

Lexi turned her attention to the man standing with Lady Twila and leaning casually on a walking stick. He didn't need it for walking. It was more for flash. This one resembled a phoenix, its orange neck curved downward to form a hook.

Sir Henry wore a relaxed smile that barely creased his skin, which was always overly tanned, and his black-framed glasses exaggerated the size of his intense, dark eyes. She loved that his suit jackets were never an expected color, and he often paired them with some kind of embellishment. Today the jacket was royal blue and accented by a silk scarf in honey gold with white polka dots. No sequins this time.

"Right as rain. I would like to congratulate you on your recent academic accomplishment. Pardon me if I cannot keep track. There have been so many."

"That's okay. I graduated from university."

"So that's it, then? No more aspirations?" He held Lexi's gaze, but not in an accusatory way. The man had a knack for putting people at ease even when he was asking difficult questions.

"As far as college pursuits, that's it for now. I'm planning to take a solo trip this summer. I'll be visiting three continents over two months."

Their eyebrows could not have moved faster, slamming into perfectly parted hairlines.

"Is that so?" said Lady Twila, her lashes fluttering like butterflies. "What an exciting prospect."

It was impossible for Lexi not to read their shock. They knew the hoops she probably had to jump through to get such an exciting prospect approved. How sad was that?

An hour later the living room was filled with mingling guests. Emily and the twins were huddled in one corner. Octavius and his sister, Diana, were already disagreeing about something, based on all the hand gestures. Burt had staked a claim near the champagne fountain (no surprise there) and Nora chatted with him as she nibbled from a plate of stuffed mushroom caps. Lexi kept her greeting with Nora brief only because her mom took issue with the woman, although she refused to say why. Lexi really needed to stop indulging her mom's pettiness.

Then there was Uncle Z, short for Zenith. He wasn't really her uncle, but had earned the title when he became her godfather. As usual, he insisted on meeting everyone at the door like he ran the place, although his linebacker physique and lumberjack beard made him look more like a bouncer than a butler.

Lexi had only expected to see the misfits this weekend, but as she watched the guests arrive, there were many faces she didn't recognize. Being the daughter of an overzealous CEO, she had become accustomed to her dad inviting unrelated guests to family gatherings. It gave him an opportunity to forge new business partnerships while plying guests with alcohol and gourmet appetizers. After the fourth group of strangers arrived, however, Lexi started to question the intent behind these random invites.

Each of the newcomers had brought their sons, all of them close to her age. She'd already been introduced to Will from Argentina, Sami and his older brother, Yash, from Kolkata, and James from somewhere in England, all of them still navigating the perils of college. After years of blocking Lexi from making any kind of love connection, her parents had laid out the choices for her like an all-you-can-eat buffet. *WTF?*

Someone grabbed her elbow, and Lexi was forced to smile at yet another boy, this one no older than eighteen and wearing that unfortunate top-heavy hairstyle that should never have caught traction. Dion was quick with the introduction.

"Hey, Lexi, I want you to meet Roderick. He and his family live in Bruges, Belgium."

"Call me Rod. And we're actually looking at property in Boston," Rod pointed out as he stared at the dandelions on Lexi's chest. "I'll be attending Harvard next year, and my parents don't want me living on campus."

"Dorm life isn't so bad," Lexi said. "I met my best friend there, and we remained roommates until graduation."

"I heard you attended Boston College. That's a much smaller campus, with half the population and a higher acceptance rate."

Lexi pretended she hadn't already made up her mind about this entitled brat and continued to smile at him. "I don't know what the acceptance rate has to do with living on campus, but I know plenty of people whose parents didn't want them in dorms. I had to beg my parents to let me. If you'll excuse me, I need to have a word with my dad."

With single-minded intent, and no remorse for cutting out on the boy from Bruges, she located her dad next to the bar talking to Cherry, a petite blond and longtime member of their live-in staff who had a knack for knowing everything. Lexi made her way over and got his attention with a pointed eyebrow lift. He nodded and finished up his conversation while Lexi helped herself to a bottle of water from the cooler.

"What's on your mind, graduate?" He threw an arm over her shoulder and took a pull from his drink. He was already over the limit, which kind of surprised her, but his alcohol intake rarely gave her an advantage during serious discussions. She knew that the trick with her dad was not to make accusations sound accusatory.

"It's just that I'm noticing there are a lot of guys my age here. Guys I'm meeting for the first time. Is it merely coincidence that the friends you've invited have sons who had nothing better to do than help some random girl celebrate her graduation?"

Lexi tipped the water bottle over her lips and gulped. She'd started to ramble, which was not out of character for her, but she couldn't afford to lose focus. Not this weekend.

Her dad shifted his weight, looking like she'd caught him switching the expensive Colombian coffee for a cheaper brand. Of course she was right about the plot.

"First of all, you're far from random. And it was your uncle Z who suggested we invite a few boys your age. Your mother and I assumed you were ready to toss in your line and see what you might catch? James was valedictorian of his high school. Did he mention that?"

Lexi frowned. Not about the valedictorian comment, which still stung. It was the sports metaphors. They always popped up whenever her dad was forced to discuss personal matters.

"That's about the lamest confession I've ever heard. I don't care whose idea it was. You all had to know that it would be obvious to me. Now I feel like I'm on parade or something."

"Don't be silly. Just think of it as a trial run for when you get out into the real world. Not that you haven't experienced the real world. But you know what I mean."

Yes. The world where there are no chaperones.

While her dad attempted to climb out of the hole he'd dug, she curbed her annoyance for the sake of not making waves. She'd been in plenty of arguments with her parents over lesser things, and many of them involved her uncle Z, who could be a big fat baby when he didn't get his way. Lexi was ready to put the final nail in the coffin of her old life, which meant letting their controlling bullshit slide off her back for now.

Instead, she surveyed the room, checking out the boys she'd been introduced to. A couple of them were cute, in a hair-gel, country-club kind of way, but she could already tell they had the emotional depth of a thimble. Was it so unreasonable to want more from a potential "catch"? How embarrassing would it be to spend an entire weekend with a house full of available men and not take advantage of at least one of them? Not that she was interested in losing her V-card over the weekend. She wasn't that desperate.

As she pondered the ramifications of allowing her parents to play matchmaker, the front door opened and another stranger walked in—an incredibly handsome stranger who appeared to be arriving alone. He was dressed like one of her dad's board members, but she'd never done a double take on any of those stuffed shirts.

This guy looked younger than those cronies, too, and she noticed right away that he hadn't bothered to button his charcoal suit jacket, which offered a lovely view of his chest. Were those ripples under the rows of tailored pleats? *Yikes.* She blinked to be sure she hadn't just imagined the smolder.

The man matched every description she'd read of a hottie with a body: wavy chestnut hair that hadn't been forced into a style, glowing olive skin, and the bone structure of Adonis. He radiated vitality, and she gripped her water bottle until the cap threatened to pop off.

Tempted to press the cool plastic against her forehead, Lexi watched the mystery man turn to her uncle Z and offer a respectful, albeit antiquated, bow. Despite the formal greeting, she saw familiarity there, which became obvious when her uncle Z scowled behind his blond beard. Who was this guy? Was he crashing her party?

No sooner had she asked herself this when the stranger's eyes found her—a blazing golden gaze that reminded her of a beach bonfire, and she was unable to move or even blink as a smile grew on his lips.

She had *not* just imagined the smolder.

Four

Uncle Z looked fit to be tied as he stormed across the room toward Lexi and her dad, with her mom hot on his heels. Something had gone down with the stranger, who now stood at the champagne table attempting to get a glass of bubbly from Burt's weaving hand.

"What's the matter, Uncle Z?" Lexi rubbed his arm to calm him, and a painful jolt shot through her body. Her brother had played that trick on her before, but it never felt like she'd been defibrillated. "Wow. You could power a small city with that much electricity."

He hopped back, looking shocked himself. "Forgive me, Lexi. I must have picked up some static on the way over."

Her mom laughed, but Uncle Z was clearly in a mood and shot her a scowl.

"What's got you so riled up?" Lexi asked. "Did that man insult you? We can ask him to leave." Even as the words left her lips she knew she didn't mean them. The man was all she could think about.

"No, he didn't insult me. Your uncle Z has the backbone of a titanium blade. I just hadn't expected him to join us here. When we last spoke he had plans to visit Asia. And regrettably, that conversation ended on less-than-friendly terms."

Lexi knew her godfather was perfectly capable of less-than-friendly conversations, and she decided the stranger didn't really pose a threat. When she glanced at her dad, she found him eyeing the man intently, just like she'd been doing a minute ago, but probably for a different reason.

"Would you like me to intervene, Z?" he asked.

"That won't be necessary, Charles. Let's not sully Lexi's graduation celebration with petty things. We'll just keep an eye on him." Uncle Z assumed his parental face and turned it on Lexi. "Except for you, young one. You keep your eyes off him. He's trouble. There are plenty of young men here who can carry on a conversation without expecting—well, I trust you to make the right choices. Now, if you'll excuse me, I have a call to make."

He stomped away, and Lexi was able to continue staring at the stranger. So he was trouble, huh? He seemed to be acting civil at the moment, sipping champagne and chatting pleasantly with Nora and Octavius. Did he know all the misfits?

The man hadn't given Lexi another glance since that first intense moment at the door, when his smile had had her gawking. Did he decide she was too naive to bother with? Maybe her uncle Z had already told him to back off.

"Do either of you know that man?"

Her parents spoke their silent language while she pretended not to notice.

"We've never formally met, but we've heard about him through your godfather," said her dad.

"What have you heard?"

"We know he's committed to his work," her mom offered blandly.

"Okay. Sounds like every other CEO I've met. Why do you think Uncle Z has a problem with him? Do they work together? Did they have a falling-out?"

"From what I understand, they work together out of duty. Not by choice."

"All right, I won't ask Uncle Z to introduce us. But that must be how he found out about my party. He's probably here to wish me well before he hops on his private jet and flies to Asia. Why don't we go over and introduce ourselves?"

Her parents reacted so suddenly, jerking their heads to blink at her, that she took a step back. "Geez, what's with everybody today?"

"Let's just leave it, for now," her dad said. "I can introduce you to that man over there." He pointed to Sami from Kolkata, a boy she'd hardly call a man.

"That guy's so shy he almost passed out while we were talking. I want to know more about the man in the suit. And if somebody doesn't give me a legitimate reason why I shouldn't talk to him, I'm going over there right now."

Her dad opened and closed his mouth as if he couldn't form a coherent sentence. It wasn't a good sign. "You want a legitimate reason? Fine. The man has a less-than-stellar reputation with women, if you understand my meaning. I hope, now, you'll heed your godfather's warning, and we can leave it at that."

Wiping his palms on his expensive slacks, he guided her mom to the bar, their heads bent in conversation. So, they were worried Lexi was going to fall for this stranger. This sexy-as-sin stranger with the less-than-stellar reputation. Would it be so bad to get close to a guy like that? Even if it didn't last?

Lexi wasn't the romantically inexperienced girl her parents had raised her to be. She'd been reading some pretty filthy romance novels. In her third year at uni she'd stolen a kiss from a guy in English lit, despite the moment being awkward and short-lived. Sure, the conversations she'd had with men of the college variety had convinced her that most of them weren't long-term material. But it would have been nice to have given them a go if her parents didn't always find ways to squash any potential romances, like the guy from English lit who'd started avoiding her like the plague afterward. She wouldn't be surprised if they'd placed spies around the campus.

Now, however, it appeared she'd been given carte blanche. And as far as she was concerned, the buffet had improved significantly.

The inane chatter that *Luke*—if he was going to label himself that—suffered through while making his rounds at the party convinced him that choosing to avoid these gatherings was a wise decision. His friends rambled on about the same things that had intrigued them the last time they spoke. After just an hour he was questioning his reasons for attending, although the look on Z's face when he walked in the door already made it worth it. Predictable, but entertaining.

"I heard you're traveling to Asia. What brings you out after such a long absence? In search of pleasure, *Luke*?" Nora let his pseudonym linger on her tongue before releasing it, and he consented to play along. The whole bloody event was a farce anyway.

"As you know, *Nora*, pleasures vary depending on who you're asking." He paused, amused by her smile, before continuing. "I thought it was time to remind my friends that I'm still around. And I *do* love Asia."

"You also love antagonizing Z, although I don't blame you. It's fun. But he can be tiresome. I only consent to his request for companionship when we come here."

"That's what I've heard. I'm glad to know my messenger is doing their job."

Nora swayed as she enjoyed his banter, gently fondling the simple dress she wore, accented with only her warmth and rosy cheeks. She had figured things out, and it reminded him of the reasons he'd used for attending.

A hand rapped him on the shoulder as Octavius joined them. His grin rarely meant anything good, but it had been a long while since they'd seen each other, and Luke hoped enough time had passed to cool his friend's ire about past disputes.

"Luke. It's been an age. How are things in the nether regions?"

"That joke never gets stale. Speaking of which, I hear you won't be competing in the games this year. Finding your humility and letting the young archers claim a prize, are you?"

"Don't act like it's the first time I've done it. Diana and I made a pact years ago. She's bowing out as well, and I always keep my word." If the smirk Octavius offered was meant as a barb, he would have to try harder.

"And Emily? Is she in on this pact?"

"Not officially, but we're all competing in the races. Z will finally have some real opponents to knock him out of the top spot."

"What makes you think Z will play fair?"

Octavius scoffed. "I forget how far out of the loop you are. The game keepers started awarding Z his own prize to appease the attention hog. So the second-place winner is awarded the first-place prize, and so on."

"Fuel for his bloated ego. That's clever."

Luke was back to questioning his reasons for making the detour to the Maxwell estate, and turned a casual eye in Lexi's direction. After a heated discussion involving Z and her parents, her brother had shown up and ushered her over to a boy with stiff hair and a perpetual smirk. Despite Lexi's fairy-tale existence, Luke felt empathy for her, along with the other young men being paraded around the room. Their lives would never be their own.

Of course, he wasn't foolish enough to think that, at twenty-two years old, Lexi was completely naive. He sensed her needs simmering beneath that practiced posture as her gaze tracked him around the room. And he didn't doubt it would be easy to command her attention. But this was not the time nor the place for it, despite the comfort he could take in her company. He'd already decided it was better to heal his wounds himself.

Lexi tried not to roll her eyes while she waited for the boy to stop talking about himself. What was his name again? Rod?

"Last year I was named captain of my rowing team," he said loudly. "And my swimming improved dramatically after my last growth spurt. I was even challenged to swim the English Channel."

Maybe they just wanted you to get lost. "Impressive. So, your parents are from Boston but you grew up in Bruges?"

"That's right. Our estate is in Bruges. I'm the youngest, so I've got more freedom than my older sisters. They didn't attend uni over here. My parents are looking at a twenty-room town house in South End. There's a hot tub installed on the patio, which is great therapy after intense workouts. Where's your Boston home located?"

"Eagle Hill."

Rod's face pinched, making him look like a pug. "Too bad. I hear the noise from air traffic has driven down real estate prices in that area."

Really? This arrogant ass was judging her based off real estate prices? He hadn't asked a single question about her. Not *What sports are you interested in?* Or *What do you do for fun?* It didn't matter to him that she enjoyed horseback riding or that she admired the works of Hemingway despite his lack of dialogue tags. This boy was rich trash, and she regretted giving him a second chance. As far as Lexi was concerned, he could fly to that twenty-room town house and soak his head in the hot tub.

She glanced over her shoulder, locating the mystery man her uncle Z was determined to keep her away from. She'd already guessed that he was in his late twenties or early thirties, since he carried himself so well and mingled like a pro. But his relaxed confidence was unlike the type-A CEOs she'd met. He seemed like a regular guy. Someone who'd come into his money honestly and now lived the life of a wealthy philanthropist who liked to spend time on his yacht and drink highballs after five o'clock.

Did he have a girlfriend who sailed with him on that yacht? Of course he had a girlfriend. He was a magnificent piece of art. Where was she tonight? Had they broken up because of his less-than-stellar reputation with women?

"Well, it's been nice talking to you again, Rod," Lexi said as she backed away from the gel head. "I have a few more people to chat with. You know, the duties of a hostess."

"Of course. Congratulations, by the way."

She let Rod talk to her back as she made a beeline for the bathroom, which she desperately needed after finishing that bottle of water. Maybe if she switched to wine the boys would get more interesting. She might even be ready to talk to the mystery man.

After handling her situation in the bathroom and a quick inspection in the mirror, Lexi rallied herself for more fake interest. Why did her parents' parties have to be so dull? They'd even managed to ruin what was supposed to be her farewell-and-fuck-you party.

As she stepped back into the hallway, she nearly collided with someone outside the door.

"Excuse me. That was my fault."

His voice came across like vanilla fudge, sweet and smooth, and Lexi's heart thudded in her ears as she faced the stranger in the charcoal suit. She quickly remembered why he'd stunned her. It was those eyes that had done it. They were like twin suns, and if she didn't look away, she'd be blinded. But she didn't want to look away. Their golden glow warmed her. She'd never seen gold eyes before. Maybe they were hazel with yellow flecks. Or amber. Did people have amber eyes?

Say something.

"I don't believe we've met," she said. "I'm Lexi Maxwell."

Of course, they hadn't met. *Damn.* She was going to ruin this before it even got started.

"Luke Carrington. It's a pleasure to finally meet you." He smiled, and the hall glowed brighter. This man had radiance exploding from his pores. "You appear to be enjoying your party. I haven't seen that smile leave your face."

He'd been watching her? How had she missed that? Had he caught her watching him? What else had he noticed? At least *his* eyes were on her face. Rod had ogled her dandelions the whole time he talked about himself.

"The party's fine. But I'm looking forward to what's happening afterward."

Why had she said that? Now, he was going to ask.

"What's happening afterward?" His eyes twinkled, like he was making his own assumptions. Or maybe she was just being dazzled.

"I'm taking a vacation. A long-awaited, extended vacation."

"That *is* something to look forward to. Vacations can be rejuvenating and put a fresh perspective on life. Is that what you're hoping for?"

Lexi blinked at him. She couldn't remember the last time anyone had asked what she hoped for. "Yes. It's not what I was thinking when I started my itinerary, but the way you've worded it makes it sound less desperate."

With some effort she redirected her gaze away from his eyes. Logically, her gaze went straight to his mouth. Why was she so nervous? She could navigate her way through any conversation. Oh right, she was talking to the man with the golden eyes. And that cologne he wore. It reminded her of spice and earth. The way the ground smelled after a good rain.

She didn't realize that all the blood traveling to her head to help her form words had abandoned her legs, and the floor suddenly felt strange under her feet, like she'd indulged in too much wine. This was embarrassing, since she hadn't indulged. She casually threw out her arm to lean against the wall and missed the landing.

Luke noticed her dilemma and his forearm shot out to catch her before she stumbled. "Do you need to sit down?"

Forgoing an answer, he slipped his hand under her arm and escorted her out of the hallway and into the living room. She couldn't decide whether this was helpful or making things worse. His touch made every hair on her body stand on end, and she quickly scanned the crowd out of habit.

Maybe her uncle Z wouldn't see Luke holding her, and Luke wouldn't have to stop doing it. This was the closest she'd ever come to feeling like a heroine in a novel. Lexi knew she could hold her own in battle, but she could also enjoy the attention of a real-life Adonis.

The sound of breaking glass had everyone turning toward the source, but Lexi ignored it. With any luck, it was one of the waitstaff and not an overbearing baby-man determined to ruin her fun.

Five

It hadn't been the waitstaff who'd dropped the champagne flute, but they were the ones cleaning it up as Lexi's godfather blew across the room like an angry storm cloud.

"What's going on here? Why does Lexi look flushed?"

"I'm fine, Uncle Z," she said as she took a seat on the couch. "It's been a long day and fatigue is setting in, that's all. Can someone get me a glass of white wine?"

"I'd be happy to do that." Luke trotted off, leaving Lexi to deal with her godfather. She knew her face was flushed. It felt flushed. But now it was *him* causing it as he hovered menacingly at her shoulder.

"What did we just talk about?" he growled.

"I was coming out of the bathroom and Luke was going in. It was serendipitous." She offered him an impish smile, and he drew his lips in tighter. "It's *my* graduation party, isn't it? Let's not sully it with petty things."

Despite the room's size—it could have held ten elephants comfortably—the mood turned chilly, like frozen-tundra, ice-on-the-walls chilly. She almost expected to see the guests' breath turn to vapor as they neglected their conversations to focus on the situation unfolding at the couch.

Dion had assumed a crossed-arm stance nearby, which Lexi had grown accustomed to, but it was the last straw for her. All these displays of machismo were pissing her off, and she was preparing her defense just as Luke appeared in her peripheral view with a glass of wine.

"I hope this helps." Although his gesture was polite, he didn't linger. In fact, he walked to the center of the room and motioned for attention.

"Greetings, *groeten*, *saudações*, and *abhivaadan*," he said. "I'm honored to be among the guests here today, and I want to extend my thanks to the Maxwells for their kind hospitality. I expect everyone who made the trip to this luxurious estate with its endless amenities and breathtaking views is here for the same thing. To celebrate Alexandra and to wish her well as she embarks on the road of life."

Luke swept his arm toward Lexi, and she offered a small wave from the couch, hoping she didn't look too thunderstruck. She was still tingling like a lightning rod.

"It's a privilege to share this moment with you, Lexi," he continued. "Focus and determination can take us many places and provide us with a sense of self-worth. I'm sure I speak for everyone here when I wish you the best in your pursuit of whatever you deem worthy."

Lexi was rarely stunned into silence. She prided herself on this fact. But she knew her face was blooming twelve shades of red, and she was grateful for the burst of applause led by Nora. She stood from the couch, embracing the moment and shrugging sheepishly at her guests. When her eyes landed on Luke, she could only smile and shake her head. If she'd read him right, and hopefully she had, he'd delivered his impromptu speech to diffuse a tense situation.

As for her uncle Z, his face had gone purple, a color that meant a storm was imminent. And she knew from experience that it was better to pretend he wasn't throwing a tantrum and get on with life. Luke retreated to a lone chair in the corner. Obviously, he knew her godfather well enough to give him time to cool off.

What was their connection? If they worked together, why hadn't her godfather mentioned Luke's name before? He loved to tell stories about how important he was. Maybe Luke had bested him at something.

"You fancy that man in the gray suit, don't you?" Nora slipped onto the couch, wearing a sly grin, and Lexi sat down beside her.

"Who wouldn't? I mean, look at him."

Nora giggled, which made Lexi feel better. Although it had always been that way with Nora. "I've never known you to mince words. And I agree with you, Luke has been blessed."

"How well do you know him?"

"Well . . ."

Nora let the moment stretch out, building anticipation, which she liked to do before delivering some flowery prose. Lexi didn't mind. She was eager to get an opinion from anyone other than her parents or her uncle Z. She'd never understood what Nora saw in her godfather. Nora was a free spirit. She reminded Lexi of a cherub, with her perfectly round face, wide blue eyes, and mess of reddish-brown curls always coiffed behind a headband. Nora sang the loudest and quoted obscure ballads that usually made somebody cry.

Uncle Z, on the other hand, was a papa bear in a flannel

shirt—cuddly one minute and grumpy the next. What was the attraction between them? Lexi's mom claimed it was the sex, which was how she explained away a lot of things.

"We've been acquainted for some time," Nora offered finally. "I'm sure you've discovered how engaging he can be. Not many women are able to resist his charms."

Lexi thought about asking how many women, but she wasn't ready to go there yet. Or maybe she didn't really care.

"Do you know how old he is?"

"His age?" Wrinkles formed between Nora's brows, as if she needed to crunch the numbers. "I couldn't say, exactly. How old do you think he is?"

"Late twenties, early thirties."

"That sounds like a fair guess."

"Do you know what he does for a living?"

"I know he's responsible for the lives of many people. I expect it's many millions by now."

"Wow. He must be motivated. He seems young to be that successful. He *is* successful, isn't he?"

"Absolutely. He's extremely good at what he does. Why don't you ask *Luke* these questions, sweetheart? He's very easy to talk to."

"Easy for you, maybe. Three minutes in the hall and I wilted like overcooked spinach."

It was those exotic eyes. They were like orbs of pure sunshine. She ventured a glance at the corner of the room where Luke sat with a lowball glass, probably filled with something strong, reclined in the chair, one leg bent casually over the other. He was the epitome of cool grace as he talked with the father of one of the boys, his head bobbing like the conversation was riveting.

Nora patted Lexi's arm like a mother would. "I've never seen you shy away from a conversation. I think you two would have plenty to talk about."

Lexi didn't doubt that. But she was imagining the other things she could do with Luke besides talk. Nora had been her confidant in the past, and she knew her friend would respect her privacy if they discussed more personal topics. Topics that probably needed to be discussed in a less public space.

Then Nora leaned in and whispered at her ear. "You haven't lost your maidenhood yet, have you?"

"My what?" Lexi's attention snapped from Luke to Nora.

"You're a virgin," Nora clarified.

"Oh. Yes, I am." Lexi's face flushed with warmth, and she took a sip of wine, which was still chilled enough to be refreshing.

"I understand your apprehension. However, if I may be so bold and offer you some advice, woman to woman—you couldn't choose a better gentleman than Luke to help you through that rite of passage. He has always struck me as someone who employs integrity and thoughtfulness in everything he does."

Nora's lips lifted into a Cheshire Cat smile, causing Lexi to blink at her. Did she know this from experience? Was Nora's name written in Luke's little black book? If so, they seemed to have parted on good terms. Or was it ongoing? Lexi didn't want to know.

"It's not that I haven't tried." The words tumbled out of Lexi's mouth like they were tired of waiting their turn. "You've been hanging around my parents long enough to know that I'm rarely alone. And *never* with boys. It makes sex kind of impossible."

Nora clicked her tongue. "That's unfortunate. Youth can be an ideal time to experiment with new things, especially when it comes to sex. I don't want to overstep, but I will say this: when there is mutual respect and both parties give themselves willingly, the first experience can be incredibly freeing. I hope you'll overcome these obstacles soon."

Lexi pressed her hand to her stomach, and her thoughts returned to the hallway, imagining herself with Luke, alone. Maybe in the bathroom, her back against the door, his hands on her hips . . . "What about love? Shouldn't I be in love with the man who takes my virginity?"

"Love?" Nora tapped her cheek with a finger, like the question required serious thought. Was she really on the fence about it? Or was she deciding on a version that would sound good to Lexi's parents if they found out she blabbed?

"Love is an emotion that often complicates matters in the bedroom. To my mind, sex is simply an act of trust and pleasure. Why put parameters on a sexual relationship by requiring that love be involved? Of course, I'm not condoning sex with random strangers. But I prefer to leave love out of it. The risk of having one's feelings dashed against the rocks is too great otherwise."

Nora finished her sermon about loveless sex with a shrug, but Lexi could read between the lines. Nora had lost a lover. Maybe more than one. Did it have something to do with her uncle Z? Or even worse, Luke? Did *Luke* feel the same as Nora about sex without love? Lexi took another swallow of wine.

"Do you know who invited Luke?"

"I expect he learned of the event through mutual friends. I'm not surprised he failed to inform anyone he was attending. He likes to antagonize your uncle Z."

"Why? What is their relationship status? I heard they work together but not by choice."

Nora made a motion of zipping her lip, and Lexi pursed hers.

"That isn't fair. You started it."

"And your uncle Z would make me sleep in the stable if he overheard us talking about him."

"Can I ask one more question?"

"You may."

"Do you know if Luke plans to stay all weekend?"

"If the gods will it."

Nora recited her favorite quote before rising and drifting away. She had given Lexi more than Lexi had bargained for, which usually happened with Nora. It was good, actually. This was Lexi's last hurrah before she told everyone to shove it, and she pictured Luke lying in one of the guest beds with his eyes lighting up the room. Did he wear boxers or briefs? Maybe he slept in the nude. What would she do to him if he was naked in *her* bed? What would he do to her?

Dinner was served, followed by more drinks, and somehow Lexi was never able to speak to Luke again. It was frustrating and a little humorous the lengths her family went to to keep them apart. But when she learned he was staying the night, she held out hope.

Lexi had no intention of tiptoeing around her godfather's moods all weekend. In fact, as she prepared for bed, she came up with a few ideas for getting Luke alone. A visit to the stable would make for a great conversation starter. There was also the trail to the gorge. This felt like the beginning of an epic battle, and she needed to be ready for whatever her family threw at her.

Swinging open the doors to her balcony, Lexi walked outside to bid good night to the sea, inhaling the salty air as it blew across the polished marble. It was one of the redeeming qualities of their castle in the sand. As she leaned over the railing, she noticed someone walking down the east-facing path—a guest enjoying a nighttime walk on the beach.

On closer inspection, she realized it was Luke, and he was naked! Completely naked! This fact became more obvious when he stepped away from the row of cypress trees and onto the sand. She couldn't see details, the Olympic-sized swimming pool and a wall of seagrass stood between them, but there was no mistaking him. And Lexi couldn't move. Rather, she was unwilling to.

He spread out a blanket and sat down, his bare legs stretched in front of him. Had he noticed her there, an accidental voyeur dressed in pink baby-doll pajamas? What would he do if he had? Would he point it out to her tomorrow? Make her relive the embarrassment? Was she hyperventilating?

He had barely been there a minute before he stood back up and walked into the surf. Even from fifty yards away she could make out the curves of his body—a physique rivaling that of Michelangelo's *David*. It was clichéd, but there was no room in her head to think any deeper, and she imagined how he might look close up, how he might feel. Then he turned and waved at her before jumping into the sea.

Shit!

Lexi scrambled inside her room and stood behind the French doors as her cheeks burned. He knew she'd been spying on him. This was worse than any awkward encounter she'd ever had. How could she explain herself tomorrow? She pounded the tiles with her bare feet, counting each breath, reining in her nerves as Luke swam amid the ocean waves, his skin slick and glowing under the moonlight.

When a fresh blush burned her cheeks, she realized something and stopped midstride. She had no reason to feel ashamed. She hadn't done anything wrong. He was the one out there flashing the fish. Luke Carrington was no different from any other man.

Had she been merciful with her debate opponents regardless of their pronouns? No. During swim meets did she give a flying flip about those tiny swimsuits the boys wore? Not once. They were usually behind her anyway.

Then Mr. Smolder had to waltz in and ruin her perfect record. How pitiful was that? Maybe she just needed to take Nora's advice and keep her emotions out of it. She could enjoy a nice romp in the hay with a handsome man who was, at that very moment, skinny-dipping in her backyard.

Lexi detoured to the balcony door and stared through the glass. Luke had finished his swim and was reaching for a towel. If the seagrass hadn't been blocking her view, she could have seen his body all wet and glistening. She wanted to touch him. To feel the burn. Was he putting on a pair of swim trunks?

Damn.

She yanked open the balcony door with confidence, which she blamed on adrenaline, and the wind swept into her room like a mini tempest. She caught the door before it slammed, and wrestled her hair behind her ears. When she glanced out at the beach, she found Luke waving at her again. But this one said *come join me.*

He wanted her to join him on the beach, at night . . . alone?

She couldn't pretend she hadn't seen him. Waving back was the polite thing to do. She waved back. He responded with another come-hither wave, and Lexi swallowed. Did he want her to come down so he could tease her about spying on him? He didn't seem like that type of guy, although she had limited evidence to support this theory.

A late-night rendezvous on the beach with a handsome man

could either be the best or the worst thing to ever happen to her. No. Losing that lacrosse match to the thundering turds from Madison was the worst thing to ever happen to her. So this would be the second worst.

Or it could be the best.

Wasn't this what she wanted? To talk to a guy without a bunch of prying eyes? If she blew it, she blew it. Life would go on. She held up a finger, a signal that she hoped he would understand.

The story just got real.

Six

It was after one o'clock, which usually meant nothing in the Maxwell household. Especially after a party. But tonight it was quiet. And with the rooms full of guests, the alarms would be off. Lexi just needed to stay on her side of the estate and use the same route she always did if she wanted to make a clean escape.

As she took the stairs to the living room, she knew exactly where to place her feet to avoid the squeaks. Then it was a hard U-turn left, a quick right, and a short jaunt down a dark hallway to her dad's study. From there she accessed the French doors onto the courtyard, and she was free.

But her relief was short-lived. As she hugged the line of cypress trees along the west-facing path, the one less traveled, her stomach clenched as she thought about the prize at the end and the risk she was taking. Would her parents nix her travel plans if she got caught? Was her reputation on the line? How much did she care about the consequences of taking such a risk?

She'd worn her black strapless beach dress to hide the yellow bikini underneath, a recent purchase in preparation for her summer trip. It was not the kind of suit she wore for swim meets. If her parents had taught her one thing, it was to be comfortable in her own skin. But good advice only went so far without opportunities to test it out.

Luke was still there and still clothed when she arrived, so it hadn't been a trick. Why did she feel like that would have been a relief? And what was hidden behind his smile as he watched her approach? It wasn't forced. She could recognize those. Was *he* feeling relief?

"Hello, Lexi. I'm glad you decided to join me. I hope you don't mind me taking advantage of your private beach. I rarely get to swim in the sea."

"Our guests are free to use the beach whenever they like. And for whatever reason they like." *Damn.* Did that sound wrong?

His smile never wavered. "It's a beautiful spot. I expect you swim a lot."

"I swam on my high-school team. We were division champs my sophomore year. I also played lacrosse for five years."

"Nice. Sports require extreme dedication to hit that level." He waved at the blanket. "Do you want to sit? Your mother insisted I have a blanket to take down with me. I enjoy the beach, but I'd rather not sit in the sand."

"Same. There's nothing worse than sand in unwanted places."

Was she rambling? Was he rambling? She was probably just projecting her own nervous habit onto him. She sat on the blanket and experimented with different positions, finally opting for crossed legs. It wasn't like she was nude under her dress. Luke arranged himself beside her, crossed-legged as well, so they were both looking at the sea. His knee came so close to hers that she could swear she felt his body heat.

"So, Lexi, what else do you enjoy besides swimming and playing lacrosse? Any hobbies?"

Now they were getting somewhere. "I ride horses. We have six here on the property. My favorite is an Arabian mare—Jackie O."

"I keep horses too. I'll ride whenever I'm not in the mood for a longer walk. It's nice to have someone to talk to besides yourself."

"I talk to my horses all the time. I'm sure they think I'm crazy, but none of them seem to hold it against me."

She laughed nervously and he smiled, turning to hit her with those amber high beams. "The fact that you believe your horses are that sentient is a testament to your character. So, any other passions?"

Passions? Why did that word make her want to blush? "I like to read. I'm a big fan of Ernest Hemingway. Although his stories always make me cry."

"I'm partial to Douglas Adams myself. But I'll pick up Steinbeck or Thoreau when I'm feeling contemplative."

"I love Douglas Adams. Did you know he was a script editor for *Doctor Who*?"

"I didn't, but I don't watch much television. Are you a fan of the show?"

"I wouldn't consider myself a fan, but I met the tenth doctor during a trip to London. I suppose that's another passion of mine—traveling. My family and I have seen a lot of the world. I started a travel journal when I was seven and just recently ran out of paper. I'm about to start a new one."

She stopped herself before she told him about her plans to burn the journal in a ritual fire, and the tilt of his lips made her think he was reading her mind.

"It seems we have a lot in common. I've traveled a good amount too. What's your favorite thing about it?"

"Oh, wow. It would be impossible to pick a favorite. I love

trying new food and meeting new people. And I'm always amazed at the different landscapes. Some of the places we've been look like they shouldn't exist on the planet."

"Agreed. Have you seen the stone forest in China? There's a cool legend attached to it about a young woman who was turned to stone after being forbidden to marry the man she loved."

"I haven't been there, but maybe I can add it to my summer itinerary. That legend reminds me of a few tragic stories from Greek mythology. If you didn't notice already, there's a whole bookshelf dedicated to the subject in the living room. The Maxwells are a little obsessed."

"I hadn't." He stared at the waves, his brows drawing in just enough to make her wonder if she'd said something to trigger a bad memory. Then he suddenly glanced over his shoulder at the path.

Lexi stiffened and jerked around like she'd been yanked by a chain. "Did you hear something?"

"No. I smell something. I think it's lemon. What's the season for citrus here?"

Really? He'd noticed that? "You're not smelling citrus trees. That's my lemon verbena body lotion. I'm sorry if it bothers you. Some people are sensitive to certain smells."

"It's nice, actually. I like lemons."

So, he liked how she smelled. That had to be good. He turned his attention back to the sea, and Lexi found her brain vacant of things to say. He was probably expecting her to ask about *him* now. Or maybe he was comfortable with silence. She was fine just enjoying his closeness. How long had she been staring at his knee?

Say something.

"How did you hear about my party?"

Crap. That sounded accusatory.

Once again an effortless smile lifted his lips, immediately putting her at ease. "I heard about it through friends of your uncle Z. You've probably already learned that he and I don't always see eye to eye."

"Uncle Z rarely sees eye to eye with anyone. What happened between you two?"

"We couldn't agree on something that had serious consequences. Two somethings, actually. And the relationship has been strained ever since."

"Did you know he was going to be here?"

"Yes. Does that bother you? I know you two are close."

He turned toward her, and the heat was back, flooding her skin and warming the breeze that was keeping them company. She should have tied her hair back, although it had been giving her cover whenever she stared at him.

"It doesn't bother me. He's someone my parents trust, so I've learned to trust him too. Despite his unpredictable moods, he *does* seem wise beyond his years. Don't ever tell him I said that."

"And inflate his ego? I wouldn't dream of it."

She chuckled. "He's definitely perfected the art of the tantrum."

"No arguments here."

He continued to look at her, right in the eyes, but he didn't let it get weird before turning his attention back to the sea.

"Nora told me you run your own business," she said. "What kind of business is it?"

"I help people with end-of-life decisions."

"Oh. Do you help them write their wills?"

"No. I act more as a counselor. People who are staring death in the face often need a bit of assurance that there's more after this life. Hopefully something good. A lot of them cling to beliefs that make them second-guess all the decisions they've ever made. I help them make peace with their choices as they transition."

"So, you're a priest?" Lexi nearly choked on the word. Would a priest skinny-dip in the ocean? His laugh reassured her.

"I'm *not* a priest. Do you believe there's an afterlife, Lexi?"

"I'm not fully committed to any one thing. Although reincarnation might be nice. We spend a huge amount of time just figuring out the basics. After a few lifetimes, I expect the hard stuff gets easier."

"Ah, you're an optimist. A fine quality."

"And you have the most selfless job I've ever heard of. You could give Mother Teresa a run for her money."

"You're giving me way too much credit."

"It's still a job not everyone would consider, getting close to people who are dying."

Luke's gaze drifted away, out over the sand, where the surf ebbed and flowed in rhythmic cadence. Hopefully she hadn't said something out of line. He seemed attached to his convictions on death.

"Where do you live?" she asked. "You said you aren't able to swim in the ocean much."

"My home is far from the sea, but I make time for an ocean visit when I need to relax."

Far from the sea? Talk about noncommittal. Maybe he didn't want people to know where he lived so they wouldn't stalk him. He was kind of stalkable. "Where are these vacation spots? I'd love to know where you go to relax."

Luke pressed his lips together in thought. *Hmm*, those lips . . .

"When I'm really missing the sea, I hit the Mediterranean coast. I also love Peru, Argentina, Singapore. The cuisine in Singapore is outstanding. Have you been to Asia?"

"Yes. Both Japan and Vietnam. Vietnam is where I fell in love with rice fields. I haven't looked at a grain of rice the same way since."

Time passed with ease, something that Lexi rarely experienced, especially with men. She was usually in a hurry to get to the good part before some killjoy ruined her fun. They talked about everything from pad thai to poetry to Luke's lifelong relationship with the violin. When she spoke, he listened to her, his expressions shifting based on the mood of each story, as if everything she said mattered to him. Nora had been right—he was easy to talk to and charming as hell. Lexi also noticed how his tousled hair seemed to give off its own light. She'd been watching a strand dry on his forehead in a gentle whorl.

The desire to reach for his hand grew stronger the longer they were out there. It rested on his knee just a few inches from hers. Could he tell she was attracted to him? Was he attracted to *her*? The guy probably had hundreds of women in his contacts list. Maybe she was barking up the wrong tree. Was his hand inching closer to hers? Did he want her to make the first move? Or was he completely unaware of it? There was one way to find out. With a single intake of breath, Lexi lifted her hand and rested it on his.

He responded with a smile and a surge of warmth that, under different circumstances, would have made her worry he was running a fever.

"This has been fun," he said. "I feel like we could talk all night. Do you want to swim? I need to warn you, the water is cold. But you probably already knew that."

Wait. Was that a brush-off? Was he trying to tell her he wasn't interested in anything more than a chat? Maybe he *was* in a committed relationship and Nora had steered her wrong. Lexi glanced at their hands, still clasped on his knee.

"I'm sorry if I overstepped," she said as she pulled away.

"Not at all." Luke caught her in his gaze, giving her permission to stare into those amber depths. "I'd like to hold your hand. I just don't think your brother would approve."

He glanced to the west, and there was Dion stomping across the sand toward them. Lexi had been so preoccupied with making a love connection she'd completely ignored her spy radar.

"Lexi! What the heck are you doing out here?"

She stood and dug her heels into the sand as she glared at her brother. "You would know, if someone had invited you. But they didn't!"

With a violent sweep of her arm, she waved him away. At the same time, a gust of wind swirled between them, stirring up a cloud of sand that blocked his path. He coughed as he stumbled backward.

"See? Even Mother Nature doesn't want you here," she said.

But he wasn't listening. Or maybe he didn't care. He dodged the sandstorm and tromped over to the blanket like Poseidon himself.

"You're supposed to be in bed," he said, eyeballing Luke as if the guy was holding a gun to her head.

"I'm not *supposed* to be doing anything. And who made you my keeper this weekend?"

Dion frowned. In fact, he had the audacity to look hurt. "Is it a crime to want to look out for my sister?"

"Your sister can look out for herself," she said.

"I believe this chance meeting is fortunate," said Luke. "Why don't you join us, Dion? Lexi and I were just talking about how much she enjoys traveling with her family."

Dion rubbed the back of his neck, looking like the wind had been sucked from his sails.

Good.

"Well, it's almost two o'clock, and there are a lot of activities planned for tomorrow . . ."

"By all means, Dion, go get some rest."

Lexi raised her eyebrows so high she felt a strain behind her eyes. After all the complaints she'd made to him about their parents micromanaging her life, here he was doing the same thing. Sometimes she felt like she was trapped in some kind of curfew hell.

Dion sighed and glanced down at the blanket while Lexi held her breath. "I suppose I could hang out for a little while."

Crap.

Apparently, hell was real.

Seven

The kitchen bell chimed as Lexi shimmied into her jeans. She knew Chef Lorraine had prepared something amazing for breakfast, and she didn't want to insult her by holding up the meal. But Lexi was preoccupied with the memory of Luke's windblown hair and his sultry voice when he had talked about Mediterranean architecture and his love of horses.

Mostly she thought about his naked body. Sure, it had been dark. Sure, he'd been on the beach and she'd been on her balcony. But when she got up close, when she saw the moonlight glinting off his skin . . . She wanted to punch Dion for interrupting them. Lexi had been hoping to hear some of Luke's poetry. Maybe even steal a kiss. If her brother didn't watch himself, he would end up on her enemies list.

Breakfast was served on the outdoor patio, a partially covered space draped in wisteria that was currently bursting with periwinkle-colored blooms and filling the air with sweet perfume. The raised deck of white marble overlooking the swimming pool and the sparkling sea beyond provided a view rivaling any Lexi had seen on her travels. If only the memories tied to it were as good as her journal entries.

She stood at the railing, sandwiched between two potted cypresses, out of sight of the gel heads, and counted twenty-six place settings split between two tables. Her mother had chosen to forgo the name cards, which left seating arrangements wide open, and Lexi was determined to sit with Luke. He had more interesting things to say than anyone else she'd met. And when *she* talked, he listened. She wondered what he'd wear today. She'd seen him at his most refined and at his most casual. Like naked.

"Good morning, Lexi." Luke's voice met her ear in a baritone whisper, as if it was delivered on a cloud, and a flutter tickled her ribs as she turned to him, tucking away an image of his naked abs.

His hair was ruffled on one side, like he hadn't been able to get a stubborn cowlick to stay down, and she had to fight the urge to reach out and fix it. He also carried that musky, worldly scent with him, mocking her like something forbidden, and she took in a deep breath, hoping he hadn't noticed but not caring if he had. All at once, the world felt right.

"Good morning to you. How did you sleep? Mom said she gave you the downstairs suite with the view. I love that room. Sometimes I open all the windows and listen to the waves."

Luke's smile arrived like a slow burn. If he was faking, he had her totally fooled. "I feel privileged. And I slept very well. What about you? According to Dion, we have a busy day ahead of us."

"I slept fine. I've never needed more than six hours. My mind just refuses to take longer breaks." Lexi realized that guests were claiming chairs, and she snatched Luke's hand, tugging him away from the trees. "Let's hurry and find seats before the tables fill up."

His chuckle reminded her that he wasn't Mara, and they weren't trying to snag a good table in the food court. But the deed was done, and Luke didn't seem to mind as she continued her trajectory toward a pair of empty chairs.

She felt her godfather's gaze from all the way across the patio, where he posed like a garden statue. Strangely, she felt no guilt. Just defiance. But if she wanted to avoid a war between him and Luke, she'd have to play it cool. When the family from Argentina swooped into the seats across from her and Luke, she smiled politely.

She'd talked to the boy briefly the night before. His name was something forgettable, like William. He seemed reasonably intelligent and had a nice accent. He'd worn his uni sweater today, despite the gorgeous sunshine, and she tried not to hold it against him. It was probably still cold in Argentina.

"So, William, where in Argentina were you born?" she asked.

"You may call me Will. I was born in Salta, where I live now. Our manor is like yours but much older. Have you been to Argentina? I heard your family has traveled to many places."

"I haven't been to Argentina, but western Patagonia has been on my bucket list for a while."

His thick eyebrows rose, as if she'd sparked his interest. How curious. "Oh, Patagonia is *hermosa* . . . beautiful."

She couldn't be sure if he was being forgetful or condescending. They had already conversed in Spanish. "Do you have any siblings?"

"Two. A younger sister and an older brother. Thankfully, he will be taking over our manor so I can pursue other things."

Will's mother gave his arm a covert pinch, and he blinked in pain. "Of course, I would never abandon my duties to the family."

It seemed Will had been experiencing the same sort of parental controls as Lexi, and she couldn't help feeling sorry for the guy.

"I visited your stable this morning," he went on. "You keep some fine horses. Did you know that Argentina is known for their superior horse breeds?"

"I did. Do you ride?"

"Only with my friends. I am too busy with important obligations to be competitive in riding. But I have been told I could jockey if I was not so muscular."

And there it was. Arrogance wrapped up in a cashmere sweater. Will's attention was drawn to the croissants being placed on the table by the waitstaff, and he flexed his arm as he reached for the basket. Too bad. She'd been rooting for him.

"I consider myself a decent rider," she said. "Would you be up for a one-on-one race on the beach after we eat?"

Will's eyes doubled in size. Clearly he hadn't expected to be challenged at breakfast. Or was it the fact that a girl had challenged him?

"To you, I will say *yes*. I cannot pass up a chance to race. I will warn you, though, I am not used to losing."

Lexi held him under the influence of her bring-it-on smile, which usually struck fear into the hearts of her opponents. "Then this will be a great opportunity to see how you handle it."

Once she'd issued the riding challenge, Will threw everything he had at her between courses, asking questions designed to stump or humiliate her. But he only humiliated himself as Lexi bantered right back while enjoying her eggs Benedict. Luke's smile never left him, even when it was time to head down to the stable.

By then Lexi was ready to be rid of the yammering pest from Salta, and she managed to pawn Will off onto Dion so she could give Luke her undivided attention. They lagged at the back of the group and made up for lost time.

"I don't really care if he wins the race," she said. "I already won the battle at the table. That preppy clod crossed the line when he started quizzing me on the origins of my own hometown. *Qué tonto.*"

Luke laughed and she laughed with him, attracting her parents' attention. At least they weren't hovering over her. She had put a stop to that when she'd turned eighteen. But her uncle Z thought manners didn't apply to him, and he snorted like a temperamental horse all the way to the stable.

Lexi guided Luke to the stall where her best friend lived—a sleek, chestnut-haired horse who eagerly greeted them, smudging Lexi's cheek with her wet upper lip.

"This is Jackie O. We've been riding together since I was twelve. Mares can be tricky in the equestrian arena, but we have an agreement. As long as I let her think she can do whatever she wants, she does whatever I ask."

"She's a beautiful specimen. What will she think of your challenge to the preppy clod? Can you talk her into a race?"

Lexi patted her horse's jaw. "Jackie O is an incredibly proud animal. She won't let another horse beat her. But she wasn't so brave when she first arrived. Don't laugh, but I told her stories about the Hippoi Athanatoi, the immortal horses of the Greek gods. I think it helped her become the fierce mare she is today."

"Clever. Not many people are familiar with those stories. It's a good thing your family has such a strong interest in the Greek myths."

Hmm. He'd remembered something about her. Luke's hit points were growing by the minute, and she smiled at him probably longer than was reasonable.

"You seem to have a close connection with your horse," he said. "Are you that way with all animals?"

"I'm not sure. I *do* love animals, but we've only kept horses.

Dad's allergic to dander." She unlatched the gate and led Jackie O out, pointing at Dion and Will as they greeted a horse two stalls down. "Looks like Dion's getting Razor ready for my opponent. Razor's a good sprinter, so this should be fun."

Lexi pulled on her riding boots and saddled up her horse while Luke observed silently, as if he didn't want to interrupt her process. She did give off a leave me alone vibe during her prep routine. When her dad walked over, she knew the speech was coming.

"I'm sure I don't have to remind you to be careful," he said as he inspected Jackie O's reins.

"I'm good, Dad."

He glanced at Luke before adding, "Just remember to keep your head in the game and not on the sidelines."

She smiled to suppress the huff that wanted to blow past her lips, then hurried to walk Jackie O out of the stable. Her mom and uncle Z stood amid the curious spectators. They didn't look happy, and Lexi was fine with that. She ignored them as she climbed into the saddle and walked her horse onto the beach.

Will the clod talked to Razor like they were old pals. He patted the horse on the neck and offered encouragement in his ear. Lexi didn't doubt the boy could ride. He appeared at ease in the saddle, but he was foolish to think he could race a strange horse and come out on top. They were on Lexi's turf, and she and Jackie O had already beaten the very horse Will was riding many times over.

"Okay, Will. Listen up," Lexi said as she brought Jackie O alongside Razor. "We're racing to that first outcropping of rocks. It's just shy of a mile." She pointed to the spot she and Dion used as their finish line. "There's plenty of beach for two horses to pass easily when the tide is ebbing, which is now. So give us some space."

She found her brother with the gathering crowd and shouted at him. "Hey, Dion. Will you do the honors?"

"My pleasure."

Dion slipped off his shirt, twisting the stiff white fabric between his hands as Lexi and her opponent lined up. A zing of excitement sent her heart into a gallop. She always got off on the adrenaline rush of competition. Making a quick search through the spectators, she found Luke appraising her with a subtle smirk. She offered a grin that wasn't at all subtle before putting on her game face.

"On your mark, get set, go!"

Dion's white flag came down, and Lexi urged Jackie O forward with a *whoop*. Razor was quicker off the mark, which Lexi had expected, but Jackie O's desire not to be left behind had the mare snorting as she caught up with her opponent. The two horses raced neck and neck for the next five hundred yards, and Lexi couldn't help chuckling at Will's strained expression. His brows crowded together like a hedgerow as he hunched behind Razor's head.

With the finish line looming, Lexi's lungs expanded and contracted powerfully, her body making very little contact with the saddle. She would have thought they were flying if it hadn't been for the sound of Jackie O's hoofbeats. She knew Will would make his move soon, and when they reached the last four hundred yards, he didn't disappoint.

As he spurred his horse faster, Lexi's endorphins skyrocketed as she called to her horse.

"Giddyap, Jackie O! Beat that gelding!"

Encouraged by Lexi's enthusiasm, Jackie O sprinted like lightning, and Lexi's muscles clenched as she held on like her life depended on it. Which it did. If she lost her grip now she'd get thrown at twenty-five miles an hour and smash her head on the rocks. Not a pretty ending to a harmless challenge.

As the finish line approached, a gust of wind seemed to carry Jackie O the last few yards, blasting them ahead of Razor and beating his arrogant rider by half a length. Jackie O's coat was glowing a vivid yellow, just like yesterday when they had raced Dion on the beach, and Lexi felt as though a current of electricity was running through her. She had to force her attention back to reality when she saw Razor weaving into them, and she quickly wiped the satisfied grin off her face as Jackie O tried to change directions and stop at the same time.

"Whoa, girl!" Lexi's balance shifted quickly, and her heart stuttered when she realized she was going down. She hurried to free her boots from the stirrups, but the shooting pain in her calf told her she wasn't fast enough as she toppled sideways off her horse.

The unforgiving wet sand came at her like a brick wall, jarring her body with a painful crunch, and she headed toward the surf in a tuck and roll maneuver. She finally came to a stop in the surf, spitting sand and saltwater from her mouth, and the shadow of a horse appeared in her peripheral view, followed by the thump of boots.

"Lexi, are you okay? Razor didn't want to—"

"What the hell?!" Lexi sat up and winced at the pain shooting through her shoulder. "Don't you know anything about racing etiquette? Reins are for steering, dumbass!"

"I'm sorry, it felt like the wind pushed us off course. I swear."

He stuttered through his lame apology, appearing more interested in something over his shoulder than in helping Lexi to her feet. If she hadn't felt like throwing up, she would have pummeled the clod into next week.

Voices carried up the beach, and she knew what was distracting Will. She watched the color drain from his face, no doubt anticipating the sting of someone's fist, as her family sprinted toward them for all they were worth. Luke and Uncle Z appeared to be engaged in their own competition, but Lexi was more concerned about her parents. They would probably forbid her from ever racing again. It was a good thing she was cutting the apron strings this weekend.

Jackie O nudged Will aside to stand next to Lexi. At least *she* knew how to be helpful, and Lexi slung her arm—the one that didn't feel like it was broken—over the horse's neck. Luke and Uncle Z reached her at the same time, and without even thinking of the consequences, she stepped into Luke's outstretched arms, ignoring her godfather completely. She already knew what a scowl looked like.

Eight

As soon as Luke was sure that Lexi had chosen him, he swept her off her feet and carried her to the estate. He couldn't decide which he enjoyed more, having Lexi fall into his arms or seeing the stupefied look on Z's face when she did. But Luke didn't waste time gloating. Lexi had a lot on her mind, and she used the trip to verbally lambaste the boy who had caused her grief.

"I have never met a more idiotic, arrogant, muscle-headed clod in my life. If you're going to brag about how competent you are at something, you damn well better prove it."

"I agree," he said.

"Why do boys have to be so full of themselves? Don't answer that. I know why. They have egos the size of Mount Everest. Too bad their brains are the size of walnuts. I swear, if they weren't so obsessed with outdoing everyone, they might realize that women have more to offer than pouty lips and child-bearing hips."

"Right again."

"I may not have a lot of experience with men, but I'm not clueless. I won't fall for just anyone. The man I choose will respect my mind and take me seriously when I say I'm going to kick his ass."

"I can't argue with that."

Lexi squeezed her eyes shut and breathed heavily through pursed lips. Luke hoped his commentary hadn't stifled her rant. He was enjoying himself immensely. He'd met too many women who were afraid to let go and show off their intense spirit. And it said a lot about Lexi that her family had not managed to smother hers.

"I apologize for going off like that," she said. "I'm not usually so whiny."

"*Whiny* is the last word I'd use to describe you. And you don't need to apologize to me. Your anger is perfectly justified. Will behaved like a clod."

The others were still trying to catch up when they arrived at the pool, and Luke delighted in Lexi's closeness, her arm wrapped around his neck and her hand gently resting on his chest. The intimacy made him acutely aware of his pulse, and an unexpected lightheadedness nearly caused him to stumble onto the deck.

"You might want to soak in a hot bath," he said. "You probably strained a few muscles breaking your fall. A medicinal oil like clary sage makes a soothing rub."

"I'll be lucky if they're just strains. But you're right. A good soak is just what I need." Lexi caught him in a gaze that mimicked the sky. Her lips were quite close. Was she aware of him looking at them? "You can drop me off here."

She pointed to a chaise next to the pool, and he set her down somewhat reluctantly. He watched her take stock of her injuries, and she grimaced when she pressed on her left shoulder. She pulled off her boots and socks, taking a moment to inspect her ankles.

"No broken bones, so that's a relief."

She stood and walked to the edge of the swimming pool,

offering him a cheeky grin before diving in, clothes and all. Luke laughed despite the seriousness of her recent trauma.

"When I said a hot bath, I wasn't thinking of the swimming pool," he said.

"*Au contraire*. It was the perfect suggestion. The pool is heated. Care to join me?" She smiled up at him, her lips glistening with moisture.

Luke needed to make some important choices, and fast. He hadn't intended to become enchanted by her, and the risks of a liaison were potentially disastrous for both of them. He recognized Lexi's fascination with him. He also noticed that she wasn't interested in following her family's directives this weekend. She was establishing her boundaries, and he was part of her battle plan.

And a battle was definitely coming for her. A battle she wasn't likely to recover from as quickly as she'd done after today's skirmish. Luke hadn't come to the party to get recruited. Rather, it was to be entertained by the warped spectacle of it all. He had to credit his insatiable curiosity, and perhaps his loneliness, for how swiftly his intentions had changed.

Lexi swam toward him, her eyelashes laden with water droplets, distracting him once again. "Don't tell me you've never gone swimming in your clothes before."

"Actually, I have. Not always on purpose."

"Well, then, what are you waiting for? Your linen shirt shouldn't need to be dry-cleaned."

He chuckled, wishing things were as uncomplicated as a ruined shirt. How nice would it be, though, to feel something again? He bent down and pulled off his shoes and socks, feeling a jolt of emotion in the process. But which one? Intrigue? Fear?

Infatuation? And Lexi laughed the whole time, joking about his leather shoes being stained by the seawater and how he would have to remain barefoot for the rest of the weekend.

Her amusement continued after he jumped in, although he *did* catch her grimacing when she swam toward him. They met in the shallows, where their feet could touch the bottom, and, for a moment, her unfiltered smile made him forget the risks.

"Thanks for carrying me home," she said. "You make a decent hero."

"If that's to be my role, I'll fulfill it to the best of my ability."

Lexi bit her lip, a seductive maneuver whether she knew it or not. Was she okay with him staring at her? Certainly other men had done it. Had desired her. How many had she desired in return? Did she want to kiss him? Did she want *him* to kiss *her*? Right now? As voices echoed up the path?

He reached for her hand and held it under the water. She used the connection to bring their bodies closer until he was able to count the droplets on her skin. Surely she heard the voices too. How willing was she to take such a risk? She tugged on his hand again, sending the water rippling away as their chests collided and their lips met.

The contact was electrifying but much too brief. Lexi's mother walked through the cypress trees and the kiss ended before it had even started.

"Lexi, are you okay? Why are you swimming in your clothes? Did you fall in?" She spoke to her daughter but her eyes were narrowed on Luke. Granted, he might have appeared guilty as he splashed away from Lexi.

"I'm okay, Mom. I just wanted to take a swim without the hassle of changing."

Luke realized Lexi's face had flushed a stunning pink just moments before she dunked her head under the water. Z arrived and scowled at Luke. It had been a while since they'd sparred, and it felt like old times. But Z was gunning for Lexi as she surfaced.

"How do you feel, young one?" Z asked her. "Did you break anything besides that poor boy's ego?"

"Nothing is broken. I'll be fine. Thanks for coming to my rescue, though."

"Well, it appears you didn't need *my* help today. But you can always call on me if anyone else tries to put you on your back."

Z pivoted on his heel and made for the estate, probably to find a bucket of ice to soak his fat head in. It took a lot of provoking and good reason before Luke entered any kind of battle. And he certainly didn't wish to do that with Z now. But his motives were changing as fast as thunder followed lightning.

He had discovered Lexi's spark, and he worried that they would try to snuff it out. He couldn't leave her to defend herself alone. It wouldn't be easy. Nothing involving Z ever was. He just hoped she wouldn't hate him when she finally learned the truth.

Will offered a formal apology to Lexi and her family before he and his parents made a run for it, after which the remaining guests embarked on a less dangerous version of horseback riding on the trails that traversed the property.

After her parents forced her out of the pool, her dad started a fire in the fireplace even though it was plenty warm, and she suspected he was exaggerating the seriousness of her trauma for the benefit of Will's family. After she changed into her fleeciest sweatpants, she snuggled under a blanket on the couch, insisting that Luke stay and keep her company. And nobody dared to give her grief about it.

Sitting at her feet, Luke paged through a book thoughtfully. Now and then he would stop to tug the blanket over her toes when they slipped free. Each time his fingers brushed her skin a fresh wave of chills would ripple up her calves. She only hoped he wouldn't discover that she was moving the blanket on purpose.

Lexi also hoped he couldn't read her mind because—holy crap!—that was the best almost kiss she'd ever had. If her family hadn't shown up she might have swooned. Luke's lips tasted like freedom, in spite of how tragically brief it was. But she couldn't help wondering if she'd been too pushy. He seemed hesitant, even though his eyes were beckoning her closer. She still didn't know about his relationship status. Was it wrong that she didn't care?

Her experience with men totaled three, which included a pop singer who occasionally made an appearance in her dreams. Were her feelings for Luke purely physical? She didn't think so. As far as she could tell, he had a brain and he knew how to use it. And he talked to her like she had one too. Was that why she wanted to tackle him right there on the couch and taste his lips again? For his brain?

She stared at him until he looked up from the book, his eyes smoldering and sexy. Did he do that on purpose or was it totally unscripted? What was he thinking? Did he appreciate her outlook on life? Her sense of humor? Did he feel the same rush when their bodies connected? Like two stars colliding?

Lexi tucked a strand of hair behind her ear, switching her attention to the crackling fire so he could get back to the book.

He'd discovered their Greek mythology collection, and when he chuckled, she hoped it was triggered by something he'd read.

"Have you read much Greek mythology, Luke?" she asked.

"I'm fairly well-versed. I find the stories fascinating."

"What do you find fascinating about them? Is it because the gods run around doing whatever the hell they please?"

Luke laughed and closed the book on his lap. "They do, don't they? I've developed my own theories on how the gods might handle things, although some of it conflicts with what's written in these books."

"Please, tell me." Lexi sat up straighter, although she was careful to keep her feet within reach of his hand. As if reading her mind, he tucked the blanket under her heels.

"Take Mnemosyne, for example. This Titan is responsible for the pool of memory in the underworld, a counterpart to the Lethe River. Those who drink from it are granted the ability to retain their memories and stop the transmigration of the soul. This is rarely mentioned anywhere. It seems obvious she spent more time in the underworld than what is written in most texts, and I believe the story and the Titan deserve more credit here."

Lexi grinned at the cute way Luke jutted his chin after he made his point. That strong, clean-shaven chin. "There's only one source I know of that references the pool of memory, which tells me you're more well-versed than you let on. What's your take on Orpheus and Eurydice?"

"Orpheus was a fool. He was asked to do one simple thing, and he blew it. Their story is the perfect example of what happens when we lack faith and don't trust others to make good on their promises."

"Sometimes people don't make good on their promises."

"True. And there are consequences to be paid on both sides. The Fates don't miss a thing."

"You talk about the gods like they're alive and well and could be living among us."

"Who's to say they aren't?" He shrugged his indifference but the twinkle in his eyes told a different tale. "Do you have a favorite myth?"

"Probably the story of Persephone. She was wooed by many gods because of her beauty and purity. But Demeter and Zeus kept her isolated because they didn't think anyone was good enough for her. Hades felt sorry for Persephone, and he fell in love with her after watching her from afar. So he took her to the underworld and made her his mate. I'm sure you already know the story. It's one of the most popular."

Luke appraised Lexi with a cocked head. Did he believe a different version of the story? She felt compelled to continue her defense.

"Most people view Hades's actions as selfish and ruthless, but I think the story is a metaphor for passion taken to the extreme. One version even says that Zeus allowed the kidnapping when he got tired of all the suitors vying for Persephone's affections."

Luke slapped the book cover and filled the room with throaty laughter. "If you've read anything about Zeus, you would know *that* version of the story is horseshit. Persephone was in love with Hades. He did her a favor by removing her from the stranglehold of her parents."

Luke's cheeks grew flushed as he argued his point, and Lexi didn't know what to think of his impassioned response. It was something she'd asked herself about her own parents' preoccupation with the gods. Before she could question him, Luke gave her one of his cure-all smiles.

"You think I'm strange, don't you? I can see it in your eyes."

"I don't think you're strange. My mom wanted the family to practice Hellenism for a while. She named me Alexandra in honor of the Olympian Hera. And my brother is named after Dionysus."

"It sounds like your parents believe there are more truths than what the world tells them. Maybe the term *myth* was invented to hide the truth that the gods really *do* exist."

Lexi wanted to humor Luke, but it was difficult. Back when she believed there was more to life, more than status and wealth and following rules, she had considered the prospect of the gods living in the modern world. But it was too far-fetched. Someone would have noticed a bunch of magical beings wandering around.

Her parents walked into the room, with Cherry hurrying to get ahead of them before they made it to the bar. They were talking about the family from Kolkata before they remembered she and Luke were there, and the gossip stopped abruptly.

"How are you feeling, Lexi?" Her dad dropped her mom off at a bar stool and continued toward the couch. "I'm glad we thought to get that fire started."

Lexi didn't think it was the fire warming her up, but she kept that to herself. "I may live to see Casablanca."

"Casablanca?"

Damn. She'd planned to wait until the weekend was over before mentioning that little addition to her travel plans. "Yes. I'm thinking of including it in my itinerary. But we can talk about that later."

A glance was exchanged between her parents, which was interrupted by Cherry handing a drink off to her mom.

"I hope you'll feel well enough to spend time with the other guests soon," said her dad. "Rod and his family are thinking about cutting their visit short too. And I would hate to think it's because you've been snubbing the young man's interest."

"Rod's only interest is property values in Eagle Hill."

"I'm sure that's not true. I know he's a swimmer. He was challenged to swim the English Channel."

Lexi snorted. "Please. Rod is no different than Will—a self-absorbed peacock. Do we have to talk about this now? I was just starting to enjoy myself."

Luke stood and carried the book back to the shelf, escaping the awkward moment like any reasonable person would, and Lexi prayed her dad would just leave it.

Fat chance.

"I think you've been spending too much time with one guest," he went on. "There are plenty of people here who would like to enjoy your company. Burt says you haven't spoken five words to him."

"Burt's here all the time adding wine to our collection. I thought this weekend was about me having fun, not about me making sure other people have fun."

In a not-so-covert maneuver, her father leaned in and spoke against Lexi's ear. "I don't want to see you disappointed. Luke may be handsome and well-spoken, but he's not the type to stick around for the ending credits. If you insist on pursuing him, we're going to have a problem."

Apparently, this *was* happening now.

"Let me get this straight—just yesterday I confronted you about the obvious scheme to set me up with some boastful, entitled gel head, and you said to throw in my line to see what I could reel in. Well, I took your advice, and I'm happy with my catch."

Her father hovered like an eagle on its perch, all narrowed eyes and laser focus, while her mom was being unusually quiet as she arrived with his drink. Lexi didn't know whether to feel relieved or neglected.

"Your godfather doesn't trust this man to have your best interests at heart, and I trust your godfather's counsel," her dad said, making no attempt to keep his voice down. "Let's not drag this out. If you're feeling better, why don't you go upstairs and change for lunch."

Lexi didn't roll her eyes, but she *really* wanted to. "None of you have ever trusted me, and I've never given you a reason not to. I've been busting my ass for excellence, and the shitty thing is, none of it has been for me. Was an all-girl boarding school *my* choice? No. Was Boston College? No. Have I ever attended a party without a chaperone? No. If I continued to leave you all in charge, which I don't plan to, I'd be an old maid at thirty!"

Her dad shook his head, as if *he* was the frustrated one. "Take a breath, baby."

Ignoring the pain, Lexi threw off the blanket and stood to face her parents. "I am not your baby anymore. I'm an adult who can make her own decisions—and her own mistakes—and learn from them, for better or worse. I'm taking a solo trip this summer and none of you are allowed to interfere, or I might do something extreme."

"Extreme? How?" her mother asked, looking concerned for the first time in a long time.

"If I told you that, you'd expect it."

Her dad's face bloomed, just like the Graham Thomas roses pressing their faces against the window behind him, as if trying to catch all the gossip. "Don't you threaten us. We work hard to make sure you have a good life. Privilege doesn't come with a guarantee. It can be revoked."

"Who's threatening who?" A rage Lexi had rarely experienced boiled beneath her skin. Or maybe it was fear. What would she do if they cut her off? Had money become her safety net? Had her privileged life made her vulnerable? Her fingers tingled, like sparks were trying to escape, but she didn't look down to confirm it.

She sensed Luke's presence behind her, just close enough to make her feel less alone. Then Nora walked in and stopped suddenly, as if the drama in the room had created an invisible wall. Her parents turned, making it clear she'd interrupted them, but Nora simply shrugged and stood her ground. Lexi appreciated that.

But this was *her* fight, and her freedom was worth more than her stock holdings, so she barreled on.

"Every time I meet an expectation, you add another one to the list. How long did you expect me to live by your rules? Forever? Would you want someone to control the way you lived? Handing out freedom only when it suited them? Try putting yourself in my shoes, for once."

Her parents did something then that she hadn't expected. They looked surprised, blinking at each other like they'd been denied sunlight for a week. Were they worried Lexi might disappear off the map until she was ready to be found? Surely, it wasn't empathy.

Her dad rallied, setting his jaw, and growling his rebuttal. "How much freedom do you think I have? Sometimes honoring commitments is more important than freedom."

"Those commitments have never been mine to honor. And the last time I checked, slavery had been abolished."

"Didn't you hear, Lexi? Privilege is the new slavery." Her mom put in her two cents before downing half the liquid in her glass.

The other guests were starting to file in, but no one seemed to notice the tension. Cherry hurried to fill drink orders, and there was talk of the extraordinary lunch being served on the patio. Lexi was grateful for the guests, and she allowed herself to get caught up in the party atmosphere. She had said her piece, which was long overdue. Regardless of the outcome, this would be her Gettysburg.

Nine

While lunch was served, Lexi went upstairs to change clothes and rub ointment on her bruises. Away from the others, she decided she needed more time before facing her parents again. They'd had plenty of arguments, and Nora had been privy to a few, but it sucked that Luke was being dragged into her melodramatic life.

Cherry brought up a plate of food, and Lexi enjoyed her summer salad and baked brie on the balcony. Her private hideaway hung over a courtyard in the southwest corner of the estate, above the French doors to her father's study. The rows of cypress trees offered her some anonymity as she watched lunch taking place on the patio.

She made a point of locating Luke first. He'd placed himself in the perfect spot for her to view him between the trees, and he seemed genuinely engaged in a conversation with Nora, which was no surprise. They were both excellent at it. But every so often she would catch him glancing at her balcony. She couldn't help wondering if the fight had convinced him to heed her parents' warning and keep his distance. Or maybe even to cut his losses and leave for Asia sooner than he'd planned.

As guests finished their meals and began to migrate inside, Luke fortified himself with a large gulp of wine then stood and left Nora with a crooked grin. Lexi lost sight of him after that, which triggered a pain in her chest that had nothing to do with her fall on the beach. Would he disappear without saying goodbye? They'd shared an almost kiss.

Lexi left her seat and moved around the balcony, trying to get another glimpse of him. With Luke gone, there would be nothing to make the party bearable, except for Nora. Maybe Nora had his cell phone number. Would it be weird if she contacted him that way? She didn't want to come off like a stalker.

"Psst."

The sound came from below, and she hurried to the opposite side of the balcony to investigate, crossing her fingers. Luke was there, standing in the courtyard, partially hidden behind a hedge. Her heart literally fluttered with relief.

"Well, hello, there," she said. "Did you enjoy your lunch?" Her voice hitched but she didn't care. Something about his posture—hands tucked into the pockets of his pleated pants, head cocked casually—immediately soothed her.

"The food was delicious but conversation at the table lacked a certain . . . unreserved point of view." He offered a simple smile, and Lexi held tighter to the railing.

"I promise not to tell Nora you said that."

He chuckled as he glanced from side to side. "I expect my movements are being monitored, but I wanted to check on you to be sure you're feeling better. How are the bruises?"

"They're a nice eggplant color. If Will had stayed I would have worn my dress with the spaghetti straps just to show them off."

"You should do whatever you like. And I support your right to fight for it."

Luke couldn't have said anything more thoughtful, and she prayed that he really meant it as she admired the way the sun played with his hair.

"Thanks, that means a lot. To be honest, it's been hard finding anyone who understands. Most people just see the money and expect me to have a perfect life. You're seeing me reach my wit's end. Lucky you."

She lowered her face, almost wishing it wasn't so easy to talk to him. He was learning all her darkest secrets before he even knew about the good stuff.

"I don't think we can give luck credit here. I like to treat these kinds of circumstances as fortunate events. Not that they're all pleasant. But even unpleasant events can bring unexpected rewards later. Your rewards seem well justified, if there's a battle to be had."

"And will you be here or in Asia for that?"

Lexi stretched farther over the balcony, looking for tells on his face through the shadows of the cypress trees. He never flinched.

"A captain needs a second, right? And Asia isn't going anywhere." He glanced around again, while she struggled to keep her feet on the ground. She wanted to be with him so badly.

"This could well be the battle of my life. What qualifications do you have? Can you help me form a battle plan?"

He made a show of scratching the back of his head. "I'm sure I packed some in my suitcase. I never leave home without them."

She let her laughter roll without worrying about possible bystanders. "I suppose there's no better time than the present, then. Meet me inside the stand of pines out front in ten minutes."

At first he appeared hesitant to help her explode her life, his forehead creasing as he gazed up at her. But it only lasted a few seconds. "Aye, aye, Captain."

Lexi opted for a button-down blouse and jeans in place of something fancier. She was taking Luke on the estate's private path, and it required sensible clothes. As for her escape plan, she might have chosen to climb off her balcony using the folding boat ladder she kept under the chaise—a gift from her brother after she'd broken her ankle jumping off the railing—but she didn't trust her injured body not to fail her. Instead, she chose to follow her usual escape route through her dad's study and hope for the best.

The first leg of her journey was a piece of cake, as everyone seemed to be outside enjoying the garden maze. When rounding the corner into the study, however, she found Cherry with her head inside the mahogany liquor cabinet. Lexi started to back out, but Cherry was a pro.

"Can I get you anything, Miss Maxwell? More food? Bandages?"

"I'm fine."

Cherry pulled out a bottle with a black-and-gold label. It looked old, and she talked as she brushed the dust off with her apron. "Have you come down to rejoin the party?"

Lexi wasn't admitting defeat yet. "Yes and no. I was cutting through my dad's study to avoid certain . . . conversations. I think I'll say hello to Jackie O first. I want to see how she's doing."

Lexi crossed the room, navigating the furniture, while Cherry continued dusting. "I understand. You'd prefer that no one knows where you are for the moment."

Taking hold of the doorknob, Lexi glanced at the clock on the wall, quickly deciding how much time she had before Cherry spilled the beans. "Yes. Thanks, Cherry."

"Just be careful. Your bruises are fresh."

No. The bruises have been there for a while. "I promise, I won't be riding."

Lexi opened the door and peeked outside. A handful of people remained on the patio, but most of them were staff. She made a quick exit, then a hard right before sprinting along the west side of the estate. Fortunately, that side held nothing of great interest, just the garages. The only person she could run into was Ham.

Lexi crossed her fingers as she stopped at the corner of the estate. A security camera blinked above her, but she knew nobody monitored them. Thankfully, the garage doors were closed, which meant Ham was helping somewhere else instead of tinkering with his limo. He treated that thing like it was his child, which she always thought was sad, since he'd never taken the time to have any.

It was an easy jaunt from there. Lexi just hugged the tree line leading to the front of the property, hiding in the shadows and avoiding protruding roots. She appreciated that some of the grounds were left unmanicured. Some things in nature were more beautiful when allowed to grow wild.

At the stand of pines, Luke was waiting.

"Good, you made it," she said. "I got busted on my way out by one of our live-in staff, Cherry."

His brows rose. "Was there trouble?"

"No, but she'll eventually have to tell someone. We have about twenty minutes before a search party is sent out."

"Did you have somewhere in mind rather than here?"

"Yes. I thought I'd show you more of the property. There's a path that leads to the stables then out to the sea."

"That sounds perfect."

She thought about taking his arm, since it had worked at breakfast, but she'd been plagued with doubts since their almost kiss. She needed to know his relationship status. Sure, she was interested in exploring the wonders of romance, but maybe not the way Nora had described them. She didn't want to end up a casualty of *that* war.

Luke waved her forward, which seemed perfectly natural and not like he was avoiding contact. It didn't take long for her to become attuned to his proximity as they trekked through the woods. The warmth he gave off never seemed to leave him, and she could almost feel the sinew of his muscles as his arm swung beside her.

"So, are you making this trip to Asia alone?" she asked.

His smile didn't give away anything, like his suspicion that she was prying. "Yes. Most of my trips are taken alone."

"Is that by design? I've heard solo travel is quite different than traveling with others."

"I have precious few vacation days, so I tend to use them as personal time. Occasionally, I'll plan to meet someone along the way."

"Oh. Is it different people each time? Or the same person?"

This time Luke grinned, but she'd expected it. She appreciated that he wasn't clueless. "Different people."

Had her question been answered? If so, how did she feel about it? Was he telling her that he wasn't committed to one person? Was he reaffirming her family's warning that he couldn't be faithful to just one? If she pursued him any further was she destined to be a one-hit wonder on his playlist?

"Since we're on the subject of travel," he said, "after this solo trip of yours, what will *you* do? Are there any job prospects in the works to go along with that political science degree?"

Lexi rolled her eyes, then regretted it. She didn't want him to feel insulted for asking such a run-of-the-mill question. "I've been headhunted already. It's just a matter of picking someone to work for."

"You don't sound too enthusiastic about it."

She chuckled. "Good. That means I hadn't been wrong about you. To be honest, the poli-sci major was part of my dad's grand design. He thought it would open the doors he could walk me through. Did you know that my mom has a doctorate? A PhD in bioengineering. She put her career on hold to raise me and Dion and live in this Brobdingnagian eyesore. I think she was fine with it when we were kids, but now . . ."

"Now what?"

Damn. How much information was too much?

"She's not happy anymore. It may not be obvious to others, but it is to me and Dion. It's not her marriage either. She and Dad are thick as thieves. I think it's because she feels like her life isn't her own. I don't want to end up like that. I refuse to."

"Even if it means doing something extreme?"

"Yep. I'm testing to see how far the boundary stretches. Who knows, maybe a compromise can be reached without bloodshed. I'm tired of fighting."

They arrived at the stable, and Lexi fed Jackie O from the treat bag, thanking her friend for teaching that preppy clod a lesson. Then they took to the trail again, since there was a high probability of being discovered by someone in an apron. Besides, she wanted to show Luke her favorite spot, where the pines opened to the ocean, which she may have rambled on about until they arrived at the clearing.

"Who wouldn't love this view?" she said, waving her arm at the sea as if she had control over its awesomeness.

"Only the blind."

As they stood together, breathing in the salty spray and watching the surf roll up the beach, Lexi wished she *did* have more control over things. Not something so outrageous as over the forces of nature, but something that most people took for granted, like over her own life.

Suddenly, the hairs on her skin rose, and she realized they were responding to the touch of Luke's hand as it drifted down her arm. Then, ever so gently, he slipped his fingers between hers. He had initiated the connection. Proof that he was interested.

Holy crap.

"How often are you able to visit the ocean?" Lexi asked, as she rode a tidal wave of hormones. Hopefully, they hadn't already covered the topic.

"Not as often as I'd like."

"That's a shame."

"Would you like to hear a couplet I wrote about the sea?"

"I'd love that."

"*Turquoise, green, and sometimes gray, emotions in and out. / Those who dare to sit and feel, will nary have a drought.* I wrote it when I realized that I'd be spending more time away from the sea than with it. It's a reminder."

She turned to smile at him as warmth spread through her limbs. "It should be a reminder to us all."

Without a bit of warning, Luke pulled her toward him, and their bodies collided. Rather than push him away, she let him secure her in his arms as he backpedaled through the trees.

"I'm sorry if I startled you," he said. "There's a snake on the path, and I didn't want us to disturb his sunbathing."

Lexi glimpsed the snake as it slithered under a fallen branch. "That's a Maritime garter snake. They're harmless. But I appreciate your concern."

"I've made your welfare my priority this weekend."

Luke released his grip, lowering his hands to her waist and leaving them there. Thanks to the snake, their proximity had improved significantly, and his breathing pulsed in time with the crashing waves. Or maybe that was *her*.

"This is nice," he said.

"Yes, it is." She took a moment to appraise his lips, imagining. He was appraising her lips too.

"Lexi, I'd like to finish what we started in the pool. Before we were interrupted."

Lexi's throat turned against her, and she swallowed hard. She refused to swoon and miss her opportunity, but her body felt like melted wax. Luke appeared to be taking the plunge, no matter the risks. What kind of risks was he taking? Were they worse than backlash from her uncle Z or banishment from the estate?

Luke held her impossibly close, his heat soothing her like she'd been touched by the sun. Something else touched her as well, against her hip.

With only her fully aroused libido to guide her, Lexi uttered her reply. "Yes, please."

With the barest tweak of his lips, Luke leaned in and pressed his mouth to hers with incredible tenderness. Her heart raced as she submitted to the rush. It was superb. His lips were superb. And she was vaguely aware of his fingers trailing up her arm to the nape of her neck, lingering there as if to savor the experience before sliding through her hair in a sudden rush.

Before the spell could be broken, she ventured further,

opening her mouth and stealing a taste with the tip of her tongue. He responded with his pelvis, pressing his hand to the small of her back to urge their bodies closer. Then his tongue joined hers, dipping into her mouth and coaxing a gasp from her throat.

They stood amid the pines and seagrass, kissing like real lovers under the spring sunshine, the surf pounding the sand beside them. An hour might have passed, but it was probably only minutes before Cherry popped out of the path like a harmless, yet unwanted, snake.

"Pardon the interruption," she said softly, her cheeks looking as if they'd been sunburned. "I followed the voices from the stable. I'm here with a message, Miss Maxwell. A game of croquet is being set up and your godfather insisted you be present. He was putting on his boots to look for you, but I volunteered to come in his stead."

Cherry often seemed torn between her allegiances, and Lexi tried not to condemn the woman for her prying nature.

"Thank you, Cherry. I'll be there shortly."

Cherry left them, and when Lexi turned to Luke, he also appeared to have been exposed to too much sun. Was it from embarrassment or the heat of their kiss? Based on what she'd seen of his confidence and charm, she doubted he was easily embarrassed.

"I guess we need to head back before my family arrives with pitchforks," she said. "I'm not ready to do battle over a missed game of croquet."

"Au contraire," he said, rebounding with a smirk. "A croquet game sounds like the perfect field on which to do battle."

Ten

Luke Carrington had to be the most amazing man on the planet. He was humble, witty, handsome, even chivalrous. And that kiss. It was better than any kiss Lexi had ever imagined. What would have happened if Cherry hadn't shown up? How far would they have taken things?

Fortunately, it was only Dion on the croquet lawn when Lexi arrived, making it easy for her to act casual and help him set up. Luke had detoured to the east-facing path, giving the impression he'd been walking on the beach.

"What did Mom and Dad say to piss you off this time? Nobody would tell me," Dion pried as he tapped a wire wicket into place with his mallet, adjusting it with a tug to form a perfect arch.

"Of course, nobody would tell you. It was *their* fault. They want me to stop spending time with Luke. Dad thinks I'm chasing off the boys he invited. Well, I say good riddance to bad rubbish."

Dion snorted. "You really showed up that tight-assed Argentinian boy. How're you feeling, by the way? Can you swing a mallet?"

Lexi rubbed her shoulder and grimaced when pins and needles

radiated down her arm. "I'll be reminded of his stupidity for the next few days. But it was worth it. Maybe he'll have a clue now."

"I doubt it."

She followed him as he counted his steps and stopped to pound in the next wicket.

"Is this guy really worth all the trouble?" he asked, his head lowered as he hammered. Was he hiding a scowl? Surely he wasn't about to pass judgment on Luke after their late-night conversation on the beach. Luke had said all the right things.

"Yes. He's the real deal. Realer than most of the people I've met. And he gets me."

"What makes you think he gets you?"

"A girl knows these things."

He looked up, his brows lifting skeptically. "I'm going to need more than that. Did something happen on the beach last night before I got there?"

"That's none of your business. I don't ask you about your personal life."

"Good. You're better off not knowing about that mess."

"What do you mean? Why is it a mess?"

Dion rarely got personal, but he seemed to be sharing more than usual this weekend, so Lexi probed as she walked to the next wicket location, which rested near the hedge that formed the south end of the garden maze.

"I understand what you're going through, that's all," he said, crouching to hammer the wicket. "Don't you ever wonder why I'm twenty-five and don't have a steady girlfriend?"

"Not really. You just turned twenty-five last month."

He gave her a pointed look. "Are we being serious here, or not?"

"Of course. I pegged you for a romantic and assumed the right girl hadn't come along. Better?"

He cracked a smile but it didn't last. Lexi shadowed him as they headed for the final wicket location. "There have been two girls I thought would be a good match for me, but it's not just me they're marrying, is it? Imagine yourself in their shoes—in Mom's shoes. It's like marrying into the mob, but without all the murdering."

"Believe it or not, I've used that metaphor before. Have you been breaking things off with girls because you don't want to ruin their lives? How altruistic of you, Dion."

"Tell no one," he said with a forced grin. "Lexi, I'm not trying to minimize your situation. The opposite, actually. I figure I only have a couple of years before I'm required to make a choice, whether I'm ready or not. Just keep that in mind when you're railing against the family's wishes. And I'd like to say one more thing."

His lips took a downward turn as he cradled the mallet in his bent elbow. "I know stuff about Luke. And Mom and Dad aren't wrong. If you keep pursuing him, shit is going to hit the fan."

Lexi held her jaw tight and relieved Dion of his mallet, speaking through clenched teeth as she hammered in the final wicket. "If you know something"—*slam*—"feel free to share it."—*slam!*—"Otherwise, shut the hell up about Luke!"—*slam!*

She stood and handed the mallet back as he eyeballed her warily. Then he knelt to adjust the wicket, which she'd hammered all the way into the ground.

"I can't tell you what I know," he said. "But you'll find out soon enough. Let's just drop it and play croquet."

"Fine by me."

Lexi walked across the lawn to greet the guests who were

beginning to arrive. She didn't want to be angry with Dion. His confession had sounded genuine. For a while she thought he'd turned spy for the family as her parents were always finding out about her missteps. But after she graduated high school he stopped checking in, even when they'd spend months apart. At the time she suspected he'd pulled away so there was less to report on her. Now she wondered if he'd just been busy managing his own version of family bullshit.

"*Buon pomeriggio*, signorina Lexi." Lady Twila's lilting voice seemed to ride the currents of the air as she sashayed through the grass like it was the red carpet.

Today, the royal beauty wore a flowing chartreuse gown that perfectly matched the new growth of leaves on the foxberry bushes. Lexi didn't doubt she had done it on purpose. Beside her, Luke and Nora had their heads bent in secrecy, while a safe distance behind them Uncle Z and Lexi's parents led the other party guests outside.

"Buon pomeriggio, signora Twila," Lexi replied, although her eyes were on Nora, who stowed a grin when she and Luke joined them next to the mallet stand. "Who's interested in a game of croquet? We can play teams or singles."

"I think your uncle Z is going to try his luck," Nora said.

"Uncle Z hates croquet. He calls it a sissy game."

Nora's grin was back as she glanced at Luke. "Well, Luke has issued Z a challenge. And we know how much your godfather loves to prove he's better than everyone else."

Still buzzing from their steamy kiss, Lexi addressed Luke without looking at his lips. "You're either a very brave soul or you don't know my uncle Z as well as you think you do. He's a poor sport and a terrible loser."

A wicked smile spread across Luke's face. "I know he is. That's why I did it."

Lexi shook her head. What made her think Luke was in control of his ego? Regardless of chivalry, he was still a man. "Let's play singles, then. I have no interest in teaming up with delinquents. It'll be me, Dion, Uncle Z, and Luke."

Lexi won the coin toss, which was not an advantage in the game of croquet. Still, she had confidence in her skills, as long as her shoulder didn't act up. While she advanced her ball to the middle wicket, she assessed the posture of her competitors. She didn't have to read Dion long. He sucked at croquet. But despite his hunched stance of resignation, she noticed a rare focus in his eyes.

Her uncle Z had begun a perimeter walk around the court. He was either trying to rattle her or had realized that his knowledge of the game was lacking. Emily joined him partway through and appeared to be offering pointers. Regardless of the weather, Emily always wore sturdy boots and a leather jacket, with fingerless gloves reinforced in thick hide that covered her knuckles, like she expected a fight to break out any minute. She wasn't far from the mark half of the time. Luke remained at a respectful yet watchful distance to Lexi's right, congratulating her position after she'd finished her turn.

When it was time for her godfather to make his play, he powered through his first two shots, which landed his ball beyond the wicket and forced him to backtrack. His growl silenced the murmur on the sidelines, and he stewed a few moments, pinching the bridge of his nose. His next move would require a light touch, something he didn't have much of. But he managed to tap his ball through the wicket, and Lexi bit her lip as she watched him take aim at hers.

While she knew he loved her like a daughter, he never gave Lexi an inch when it came to competition. Delivering a power-packed swing, he slammed his ball into Lexi's and sent it careening across the grass into the center of the court.

"Oh, that's going to cost you, Miss Maxwell." He grinned as he swung his mallet around like a toddler. It was tempting to banter back. He'd been pushing her buttons this weekend. But she couldn't afford to get sidetracked.

It was Dion's turn next, and it took him extra time to play through. But he did well on his first go, coming within a foot of Lexi's ball. This gave Luke a clear advantage, and his lips remained set as he navigated through the first three wickets in three clean shots. Lexi was so shocked that she broke her own rule about in-game banter.

"You didn't tell me you could play croquet, Luke."

"You didn't ask."

It made sense now why he had challenged her godfather, and she was tempted to comment on it. But the smile Luke offered was already ramping up her heart rate. Instead, she was forced to watch him target the two balls sitting helplessly in center court. Would he go after her or Dion?

He performed his next shot with calm resolve, and his ball seemed to move in slow motion as it rolled up to Lexi's and tapped it ever so gently. Was he trying to piss her off? Or was he reminding her of their amazing kiss among the pines?

"Pardon me, *mon ami*," he said with an innocent shrug. "We are on a battlefield, are we not?"

"Just remember that when I'm taking you down," Lexi retorted.

"I look forward to it."

"Enough talk! Get on with it, already!"

Uncle Z's grizzly bear–like voice shushed everyone, but Luke showed no sign that he was rattled. He continued to guide his ball easily through the middle wicket, earning another shot. Without a hint of hesitation, he sent his ball into Uncle Z's and knocked it out of bounds. He was now in the lead.

There was no doubt in Lexi's mind that Luke wanted to beat her godfather. He'd issued the challenge, which meant he had to win to save face. Even Lexi wanted Luke to beat him. But would Luke try to beat her?

She had no idea how competitive Luke was, although she was beginning to form a hypothesis as she watched the two men stare at each other across the lawn. If she had to guess, their history went a lot deeper than anyone had let on.

Luke's pulse hummed in time with his movements, carrying him through the game without drawing attention to the fact that he was using power beyond the realm of human perception. He knew Z was employing the same tactics, although with less finesse. As for Lexi, she had an advantage over everyone without any help.

Risking his edge, he glanced at her standing alone outside the boundary line. She held herself with easy poise, confident even under stress. What was she thinking of him as he battled with her godfather? Was their longtime rivalry obvious? Nora's unrestrained grin said yes.

Luke had two choices as he assessed the field: send Lexi's ball out of play and claim an easy victory over Z, or target Z and give Lexi an easy victory over everyone. Either choice held consequences, and as he weighed them, he was reminded of the kiss.

But not just the kiss. The delicate fragrance that sweetened Lexi's skin and the way her heart raced as she responded to him. He knew the rush was sublime. He'd felt it, too, as he tangled his fingers in her hair.

Of course, logic told him to stop encouraging Lexi's affection. She had torn down his wall and enchanted her way into his heart, which was a precarious place for anyone to be. He knew the sensible move was to send her ball and her infatuation flying. But it had been so long since he'd felt that kind of connection. Since he'd felt hopeful. Did it make him a fool to encourage it? Or was he a fool to ignore it?

"We're all looking forward to the big finale," Lexi said, pointing at the final pair of wickets, as if offering herself up as a casualty in his war.

Luke chose to follow his instincts, which had successfully carried him through many sticky situations, consequences be damned. He drew back his weapon and shot his ball into the one belonging to his nemesis. Z's ball bounced farther out of bounds, enough to give Lexi the advantage, and the audience drew in a collective breath as Z threw up his arms and roared. A powerful gust of wind followed the gesture, and everyone glanced anxiously at the sky, as if they were looking for lightning to follow. It wasn't far from the truth.

But Luke still had another shot, which could be his last if he didn't hit Lexi's ball out of play. Once again, he considered the outcome of a win. She'd been a worthy and gracious opponent, and he expected her to recover with no long-term resentment—unlike Z.

As he watched Lexi worry her lip, he decided that if this was to be his last move, he wanted it to be an honest one. So he chose not to use the laws of nature as he brought his mallet down. His ball took an eternity to move across the lawn, causing the spectators to go silent as it approached and missed Lexi's ball by the width of a dragonfly's wing.

Lexi clenched her fist at her side, although it looked like she wanted to raise it in triumph, and Luke stepped off the playing field, bowing humbly to her as he accepted the defeat. The onlookers drew close as Lexi aimed her mallet and drove her ball through the last two wickets, sealing her win with a resounding *clank* against the dowel.

Voices rose as the court quickly crowded with well-wishers, patting Lexi on the back and praising her skill. Luke listened to her engage with each person, offering grateful thanks along with a humble smile.

"Lexi has a strong spirit," Z said as he appeared beside Luke.

"On this, I will agree with you. I suppose you want to take credit for that."

"I take only the credit that is due me. Lexi is fearless on her own. She doesn't care whether she wins or loses. She's inspired by the challenge. You don't find many with such exemplary traits."

Luke nodded, wondering why Z wasn't grabbing him by the collar and throttling him. Of course, it would have drawn too much attention.

"I expect you'll be present when we tell Lexi the truth?" Z said.

"Yes. I believe she's aware there's a storm brewing. I'd hate to see her outnumbered."

Z's face pinched like he'd stumbled into a hornets' nest, and Luke almost felt reassured. A quiet opponent was often the deadliest. "If you take advantage of her vulnerability, I will crush you," Z growled.

Luke met Z's scowl without difficulty. "There's no need for threats, brother. I'm just saying there's more at stake than simply dashing her dreams, and I'm curious to learn what you consider to be 'the truth.' I've seen the signs, and you have too. It's obvious to everyone but her, which leads to accidents. Like the one today."

"The stakes are not your concern."

"They *are* my concern while I'm here." Luke stopped there. He knew his brother's limits, but that didn't make it easy to watch the sneer twist the tangles of hair that framed Z's mouth; the mask he never removed.

"I'm not denying that. But I want to make this as painless for Lexi as possible. In other words, one damn thing at a time."

Z walked away, shouldering his mallet like a sword, and Luke took it as a mercy. Of course, that didn't mean the threats weren't still there, waiting to land the next blow. Luke rarely felt the sting of regret, but he was beginning to wonder if the Fates were the ones really in control here.

Eleven

After the epic round of croquet, the wind picked up significantly, destroying hairstyles and making it difficult for other guests to play a proper game. Dinner service had to be brought indoors, which Chef Lorraine and her team easily adapted to. They'd prepared two free-range turkeys and a cornucopia of veggies, making the table look like it was fit for the gods.

Lexi had been floating on cloud nine ever since the kiss, and her win on the lawn had put a permanent smile on her face. So she didn't mind when her dad seated her next to James from Yorkshire, a boy she had barely spoken to. Luke claimed the seat opposite her, which gave her some reassurance. He had gone quiet after his congratulatory handshake, and she suspected he needed time to heal his ego before he would be ready to talk again. As she and Luke exchanged smiles behind their water goblets, James made his move.

"You were brilliant on the croquet court today, Lexi." His British accent triggered a memory of a bartender she'd spoken to at a London pub, before her father had rudely interrupted them.

"Thank you. Do you play?"

"I haven't played enough to get where you are, but I enjoy the strategy of it. It's not unlike backgammon in that way. Do you play backgammon?"

"My brother and I used to play a lot before he started working for the man. I take it you prefer backgammon to croquet?"

"Guilty as charged. I grew up playing with my brother, same as you. Now I play with my mates at Oxford."

"Oxford University? I wanted to apply there. But it wasn't in the cards." She glanced down the table at her parents and uncle Z—the reasons she didn't go to Oxford. They were the ones who held all of Lexi's cards.

"Can I interest you in a game after tea?" James asked.

Lexi didn't need to be told he meant dinner as she considered his offer. Three challenges in one day had to be a record for her. "Sure, why not? I appear to be on a roll today."

"Let's hope the dice rolls in your favor." James raised his glass to toast her, and his smile came across more genuinely than she'd expected.

His easy humor caused Lexi to grin back, and she gave the boy a more thorough inspection. She'd already noticed that James was on the taller side, with dark-blond hair that hung loose over his forehead without the aid of sticky products, and his brown eyes held a gleam of intelligent curiosity. A fine specimen by anyone's measure. It was a credit to Luke's overwhelming sex appeal that Lexi had dismissed James from Yorkshire.

As dinner was served, Lexi decided to give him another opportunity to prove he wasn't a one-hit wonder, and he managed to impress her with his knowledge on the sociology of gameplay, a subject she'd researched in college. She nearly forgot about the rest of the table until the toe of Nora's shoe made contact with her leg, and Nora offered a subtle chin jut toward Luke.

His eyes were narrowed on James, and he was stabbing his turkey breast mercilessly. Did Luke consider the Oxford boy with the British accent to be a threat? Lexi's diplomatic side decided to swoop in and try to smooth things over.

"You should sample Chef Lorraine's gravy, Luke. She uses buttermilk to thicken it. *C'est magnifique.*" She pushed the gravy boat across the table, directing Luke's focus away from mutilating his dinner. Somehow, he made it look casual.

"Thank you. Your chef is a credit to her profession. I'll extend my compliments after the meal."

He accepted her offer, and the exchange diverted Lexi's attention to their fingers as they met on the gravy boat. It was embarrassing how her hormones pulled her under like a riptide at such a simple touch.

Dessert arrived, a divine watermelon and strawberry sorbet served with lemon wafers, after which the guests were invited to enjoy cocktails at the bar. Luke hung back, waiting to pull out Lexi's chair.

"I was hoping you could introduce me to Chef Lorraine," he said. "I'd like to give her my compliments."

"Lexi, let's set up the backgammon board before all the good seats are taken." James made his own request as if Luke's comment didn't register.

It seemed diplomacy would be needed again, and Lexi did her best to assess the urgency of their expressions. She couldn't deny that she'd been a beast to all the boys since the weekend started, and she ought to be civil to at least one of them. James had earned points just by making it through dinner without annoying her, but she also wanted to nurse Luke's ego back to health after that blow on the croquet court.

Ultimately, it was her dad's CEO advice that she decided to follow: *If you try to please all the people all of the time, you end up pissing everyone off. It's best to choose what works for you.*

Lexi gave Luke her undivided attention. "I would love to introduce you to Chef Lorraine. But timing is important with the chef. If I bring in a guest before the staff has cleaned up, she'll mount my head in the meat cellar. Would you mind waiting through a game of backgammon?"

Luke smiled, showing no sign that he'd been put out. "Well played, once again. The kitchen tour can wait."

Riding the wave of another success, Lexi ushered James into the living room, and they set up the backgammon board on a high-top table. James took Lexi's drink order and walked over to chat with Cherry, who poured him something from the bottle she'd retrieved from the study. With a wineglass in one hand and something stronger in the other, he slipped onto the bar stool across from Lexi.

"What is that you're drinking?" she asked. "I noticed it came from my dad's special occasion cabinet."

James bit the edge of his lip as if ashamed of the contents in his glass. "It seems my dad and your dad both appreciate scotch whiskey. I've been drinking this brand for about three years."

"Wow. There are a lot of scotch whiskeys on the market. What are the odds he'd have your brand in his collection?"

"It was your dad who recommended it to my dad way back when. They've known each other as long as I can remember."

"Really?"

Lexi tried to avoid situations that made her feel stupid. She managed this by paying attention to her surroundings. So, why hadn't she heard of James and his family? Had their names just blended in with the random names that echoed out of her dad's study? She knew his web stretched pretty far. Even Rod had mentioned something about their dads investing in stocks that were finally paying off twenty years later.

"So, is it just you and your brother at home?" she asked.

"And a sister. They're both older. You might say I'm the spare." He laughed nervously as he fiddled with the game pieces.

"I'm sure that's not true. Your parents brought you all the way across the ocean for a party. I'm sure they did that for good reason."

When Lexi noticed the blush coloring his cheeks, she realized he must have figured out the reason, just like she had, and she hurried to roll her die so they could start the game. As fate would have it, she won the opening move, and she took full advantage of the six-five count.

During James's turn, she made a quick check over her shoulder to locate Luke. He'd taken a seat next to Nora. Lexi noticed he spent more time with her than any of the others. Who wouldn't? Nora never ran out of interesting things to say. Exactly the reason Lexi liked her. So, why was she imagining Nora on a runaway horse bound for the gorge?

James made his move, and Lexi had to force herself to focus on the game. Despite what James believed, the strategies needed for croquet were not the same as for backgammon, and he moved deftly across the board, leaving her struggling to keep up. It was especially difficult with Nora's singsongy voice tinkling above the drone of conversation.

James picked up a pip and tapped against the board it as he studied his options, a determined and admittedly attractive set to his lips. If she wasn't already infatuated with someone else, Lexi would have given him serious consideration—a thought that lasted only a second before her attention wandered back to the couch.

"Hey, Lexi. It's your turn," James said, and Lexi failed to suppress a flush of heat that took over her cheeks as she turned back to the table. "You seem distracted. I understand if you want to stop and give Luke a tour of the kitchen."

"No, no. I'm sorry. It's unforgivably rude of me to neglect you, James."

Lexi rolled the dice, shaking her head at the terrible position she'd put herself in. Dion would have eaten her alive by now. He was much better at backgammon than croquet.

Alas, Lexi's obsession with the sexy Luke Carrington ultimately caused her to break her streak, and three moves later, James finished with the win. But rather than gloat, he offered an apologetic shrug as he reached his hand across the table.

"You're a tough competitor, Lexi. I've been watching you take down your opponents one by one. I have to admit, when you ran that race against Will, it looked like you and your horse flew across the finish line. That is, before you really *did* fly. How are you feeling now?"

"Sore, but I'll heal."

"Unlike Will's ego." James chuckled. "He'll come up with some reason to excuse his behavior. I might have to miss his calls until he's had time to cool off and think about it."

"You and Will are friends?"

"Yeah. We've known each other a while." His gaze flicked to his father standing with her dad, likely bonding over their appreciation of scotch whiskey.

James put away the backgammon pieces while Lexi sipped her wine and put her thinking cap back on. Something covert was happening. It felt like a scheme that everyone was in on except her. Although James seemed like a reasonable person, with manners the other boys didn't have, that didn't mean he wasn't involved. It seemed her parents' plot went deeper than she'd initially thought. And she was going to get to the bottom of it, one way or another.

Luke had a difficult time controlling the burning sensation in his chest as he watched Lexi and James make a love connection. He knew it was the best course of action for her. It was high time she enjoyed herself fully. Perhaps, if she'd been allowed to date sooner, she would have men at her beck and call, possibly snubbing him for a more practical choice. She deserved a man who could stick around longer than an extended weekend. Someone to adore her. To nurture her.

Was Z right to suggest that Luke was taking advantage of her vulnerability? Was he letting his own feelings win over practicality? Would it even matter after tonight? He feared Lexi's feelings would be severely tested when she learned what he really did for a living. She could very well tell him to go to hell and stay there.

Luke waited for Nora to reach the end of her retelling of Antony and Cleopatra in verse form before he excused himself to visit the bar. The route he chose took him past Lexi and her new admirer. She offered him a wave and a half shrug, which looked like an apology. Did she feel guilty for enjoying the company of another man?

Luke cursed himself for his impatience before presenting a smile to Cherry. "Gin and tonic, two limes, no ice."

He knew Cherry was clued in, and almost certainly knew who he was as she handed him his drink with a shy smile that was anything but. He considered making conversation with her to give Lexi and James more time, but Lexi appeared at his shoulder.

"Thanks for being so patient, Luke. Are you ready for that tour?"

Lexi's enchanting eyes had him blinking over his glass, and he drank deeply, giving his body a rejuvenating blast of alcohol.

"Only if *you* are. Don't cut your conversation short on my account."

"It's fine. James and I can talk later. We ended up having more in common than I thought. Let's go see what Chef Lorraine is up to."

Lexi threaded her arm through Luke's elbow, guiding him as she spoke about the chef's illustrious career in France before she accepted the position with the Maxwells. Lexi's growing comfort level around him was amusing. Had she been emboldened by their kiss?

Inside the kitchen they found the chef hunched over a cookbook, commanding her staff of white aprons from a stool. "Are the potatoes fresh? We need two dozen for the hash browns."

"Oui, Chef," came a reply from the depths of a walk-in pantry.

Chef Lorraine glanced up when she noticed them, and a broad smile quickly replaced the serious expression she wore for her staff. *"Ah, mademoiselle Lexi. Avez-vous apprécié le repas?"*

"Oui, beaucoup, Chef. The meal was excellent, as usual. I would like to introduce you to my new friend, Luke Carrington."

Luke offered a polite nod to the petite woman, who barely stood higher than the countertops. She reminded him of his own head chef at home, and he tried not to stare at the blotch of flour on her cheek.

"I want to give my compliments on a superb meal. *Trés délicieux.*"

She blinked at him, possibly in recognition, although he didn't recognize her. "*Merci.* Do not hesitate to compliment my fine apprentices. One person cannot accomplish such greatness alone." She waved an arm toward the bodies, then barked again. "Tomas, what of the eggs? Can we make six quiches?"

A man with his body half inside a refrigerator called back, "*Oui, Chef.*"

"I can see you're busy with tomorrow's preparations," Lexi said. "We'll leave you to it." She leaned into the chef's face and kissed both cheeks. Then she wiped the smudge of flour off with her thumb.

The chef shook her head as her cheeks reddened. "You are growing up too fast, *petite fille.*"

"Feels like an eternity to me."

Lexi left the chef with a playful smile that stayed with her until they reached the formal dining room. All evidence of the evening meal had been cleared from the table, and lively chatter echoed through a closed door at the other end. They were quite alone.

Twelve

Lexi led Luke into the dining room in the hopes it would be empty of staff, and they walked to the large picture window. It offered the best view of the estate's vast hedgerow maze. She'd lost herself inside it many times, often on purpose. And this time of evening the setting sun lit up the trees like flaming torches. The window also provided a partial view of the croquet lawn.

Thinking back, her win on the court paled in comparison to the show she'd witnessed between Luke and her uncle Z. After her failed attempts to learn anything of value about their relationship, their unspoken banter during the game played out like a one-act drama.

"That was quite a game," she said.

"I swallowed a dose of humility today."

"So did my godfather, although you won't hear *him* admitting it."

"I'm well acquainted with his breaches of decorum."

Lexi smiled at his flowery speech. She could see Luke counseling the dying and saying all the right things. "Why does he always look like he wants to pummel you?"

"What can I say? We're both hardheaded. He likes telling people what to do, and I don't like being told what to do."

She laughed, but her amusement was short lived. Lexi was certain that her graduation party had been a setup, and she had no doubt that her godfather had helped devise the plot. It was probably the reason he threw that tantrum when Luke arrived to distract her. Maybe if she learned more about the Uncle Z she didn't know, she'd finally have an advantage.

"Why does it feel like every time I ask about your relationship with him, I get the runaround?"

She smiled to soften the accusation, hoping he'd take it that way. He responded with a sigh that didn't bode well.

"Lexi, one day I will answer all your questions about your godfather. I've kept a detailed account of my long, tumultuous relationship with him. Not only will the stories entertain, but they'll give you better insight into the reasons he behaves like he's the king of the world."

"I'd appreciate that. He acts more like he's royalty than a business investor."

"Is that what he told you?"

She squared her jaw and looked at him, preparing for more bad news. "Is that not true? Has he been lying to us?"

"No. He hasn't been lying about that. He does have a lot of irons in a lot of fires. But that's really all I'm at liberty to say. I've been given vociferous instructions to keep you in the dark until *he* is ready to tell you more."

"That's bullshit."

"Agreed."

"Well, he's not leaving this estate until we talk about why he has a problem with you. This is *my* home, too, and I want you to feel like you're welcome here."

"I would very much like that."

Lexi knew it was adrenaline that prompted her to turn and press her hand to his chest. If she couldn't get information about the plot, she could still use their solitude to see if he was up for something else. Luke's pulse fluttered beneath her hand. A good sign.

"Given all that's happened since you arrived," she said, hoping she wasn't about to ruin the mood, "I'd like to clear the air about something. For my peace of mind. And maybe yours."

"Call me intrigued."

"Your current relationship status. It hasn't been well defined. I'm unattached, by the way. If that hasn't become painfully obvious by now."

He smiled. "If you weren't, you'd have one jealous boyfriend to manage. And I apologize if I've given you the wrong impression of my character. I'm not currently engaged in a romantic relationship."

So, that settled that.

"And since we're making things perfectly clear," he went on, "any hesitation on my part is in no way a rejection. You're the reason I've stayed this long. But in deference to Z and your parents, I think any future liaisons between us should be held in secret. That is, if you want them to continue."

Lexi gave Luke's admission careful consideration, parsing out each section, because each one had significance. First, he was basically admitting that he liked her, which made her want to kiss him on the spot. The part about his deference to her godfather and his control issues was bullshit, but she'd do whatever it took to spend more time with Luke. So, *yes* to the secret liaisons.

"I'll admit, Uncle Z has been pissing me off more than usual this weekend, and I can't make any promises that I won't try to piss him off right back. But I'll let you do the honorable thing, and I'll try to do the same. When you live your life under a microscope, you learn how to make yourself scarce."

"I don't think you could get any scarcer. You're like a rare flower. One that blooms even under harsh conditions."

Luke brought his fingers to her face, and goose bumps followed his thumb as it drifted across her lips. She tried not to blink as his eyes talked to her, telling her to jump in. She had decided they were amber, liquid amber. Was she gaping at him? Her mouth had suddenly gone dry.

Just as suddenly, the mood switched from tender to fierce, as he leaned in to kiss her, his mouth open in a passionate possession, like he was desperate to take advantage of their moment alone.

Lexi slid her arm around his waist, and he pressed into her hips to share his need. How long had he been wanting this? She lowered her hand to his backside, and a moan rumbled in his chest as his fingers dug through her hair.

Then his lips left her mouth to explore her throat, chasing her galloping pulse down her neck. He kissed the lobe of her ear, twisting the delicate pearl earring with the tip of his tongue and triggering a shudder that rocketed straight to her groin. She dropped her head back, inviting him to explore, and a moan nearly escaped her too.

When he reached her chest, he pressed his lips at the V of her blouse, and the contact dazed her like a shot of tequila. The room echoed with their heavy breathing, and she pretended she couldn't hear the chime of voices outside the door and the high pitch of a piccolo as Octavius showed off for his audience.

Just when she thought her body might explode, Luke gently

pulled back, leaving a final soft kiss on her lips. She knew he was following his instincts to stop while they were ahead, but she would have risked everything to keep going.

"I wish we could never leave this room," he said. "But my conscience is telling me otherwise."

"At least one of us has a conscience this weekend."

Whatever Luke had planned with regards to deference, Lexi's plan was to have the time of her life right under her family's nose, and it was hard to wipe the goofy grin off her face as she and Luke rejoined the party.

They found Burt and listened to him hiccup through a description of the sparkling wine he'd picked up on a visit to a local winery, and not five minutes went by before James invited himself into their trio. Lexi had to give the boy credit for his bold move. It was especially entertaining when he started quizzing Burt about the bouquet of a certain French Chardonnay.

"You have discerning taste buds, Burt," James said. "What do you think defines the bouquet of French Chardonnay? There are so many regions where Chardonnay is produced."

Burt flung his hands onto his hips, as if it might stop him from swaying. "It must come from Burgundy, of course. I've sampled every wine from that area of France."

"Do you live in France?" James asked. "Your accent is hard to place. It sounds like postclassical ancient Greek. But I suspect it's modern Greek, possibly influenced by Corsican."

Everyone stared at James as he spouted his scholarly wisdom. Greek had always baffled Lexi. The alphabet alone was enough to scare off the most ardent language enthusiast.

"Do you speak Greek?" she asked him.

James nodded. *"Nai. Miláo ellinkiká?"*

Lexi raised her hands in surrender. "I only know enough to tell you that I don't speak Greek. But I'm impressed. You didn't tell me you were interested in languages."

"I did, but I don't think you were paying attention at the time."

Lexi's face went up in flames, which seemed to be happening a lot lately. "I'm sorry. That's horrible of me. I thought you were studying political history."

"I am, with a minor in European and Middle Eastern languages."

"I live in Corsica, if you're still interested, James," Burt interrupted them with a disgruntled huff. Then he eyeballed a bottle of champagne on a serving cart and tottered off.

As the evening grew later, the room gradually emptied, and it was near midnight when Lexi realized that only the misfits were left, plus James, who had spent half the evening shadowing Lexi and Luke. When he finally threw in the towel, he found Lexi at the bar pouring herself a glass of water.

"This has been a fun weekend, Lexi. I'm glad my parents asked me to come."

"I'm glad they did too." Lexi was dying to know if he'd been asked by his parents or forced into it, but prying would have made him uncomfortable, and he didn't deserve that. She already had the impression that he and his siblings were kept on tight leashes, just like she and Dion were.

"I wanted to let you know that I have to leave in the morning after breakfast. I have an important engagement on Monday that I can't get out of."

Lexi felt a pang of disappointment for wasting so much time ignoring James. He'd flown all the way from Europe to attend her party, and she'd almost totally blown him off. Luke and his golden eyes had done a good job of distracting her. No wonder they called it love-struck. It struck a person in the head and rendered them clueless.

"Let me get your number." She pulled her cell phone out of her jeans and swiped the screen. "I promise not to pester you. I know where to draw the line between friend and that annoying person who calls too much."

"I can't imagine you being annoying. Anyone who can fly a horse sounds pretty cool to me."

She laughed. "Thanks."

It felt strange sharing her number with a guy, but Lexi figured this was what her parents wanted. It was a miracle she'd connected with any of the boys they'd invited.

After pocketing his phone, James seemed uncertain, and his brows quirked inward. He glanced at Luke, who was across the room talking to Diana. Did he feel threatened by Luke? Was he going to do something about it? A second later, he bolted toward the stairs like a bee had stung him. As Lexi tried to puzzle out the strange behaviors of men, her uncle Z arrived wearing a grin.

"It looks like you're making good use of the weekend, Lexi. James comes from a high-achieving family. Did you know he was valedictorian?"

It was interesting to her that everyone except James had mentioned his valedictorian status. "Yes. And he seems like a decent person despite his high-achieving family."

Her godfather's grin turned into a smirk. James must have improved his mood. "Well, I'm glad you two are hitting it off. Do you mind joining me and your parents in your father's study? There's something we want to share with you."

Hmm. Was this another graduation surprise? After two parties, she hadn't expected anything else. They still needed to approve her itinerary. Maybe that was it. The way they'd been behaving this weekend, they owed her. But they'd have to do better than a new set of luggage.

Thirteen

Lexi knew something strange was up when the whole group of misfits followed her into the study. Even Luke joined them, and she watched him take a seat in the old wingback and massage his temples. On the other side of the room her parents stood in solidarity, mute and stiff-backed. When her uncle Z shut the door, it felt like the air had been siphoned out. She no longer believed they were presenting her with luggage.

"Let me be the first to tell you how proud I am of you, Alexandra," he said. "You have grown into a capable, intelligent, and self-assured woman."

Heads bobbed around the room as he shepherded Lexi toward her dad's mahogany desk, leaving her in front of it as he barreled on, talking more to his audience than to her.

"We've watched you blossom like a well-tended rose, and we all feel you're ready to receive our endowment. A passing of the torch, if you will. Your brother gained certain privileged information when he came of age, and now we can bestow the same privilege on you."

"What kind of endowment?" She glanced at her parents,

joined at the hip. No doubt they had been told to give her uncle Z the floor.

"Your parents have been providing us refuge here, Lexi. Everyone present, and the others who were unable to attend this event. We all share a kinship. Without your parents' gracious hospitality, we couldn't enjoy the fruits of your world in the way that we do. Of course, it used to be *our* world—a long, long time ago—until it became too troublesome for the gods to live among the mortals."

Lexi squeezed the edge of the desk as the sensation of losing consciousness swept over her. What was he saying?

"What gods would those be?" she asked.

While she focused on her breathing, he turned his attention to her parents, who nodded submissively.

"The gods from your books of mythology," he said plainly. "We are them. And we are anything but myths."

For a moment Lexi held her breath. Then she burst out laughing. She'd never understood her godfather's humor, but this was a stunt she could easily picture him pulling.

"Nice try, Uncle Z. You might have been able to fool me when I was younger, but I'm too old for that now. I'm afraid you'll have to try harder than that."

He grinned. "I thought you might say that. Allow me to provide you with some evidence."

He gestured to Lady Twila, who stood and opened the French doors leading to the courtyard. The wind rattled the doors on their hinges and quickly flung them back toward the frame. Her godfather raised an arm, stopping both doors abruptly before they slammed. She didn't know how he was doing it, but the effects were clear. Some invisible force was holding the doors in place, and they creaked and shuddered against the strain.

Meanwhile, the wind swirled around the room, lifting papers off the desk and whipping the curtains like unlashed sails. To add to the mayhem, he released a bolt of what appeared to be lightning that rocketed between the open doors. A snap of thunder pursued it, and Nora squealed with delight.

With a flamboyant sweep of his arm, he commanded the doors closed again, and the curtains fluttered back into place. The air tasted of electricity, metallic and tangy, and Lexi ran her fingers through her hair, sending pinpricks skittering across her skin.

"That was impressive, but I'll bet I can explain everything that just happened with a little research on the internet," she said.

His eyes popped in surprise, as if he'd truly thought his trick would deceive her. "You've become more skeptical in your old age. I suppose I'll have to try harder."

He turned to Emily and Diana, motioning them to opposite sides of the room. Emily wore an eager smile, and wiggled her eyebrows at Lexi almost tauntingly. However, Diana's pinched lips said she was less pleased with being ordered around.

"Don't take your eyes off these two, Lexi. Diana has agreed to only one demonstration of her skill."

Lexi knew that Diana was a master archer, but there was no bow or arrows in sight, and she was completely unprepared when the two women changed before her eyes. Emily took the form of Diana and Diana now looked exactly like Emily, right down to her fingerless gloves. After a few moments of trying to convince herself not to believe what she was witnessing, Lexi abandoned the desk to stand with her parents. The two women waited until her focus was on them again before they shifted back to their original forms.

Uncle Z made no attempt to hide his sense of triumph as he beamed a big smile around the room. "I hope that satisfies your cynical mind. I don't want to resort to asking Sir Henry to show you what he really uses that staff for."

Lexi glanced at Sir Henry, who flourished his walking stick as he offered her a bow.

"Well, what do you say now, Miss Maxwell?" said her godfather, failing to hide the pride behind his pursed lips.

She could only nod.

"I know this news comes as a shock, and I don't expect you to believe everything that comes from your boisterous uncle Z's mouth. That's why I prepared these demonstrations."

He was right about one thing, Lexi sure as hell hadn't expected this news, and she was having a hard time keeping her legs from buckling when Lady Twila sashayed over with well-practiced grace to bestow a guiltless smile on her.

"Signorina Lexi, please forgive me for misleading you all these years. I wish to formally introduce myself to you now. My name is Aphrodite, and I very much hope we can remain friends."

Aphro-fucking-dite?

That was all it took for Lexi's knees to betray her, and her mother caught her by the arm as she started to go down. Across the room, Luke flew out of his seat.

"Why don't you sit down, Lexi," said her mom as she walked Lexi to the leather sofa. "There's a spot next to Nora. How appropriate."

Lexi nodded, barely registering her mother's hostility as Nora greeted her with an outstretched hand.

"It's all right, Lexi," Nora said sweetly. "We all love you like our own flesh and blood. You have nothing to fear from us."

With her focus on making a safe landing and her eyes trained on Nora's face, Lexi's brain barely had room to make guesses on who she might be. "Your name isn't really Nora, is it?"

"No. But it *does* have a nice, breathy cadence, don't you think? Like the final words to a song. My true name is Mnemosyne. I gave birth to the muses, compliments of your godfather."

Holy Titan.

Uncle Z knelt in front of Lexi, which somehow made him look more imposing. As she forced herself to hold his gaze, her chin quivered, and she hated herself for it.

"I'm sorry I had to lie to you for so long," he said with a much-too-casual tone. "The *Z* doesn't stand for Zenith. It stands for Zeus. But you can still call me Uncle Z. In fact, I prefer it."

Tears had started to form on her lower lids, and she didn't try to stop them from falling. Sir Henry stepped forward and she took in his watery face.

"I'm Hermes," he said. "Herald to the gods, as well as mortals, when they're in need of it."

He lifted his walking stick as if to toast the room, and she expected sparks to fly from the tip. But according to the stories of Hermes, he only used his staff to help him appear human when visiting the mortal world. Octavius spoke next.

"I'm Apollo. I'm sure I don't have to demonstrate my godly powers. You've probably been wondering how I can be skilled at so many things." He flashed a smile with enough bravado that Lexi was sure he'd done something to make himself shimmer, and she blinked rapidly. He chuckled then clapped a hand on Diana's shoulder. "This is my sister, Artemis."

Lexi couldn't believe she'd missed something so obvious. Diana was the namesake the Romans chose for Artemis. She could picture Diana adopting that pseudonym and thinking it was clever.

Emily stepped forward and joined the list of liars. "I'm Athena. Goddess of wisdom and protection."

"Don't be modest, Athena. You're a warrior, and Ares can suck it," said Diana.

They broke into laughter until Uncle Z silenced them with a look. Then he waved Burt forward, although Burt looked like he'd become affixed to the bookshelf and didn't appear capable of leaving his position. Lexi didn't have to think hard to guess *his* true identity.

"Don't bother, Burt," she said. "I mean, Dionysus."

A few more chuckles erupted as Burt nodded like a bobble-head doll, but the mood remained subdued. There was only one person remaining. Someone who claimed to belong to this circle of misfits. Someone who had been a stranger before the weekend began. Lexi turned her gaze on Luke. Was he also a god? Or was he just privy to their secrets?

Lexi wiped the tears from her eyes, and the room fell silent as a list of Greek gods scrolled through her brain. Was he Ares, god of war and bloodshed? How disturbing would that be? Or Poseidon, god of the sea? Luke said he loved the ocean, but he claimed he rarely visited. Maybe he was a Titan, like Mnemosyne.

"What about you, Luke Carrington?" she said. "Who are you really?"

Surely he'd known this was coming. He had told her in his own way. And the grace that she'd come to expect didn't leave him as the gold in his eyes softened to a warm buttercup. He leaned forward in his chair, never losing sight of her, resolved and maybe even regretful.

"I'm Zeus's brother, Hades."

Lexi couldn't look away, even as an image of the underworld appeared in her mind's eye: horned demons, fiery infernos, the screams of the doomed. Hades was often portrayed as a wicked trickster who wielded a two-pronged staff and commanded a vicious three-headed dog. But she'd chosen not to see Hades that way. She wanted to believe he'd been kind to Persephone.

And the impression Lexi had of Luke fit this less popular description of Hades as a peaceful, objective god. Luke was funny and worldly and compassionate. And he treated her like something precious, especially when he offered her his lips. Why was Hades attracted to her? Did he have an end goal? Had he been playing some elaborate trick to conquer the virgin before returning to his palace of the damned? Was that why her godfather didn't want him around her?

Lexi's mind raced as more pieces fell into place. Lady Twila and Sir Henry never hosted parties at their Italian manor because they didn't live in Italy. Nora didn't like to mix love and sex because that was the nature of the gods. Lexi's stomach felt heavy and her head felt light as she turned to look at her godfather with new eyes.

"There's something else I need to tell you, Lexi," he said. "Then you can take your grievances out on Hades."

He crossed his arms like he was delivering a commandment, while Lexi stared up at him, her vision glazed, still not fully believing what was happening.

"Your parents are not the owners of this estate. It has been placed in their name for legal purposes, but it belongs to the gods. The Maxwell family is one of many families who inhabit our homes across various locations: Argentina, Kolkata, Yorkshire. This is done so we can enjoy the mortal world at our leisure. I ask you, have you not appreciated the benefits of living with unlimited resources? The sea at your door? A stable of horses? Delicious food and drink? Have your parents not provided you with the best education and experiences?"

"Um, yes. I'm aware that I've lived a blessed life." Lexi sputtered her reply as more clarity seeped in. She'd been living a life subsidized by the gods. So, was she beholden to them too? Was this why her godfather always had his nose in her business?

"I'm glad to hear you say that. Your family is the first of their generation to host the gods here. And you may continue taking advantage of it as long as you uphold the post of this estate and serve the gods as your parents have done so loyally. We consider you to be ambassadors, which is a lofty position, indeed. It's an endowment from the gods to you."

He paced the room, a tactic he used when he expected retaliation. And, boy, was he going to get it. All this time she had believed he had her best interests at heart. That he loved her. But she had merely been part of a business transaction. She wasn't his goddaughter. She was an asset.

"I must be misunderstanding you, Uncle Z. What exactly do you mean when you say *serve*?"

He looked affronted as he stared down his nose at her. "We prefer to use the term *ambassador*."

"Of course you do. Because who wants to be a servant?"

"The gods have spared no expense to give you and your family everything to enhance your life," he argued. "Only a handful of mortals have access to such luxuries. And there is also the benefit of spending time in the presence of the gods." He smiled importantly as he glanced at the others scattered around the room. "We cannot go waltzing into a resort without proper identification, especially in these times of suspicion and distrust. And we certainly cannot be ourselves in such a public space."

Something clicked inside Lexi's muddled mind then, and she

turned to her mom as a mixture of sadness and pity rose up her throat.

"Is this why you've stayed here all these years letting your degree collect cobwebs while Dad enjoys his career in Boston?" Lexi pointed to a framed document bearing her mother's name. "That paper is just a reminder of what you could have accomplished if you hadn't agreed to serve the gods, isn't it?"

Her mom offered a miserable look, biting her lip as if to stop herself from saying something she might regret, but this only brought more truth to the surface.

"Wait. You didn't know about all this when you married Dad, did you? The big reveal came afterward. And by then it was too late. They probably made it sound amazing and you thought you'd hit the jackpot."

Lexi stopped to run the numbers in her head, then a violent rush of blood flooded her veins as her pity turned into fury, and she unleashed a vicious glare on her dad. "It was you. You started all of this before you met Mom. Back when you were too young to know better. You sold yourself and your future generations to the gods."

"There are compromises inherent in every promise," he said flatly. "I considered it carefully, as I've done with every transaction I've made."

"Don't throw your CEO logic at me. This goes deeper than a business transaction. We're talking about people's lives. Their freedom."

"We have freedom, Lexi. How many trips have we taken together? And your mother has a strong online presence with her peers at a number of universities."

Her dad offered his lame explanation, although he *did* look just as miserable as her mom, mechanically reciting the words like he'd spent the whole night memorizing them. Was he regretting his decision to say yes? How much coercion took place between the gods and their lowly mortal counterparts?

"A vacation is not a career," she said. "You of all people should know how important a sense of purpose is. Dion and I have heard that speech a million times."

When Lexi glanced at Dion for validation, she found him standing half-hidden behind the drapes of the French doors, and the memory of their conversation on the beach flooded back, when he'd told her that her version of reality was about to be fucked up.

"What about Dion? Is he being forced to abandon his career to serve champagne and cocktail weenies?"

No one spoke. In fact, everyone seemed to be waiting for her uncle Z to continue asserting his dominance. Luke, for his part, observed Lexi with cautious intensity. The color in his eyes had returned in full force, shimmering like coins in a fountain.

"Lexi, honey." Her dad's voice came out like a whimper; quieter than she'd ever heard it, and it rattled her nearly as much as her uncle Z's announcement. "We're just asking you to have a presence here while your brother helps me maintain the business in Boston for a while. He'll need to know what to do when I'm gone. It's our responsibility to the shareholders to keep—"

"Fuck the shareholders!" Lexi had heard enough. She flew out of her seat, knocking knees with Nora on her way up. If she could have spit fire no one would have been safe. "I'm nothing but an asset to you, aren't I? An investment you've been sitting on until it matured. You don't have any interest in what I want for my life. You never have. None of you have!"

Lexi stomped to the French doors. She had too much to say

and only seconds before she exploded. Escaping was the only safe option. She threw open the doors and they slammed into the walls, shaking the glass in their frames and causing more racket than her godfather's trick.

The wind gusted like a whirling dervish, blowing her hair around her head as she glared at the shocked faces, at everyone she had called family. Did they really expect her to be okay with this?

"If you think money can buy my allegiance, then you're going to find yourself short one ambassador. I'm done listening to this bullshit. Don't anyone try to follow me."

"Lexi!" Her godfather snarled as she turned her back on them. "I understand you're angry, but I advise you to seriously consider the consequences of your actions."

Lexi hesitated long enough to speak clearly and succinctly over her shoulder. "I think it's high time I stopped considering the fucking consequences!"

Fourteen

Dion closed the French doors on the howling wind, plunging the study into a sober silence. His face had paled to a chalky white, and he fisted the draperies as he stared through the glass.

"Lexi is going to hate me for the rest of her life. I can't live with that guilt."

Z strode across the room and dropped his arm on Dion's shoulder. "Lexi will come around. She didn't let me finish. Once she finds out that we've approved her summer itinerary, she'll see the light."

Hades's blood pressure rose as he watched Z placate the Maxwells. The gods were a selfish lot, but they were bound by a code of ethics with rules against manipulation of free will. The ambassador families and their commitments to the gods had always stretched the boundaries of those rules. The collaboration depended upon human greed and desperation, with the gods making their offer when a mortal was at their most vulnerable.

Ultimately, it was Lexi's choice to submit to their whims or tell them to go to hell. She hadn't made the promise herself. That was on her father, and he'd be held accountable should his commitment fail to be met, even by his offspring. While Hades hadn't planned on intervening, he felt compelled to share his views, and he rose from his chair to invite himself into the conversation.

"If I may ask, when is Lexi expected to take over the post here? Has this already been decided for her? Or will you allow *her* to make the choice?"

He offered Charles and Lilith the opportunity to answer, hoping Z wouldn't bully them into censoring their response.

"Well, once Lexi returns from her travels, Lilith was hoping she would choose to live here for a while," Charles said. "That way Lilith can finally enjoy her career. They're making great strides in her field, and she has an opportunity to spend time in Sweden this fall as a guest professor. There's a possibility she could stay on longer."

"I see. So, if I'm interpreting things correctly, Lexi was allowed to attain her degree but will now be asked to put her career on hold, just as Lilith did."

Charles drew in a breath, as if preparing himself for a storm. "I suppose I could stay here and work remotely. Give Dion more responsibilities in Boston. That way both Lilith and Lexi would have time to enjoy their careers. I don't want to keep telling them no."

Lexi's parents turned to each other, their hands clasped and their doubts playing out through the sheen in their eyes, while Z shook his head, looking ready to burst.

"You've already told me that your presence is needed in Boston," Z said. "And so is Dion's if he is to continue the success of your company. It's a sound practice for ruling any empire. Do I have to remind you, Charles, that you knew the long-term commitments of accepting this life? We provide you with everything you need to build your business and your wealth. We send healers when your family is sick. When you need favors outside the realm of human capability, we're at your service. In return, you see to it that your legacy continues to support the gods here."

With his attention still on his wife, Charles countered, "We both wanted a big family to continue that legacy, but how were we to know that Lilith would have such difficulties in childbirth?"

"Well, you saw your way around that one, didn't you?" Z shot back before turning his glare on Mnemosyne. The Titan only responded with an unperturbed shrug.

Hades stepped in before any more tempests could be unleashed. "We can all agree that Lexi's path isn't like Dion's. I suggest we consider that as we devise an approach to fit her situation better. Frankly, I'm surprised that nothing has been considered yet."

"We are not making exceptions for Lexi," Z said. "Not until it's absolutely necessary. We'll give her time to cool off and come to her senses."

"And what senses will those be?" Hades asked. "Will you wait until her senses cause her to destroy property? Or cause serious injury? What she doesn't know could make her a danger to herself and others."

"Enough!" The air crackled with static as Z's fist came down on the desk.

Mnemosyne left her seat and walked up to Z, nudging him gently. "I think we could all use some cooling-off time. It's been a long day, and even the gods need rest."

A murmur of agreement spread through the room as bodies vacated chairs. Lilith stared at the door where Lexi had made her dramatic exit. Hades wondered what kind of bond the woman had with her daughter. Had resentment festered over the years?

"I'll keep an eye on her, Lilith," Hades offered. "Like Z said, Lexi will probably take her grievances out on me. And I have no qualms bearing the brunt of the abuse if it will lessen her anger toward her family."

"That's horseshit!" Z puffed up his chest and stuck it in Hades's face. "Your only reason for attending this celebration was to snatch Lexi's virtue. Persephone has barely been gone from your bed, and you're already looking to satisfy your urges. Well, I won't have it! Not here. And not with Lexi."

Hades couldn't argue that his travels away from home only happened when Persephone returned to Olympus, when he was at his loneliest. But not this season. There was more to it than saying goodbye to a lover until the next snowfall. This time, he worried that the next snowfall would come but Persephone would not.

However, he would sooner spend a fortnight in Cerberus's doghouse than admit that to Z, so he chose his next words carefully. "On my honor as a god and as an Olympian, I will not attempt to seduce Lexi tonight. That is, if she chooses to speak to me at all."

Z narrowed his gaze until only a sliver of gray could be seen, and he assumed a pose as unbending as an oak, his lips bleached white from pursing them. Hades knew this stance well, and he waited for an insult to spew from his brother's mouth. With her usual superb timing, Mnemosyne whispered into Z's ear, and his shoulders softened. Hades didn't have to guess what the clever Titan had said. The pleasure of sex was the only thing the two had in common.

A gale-force wind assaulted Hades as he exited through the French doors. He didn't doubt his stubborn brother had something to do with the deteriorating weather. Dion had worn a confused frown as Hades left the study, and it stood to reason that the young Maxwell was hearing a few things for the first time himself.

Taking a shortcut across the patio, Hades made for the path. He had a hunch where he might find Lexi, and when an angry voice reached him from the direction of the sea, he felt the urge to run. When he found Lexi, she had her pants rolled up to her knees and was wading into the water to curse at the waves.

"Show yourself, Poseidon, damn it! We need to talk about your idiotic brothers! Maybe you're the reasonable one and you don't look down on humans like dirt!"

Lexi's voice sounded raw, like she'd been shouting for a while. A wave slapped her in the chest, but she just laughed. "Is that the best you can do? What kind of god are you? Too weak to stand up and fight?"

Hades didn't expect Poseidon to be monitoring the situation at the Maxwell estate, but he'd already seen Lexi create her own consequences, even if she didn't recognize them. Although he'd planned to stay incognito, intervening seemed prudent, and he stepped out of the seagrass.

"If my brother wanted to fight, you wouldn't be standing. You'd be floating face down."

Lexi wheeled around and screamed at him. "I told you I wanted to be left alone!" She sloshed through the water, retreating farther down the beach.

"I *was* leaving you alone, until I heard you cursing Poseidon. I wanted to stop you before the waves pulled you under to teach you a lesson. I may oversee the dead, but I can't bring them back to life."

"What do you care, anyway? You're just like the others. Big fat liars with egos the size of . . . of . . . Zeus's head. Did he really believe I would roll over and accept this? Have all the years of treating me like a daughter meant nothing to him? Worst! Party! Ever!"

Hades followed her as she stomped across the wet sand. She'd begun to cry openly, the wind carrying her sobs out to sea. He couldn't blame her. He would have been angry too. He'd been furious when his brothers took away his freedom, imprisoning him in the underworld when they were convinced it was Gaia's will.

He'd spent the first two decades tearing the place apart. Funny thing about eternity, though—after a while the rough edges got smoother, and he learned to embrace his fate. Lexi had the opportunity to do the same, but he knew this wasn't the time to try to convince her of that.

Instead, he chose to keep a respectful distance as she walked farther from the estate, closing in on the outcropping of rocks where Will the clod had taken the brunt of her anger that morning. Lexi had no inkling that it was *she* who had unintentionally caused the accident. They were all fortunate it hadn't been worse.

Lexi finally stopped her determined marching, wiping tears off her cheeks as her hair wheeled around her head like Medusa's serpents. When she turned to glare at him, he almost flinched.

"I have nothing to say to you, so I don't know why you're following me."

"We don't have to talk, but will you allow me to walk you back to the estate? Your family is worried."

"Hah! I'm sure they are. They wouldn't want anything bad to happen to their precious investment."

"I'm very sorry for the role I've played this weekend, Lexi. I'll admit that I've spent very little time around the ambassador families, with only an inkling of the effect it has on each generation. It was my curiosity that brought me here."

"So, you had no interest in getting to know me when you arrived?"

"I wouldn't say that. Your situation is unique, which I was curious about. But I'm afraid I can't divulge why."

"Let me guess. Zeus doesn't want me to know why."

"Zeus keeps his cards close to his chest. It makes him feel more in control. But I wasn't lying when I said I was attracted to you. You've enchanted me, body and soul." He extended his hand. "Please, can I walk you back?"

Lexi held his gaze through watery blue eyes. They were as determined as the sea that lashed the shore. "I'm not ready to go back. But I appreciate your honesty. And I really need to be alone. Don't worry, I won't yell at Poseidon anymore."

A short laugh escaped her, and she shook her head at the waves. Likely she was processing something she'd thought to be impossible before. Hades knew the best course of action was to honor her wishes, so he offered a humble bow and walked away.

He'd already seen her face challenges with ferocity, and he had no doubt she would overcome this one too. It was probably in everyone's best interest to leave her alone if they wanted to avoid any more unintended consequences.

Fifteen

It was after one o'clock when Lexi finally snuck into the estate and discovered a text from Mara waiting on her cell phone:

Are you enjoying the graduation merriment?

Lexi needed a hot shower before tackling that conversation, and after she'd washed away the salt from the sea and her angry tears, she sat on her bed in an oversized T-shirt and typed out a response.

Crazy weekend so far. You won't believe it when I tell you. Unfortunately, I can't tell you the craziest part

Because no one would believe it.

She figured Mara would be in bed, even on a Saturday night, so she didn't expect a reply until morning. The girl rarely gave into urges past the ones involving overly sweet desserts. Lexi wasn't in the mood for talking anyway. The only person she couldn't stop thinking about was Luke, also known as Hades. So, not a person. A god.

It was going to take a while for that revelation to sink in. But a bunch of things made more sense now, like her parents' ridiculously large collection of books about the Greek gods making bad choices. She was tempted to go downstairs and grab everything she could find on Hades, although how much of it would be the truth?

She really didn't want to hate him. He hadn't been involved in the years-long betrayal that led up to the big reveal in her dad's study, and that meant something. Had they kept her in the dark about the ambassador families because they didn't want her to figure things out? Were they expecting her to marry one of these sons of ambassadors? Wouldn't those boys need to stay and serve the gods from their own estate? Maybe those families had kids to spare, like James.

Ugh.

And how could she deny the show put on by the misfits? It was one thing to claim to be a god, but it was quite another to command nature or shape-shift into something else. It seemed the books had gotten that part right. Was it some kind of pagan magic? She'd seen incredible feats of magic performed before, but it was all done onstage where the illusions could be hidden. When she wasn't so pissed off, she would have to ask.

Despite her exhaustion Lexi couldn't shut off her brain, and after tossing and turning for a while, she decided that some light reading wasn't a bad idea. She might as well learn something, even if the myths had been watered down by humans.

The soft glow of ambient light led her to the bottom of the stairs, although she didn't need it. She just needed her ears to hear if the staff was still awake. They had tells: a creaking door, the running of a faucet, hushed whispers. Lucky for her, the whole mansion seemed to have powered down.

She stood in front of the bookshelf, but her body was pulling her to the other side of the estate, where the guests slept.

Was Hades tucked in? Asleep and dreaming of things only gods dreamed of? Was he dreaming of Persephone?

What had he said when she asked about his relationship status? *I'm not currently engaged in a romantic relationship.* If certain parts of that myth were true, Persephone would be in Olympus now.

The sly dog.

Abandoning the bookshelf, she crept across the house, stopping to listen at the kitchen door. Chef Lorraine would often wake up after dreaming of a recipe and have to check if the ingredients were available. However, not even the obsessive chef seemed to be stirring.

The hallway led her into the guest wing, and she slowed to a stop in front of the room where the god of the underworld slept. No sound came from there either. Did gods snore? Did they even sleep? Surely their bodies operated similarly to humans, since they were just humans with godly powers.

What would Hades think if he knew she was creeping around like a stalker? Would he swing the door wide and invite her in? Would she say yes? The idea of being intimate with him now left a different taste on her tongue than before she'd learned the truth. She had kissed Hades. Desired him. Wanted to sleep with him.

Damn.

Lexi left him to do whatever a god did at night and returned to the bookshelf. She had read most of the stories about Hades and Persephone, but now that she knew the gods really existed . . . She startled at a noise behind her. It wasn't a loud noise, like a crash. It was the soft brush of feet against floor tiles. When she turned, Hades was standing at the glass doors to the patio, taking in the view.

A smile came to her despite the rawness of her wounds. It was probably just because he'd decided not to put on a shirt before he left his room. Whether or not that was by design, she wouldn't let his bare skin seduce her. Their relationship had been damaged, and no amount of sex appeal could change that. She told herself this as he spoke to the glass.

"I didn't think I would see you again until breakfast. And maybe not even then."

"Really? You didn't think I would plan some extravagant way to exact my revenge on everyone?"

A smile tweaked his lips, and he brought his face around to share it with her as she walked over. "Would you think less of me if I had?"

"I suppose I couldn't. From what I've read, the gods spend a lot of time planning their revenge. Unless the humans got that wrong too."

"No. That part's right."

Lexi swayed slightly, which could have been exhaustion, or it could have been the moon's reflection shining through the glass and highlighting the contours of his face. He certainly had the bone structure of a god, and she held her attention there instead of letting her eyes drift to the structure of his bare chest.

"I understand why you couldn't tell me the truth about your real identity. So I'm not going to hold that part against you."

"I'm relieved to hear that."

"I probably wouldn't have believed you anyway."

"No doubt."

"It would have been nice to have had a heads-up about the whole servant-to-the-gods bit. But I don't see how preparing for that would have benefited either of us. So—" She met his eyes, letting herself be taken in so she could look for something that might reveal an illusion. Something about the set of his lips, slightly parted as if anticipating the next words she would speak, and the softness in his gaze, reassured her. "Can we maybe try to start fresh?"

"I'm willing to do whatever it takes for you to feel better about us. Would you like to start now or wait until morning?"

Lexi gestured to the couch and shuffled over to it. As Hades followed, whether he knew it or not, their proximity kept her warm. Was that part of his godly nature? A soothing balm for the souls he welcomed into his domain? Hopefully he covered his bare chest when he greeted them. It had her heart racing, even as she tried to avoid looking at it.

"I need you to fill me in on a few things," she said as they tucked into the cushions. "You told me that you help people make end-of-life decisions. How true is that?"

"I believe it to be true. It's my job to help mortals transition from the life they've always known to the afterlife. Many are confused, and some don't even realize they're dead. Each one requires a different approach to help them move on."

"What happens when you're not there to help them? Like now?"

"There are other gods who assist. Hecate usually takes up the post. There's also Melinoe and Thanatos, although neither of them are gifted in compassion nor subtlety. You're familiar with these gods, I'm sure." He pointed to the crowded bookshelf. "Despite a few grievous exaggerations due to mortal ignorance and the passage of time, the gods and their duties are well represented. We used to roam the human realm freely."

"Did we get your powers right?"

"For the most part, yes. It's a combination of nature and will, although our power is less potent here."

"That seems logical." Lexi appreciated when things made sense, and she scooted closer to him as his answers reignited her interest, and perhaps her trust. "Do you like your job? I might have asked this before, but the context has changed."

He smiled. "It took time for me to find my stride. To be honest, I was a brute back then. Resentful more than helpful. None of my peers were interested in spending time in the underworld, so I had very little support in the early years. But, eventually, I realized the benefits of being a god outweighed the sacrifices I made to fulfill my duties. That's the long answer. The short answer is, I've made peace with it."

"It sounds like the stories about you being a troublemaker came from those early years. Did you hate being in the underworld because it was so unpleasant?"

"Actually, that's where mortals have it wrong. They paint a grim picture of the underworld because they have a grim picture of death. It's not the dark and fearful place they've imagined. There are flowering fields, pristine rivers, and wildlife unlike anything you have here. The only thing it doesn't have is an ocean, not anymore."

"Wow. So you come *here* to skinny-dip in the ocean then?" She delivered the full-fat version of a smirk, and he laughed.

"That's not the only reason I visit."

"Then why do you visit? Wait, let me guess. You enjoy talking to humans who are still living?"

"That's a large part of why I do it. Mortals have a completely different outlook on life because they know it's finite."

"Well, I'm glad you chose to visit *this* ocean. My dad used to call me his little minnow because I was always swimming. Which reminds me, is this your true form? That trick Diana—I mean Artemis—pulled in the study was the tipping point for me. But I've read that she's not the only one who can shape-shift."

Lexi blocked out any images that weren't helpful and swore she wouldn't judge him harshly regardless of his answer. Or the size of his hooves.

"Yes, this is my true form. I'll always maintain the health and vitality of a thirty-year-old human in mortal years. But I can also take the form of a dog, which comes in handy during my visits to Tartarus."

"Tartarus is real too? I think I'll skip the pits-of-hell conversation. Oh wait, was that insensitive?"

He leaned in and swept a strand of hair off her face. Tonight he smelled like frankincense and myrrh. "I'm not offended. Everyone calls it hell. Sometimes even I do. Any more burning questions?"

The wall clock was suddenly the loudest thing in the room as Lexi fell into his eyes, not caring how far down the bottom was. "I have a million, but I'm not sure I want to know the answers to all of them."

"We have time."

He reached his arm across her back and tucked her into his shoulder, being careful of her bruises. His breath warmed the crown of her head, and just like that, her worries floated away on a cloud. Unfortunately, not every worry, but she let the moment stretch while she wrestled with the question that she knew needed to come next.

"Okay, I have to ask the obvious one. What about Persephone? I assume you two are still a couple."

His chest lifted, as if preparing for a sigh, and he released his breath as he spoke. "Yes. Although she is only at the palace three months of the year. Hers is a special case, as you know."

"So, when you're not together in a romantic relationship, you see other people? Or other gods?"

"Many of us do, yes."

"I guess immortality makes it difficult to stay committed to just one."

"Commitment can mean many things. And I'm not saying that to justify anything. The immortals simply live by rules that are slightly askew from mortals'."

Lexi knew she was sliding down a slippery slope, but she needed a clear conscience before taking her infatuation any further.

"Are you using your powers to seduce me?"

He pressed his cheek to her head, as if he wanted to feel her one last time before dashing her hopes. "All gods possess enhanced qualities over their human counterparts. Our heightened senses. Our command of an audience. Our natural ability to excel at every challenge we accept. But we don't possess an inhuman power to manipulate free will. Whatever feelings you have toward me are purely your own."

"All right, then. Good to know. I probably should have led with that question."

Hades stifled his laughter against her hair. "These are all great questions. I've noticed you look at life based on how you imagine it serving you. That's a healthy outlook. And I don't say that to just anyone."

"I don't know if that's a compliment, coming from someone who talks to dead people all the time."

His body shook with more contained laughter, and Lexi

leaned into his warmth, resting her cheek on his bare chest where his pulse thumped in a comforting rhythm. If this was free will, she didn't seem to be in control of it. In fact, she realized that his recently upgraded status to immortal had made him more desirable.

"Your heartbeat makes you seem more human," she said. "And I don't mean that in a bad way."

"You bring out the human in me, which is a precarious position for a god. But, with you, I don't mind."

Lexi took advantage of the intimate moment, despite the possibility that they could be discovered. She didn't want to think too hard about the gravity of her situation, being infatuated with the god of the underworld. She also didn't really care if they were discovered.

Hades's fingers drifted up and down her arm, grazing the contour of her breast with each pass, and she wondered if he felt her arousal under the fabric of her shirt. Would he consider their current location "secret"? Probably not.

Surely he knew that if anyone had seen them—anyone of consequence—the alarm would have sounded already. How much time did they have before he left for Asia? Did he believe he was no longer obligated to stay for support? As far as she was concerned, the scene in the study had just been a skirmish. Her battle was far from over.

"I wish we could stay like this until morning," she said.

"I would enjoy that."

Lexi let her eyes close, pretending they were anywhere else but the estate. It wasn't home. It wasn't designed as one. It was a showplace. A house of mirrors, reflecting the glamour of the people inside. Had the gods been in control of that too? It was probably a good thing Hades didn't spend much time around his peers. He wouldn't have developed his humility.

A whisper brought Lexi out of her thoughts, and she blinked to find herself alone on the couch with Hades crouched beside her.

"Lexi, you need to go to bed." He spoke softly, like he hated to wake her, and she lifted her head off a cushion that wasn't there before.

"Did I fall asleep?"

"You did. And I was enjoying it so much I didn't realize we had been discovered until it was too late." He glanced past Lexi's shoulder, and she turned to find Cherry standing behind the couch.

"Don't worry, Miss Maxwell," said the woman as she tucked her messy blond hair under her sleeping cap. "I won't breathe a word."

Sixteen

Despite a lack of sleep and her family's betrayal weighing on her mind, Lexi woke up smiling. Granted, she and Hades had been busted, but Cherry had kept some of Lexi's secrets in the past. And Lexi knew Cherry liked riding horses naked when she thought no one was looking, so there was leverage in case Lexi needed it.

Mara's text begging Lexi to call had been the first thing to greet her, and they talked while Lexi prepared for another day in paradise. She told Mara about the lineup of boys who had been invited to woo her with their selfish deeds and abysmal riding skills. Only one of them, James from Yorkshire, didn't make her want to throw herself off the balcony.

Then she gushed about Luke, the stranger who had crashed her party and caused her godfather to lose his shit. He was the only man who listened to her, and had given her the kiss of her life. But as soon as Lexi admitted that she was thinking about going all the way with him, Mara got weird and had to hang up. Not a surprise from her friend who acted like men carried the plague.

Of course, Lexi couldn't tell her that Luke was more than just a man, or the fact that her family's best friends were all gods from the Greek pantheon. Lexi was still processing that herself.

When it came time to dress, she stood in front of her closet and wondered what Hades's favorite color was. Did he like pink? Lexi was in the mood for something bright and fun and a little bit deviant, so she chose a pale-pink button-front cardigan, which she wore over a white tee with a sugar skull design. It also felt like a black miniskirt day, so she slipped on her pleated one, pairing it with rosebud-embroidered thigh-high stockings and three-inch peep toe shoes. She'd seen a stylist wear the ensemble once and didn't care that it was two seasons ago.

After donning a diamond-studded necklace and matching earrings, the bling she'd received from her parents on her eighteenth birthday, she sashayed into the dining room owning every inch of those heels.

"*Sei magnifica*, signorina Lexi." Lady Twila greeted her first, swishing over in a formfitting gown made of black-and-white damask. The fabric reminded Lexi of the curtains hanging in her dad's study. Royalty could pull off anything.

"I'll never be able to match your grace and beauty, signora Twila. That is, um . . ."

Lexi hid her embarrassment with a curtsy as the previous night's drama replayed in her head. She wasn't exchanging pleasantries with royalty. This was Aphrodite, the goddess of love and beauty.

"There will be plenty of time to practice," Aphrodite said with a tinkling laugh.

A chair was pulled out beside Lexi as Hades's velvety voice spread over her like warm sheets. "Can I offer you a seat, my lady?"

"I'm honored."

As she sat, she quickly patted the chair next to her, and he obliged. As if on cue, James appeared across the table, and as he took a seat, he slid a white shirt box toward her.

"This is for you, Lexi. After our conversation last night, I thought you might like it."

His gaze flicked to Hades, and Lexi felt a pang of guilt for always showing him preferential treatment. James had plenty to offer, despite his unfortunate position as a toy for the gods. Did he know who "Luke" really was?

"That's so nice of you. Should I open it now?"

"Yeah, sure."

Properly intrigued, Lexi pulled the lid off the box and lifted the tissue paper, uncovering a University of Oxford sweatshirt. "Oh wow. This is amazing."

"I bought it before I flew over for the weekend, so it's never been worn. When you told me Oxford was one of your choices but that it didn't work out, I decided it would serve you better."

"I don't know what to say, James. This is a really thoughtful gift. Thank you." Lexi was glad the waitstaff had started setting out breakfast trays, because she knew her cheeks were lighting up.

She slid the box under her chair, and the meal commenced. Thankfully, her parents and godfather were giving her space. She assumed that had everything to do with James. Maybe they'd even provided the box for his thoughtful gift. She could picture them crossing their fingers and hoping he would be the lucky bachelor she chose.

When the serving dishes had been cleared, her dad toasted her with the dregs of his orange juice. "This is your weekend, Lexi. How can we accommodate you?"

Lexi had already decided what she wanted to do: dance to loud music and beat everyone at billiards. She glanced at each expectant face, making them wait just like they had made *her* wait.

"I thought we could hang out upstairs in the billiard room. It has the best sound system."

Her godfather stood and raised his water goblet above his head. "To the billiard room!"

While bodies flowed through the door, Lexi remained behind to give her gift a closer inspection. She appreciated the large size. Most of her sweatshirts were large on purpose. She would have put it on right then, but she was killing it in her sugar skull.

When only the waitstaff was left, she realized that James and Hades had hung back too. Lexi knew that James had to leave, and she wanted to say goodbye properly, but she found herself in the same predicament as the night before, with two men vying for her attention. How did people manage relationships at all?

Hades made his move first, pulling out her seat as she prepared to stand. "I'll see you upstairs after you say goodbye to James." Then he offered James a handshake, saying something to him in Greek. James looked taken aback, blinking as he watched Hades leave the room.

To his credit, James quickly recovered with a friendly smile and took a few determined steps toward her. "I hate that I can't join you for a game of billiards. I'm sure you'd make it fun. But I really must get to the airport."

"And I apologize for being distracted during your visit. I've been a little annoyed with my parents for inviting strangers to my graduation party. They think they know what's best for me, but that's not your fault. I'm glad you and I got to know each other."

"Me too. I'm no stranger to overprotective parenting. I

attended an all-boys prep school. It made for a rude awakening when I started college."

"How so?" Lexi tried to find something else to stare at besides his mouth. This was her usual point of focus during debates, but that strategy had been failing her over the course of the weekend, mostly with Hades.

"In college, everyone expects you to know the ropes when it comes to dating. Even my older brother was no help. So it was a rough first year for me."

"I can't imagine you having trouble finding a date."

"Believe me, it's harder for guys than girls. Our fragile egos are on the line every time we ask for a phone number."

Lexi suppressed her shock. It seemed he'd learned some humility despite his upbringing. "Well, if a girl can't see when a guy is the genuine article, she isn't worth talking to."

James glanced at his watch, maybe trying to hide the blush tinting his cheeks. "I really need to go. I hope you enjoy the rest of your weekend. And have fun on your big solo adventure. Call or text me whenever the mood strikes."

"Thanks for the amazing gift. I'll send you a picture of me wearing it while I'm sipping a limoncello in Italy."

"I'd love a picture of you."

They stared at each other for a second before Lexi inserted one more thing. "Can I ask what Luke said to you before he left?"

A flash of uncertainty drew James's brows together, but he never lost eye contact with her. "He said a treasure worth keeping is the hardest to find. I have to agree with him on that."

The last staff member vanished, leaving Lexi and James alone with his innuendo, and she couldn't help reminiscing about the kiss Hades had given her in that very room. Just the thought of him made her insides melt. But she wasn't so love-struck not to see the logical side of the equation.

Hades was a god relegated to living in the underworld, while James was an average human, like her. At least, nobody had told her otherwise. But he was still a cog in the gods' grand scheme . . . who had proven that he wasn't a total butthead.

Lexi decided to give James a gift in return, as well as a chance to leave with his ego intact. She leaned forward and kissed him on the mouth. It wasn't a passionate kiss, but it wasn't a sterile peck either. She was making her own choices now, regardless of her family's approval. And if they tried to fight her again, she'd just keep fighting back.

As Lexi headed upstairs to the billiard room, she caught a glimpse of Hades hurrying out of sight. Had he been curious about what happened between her and James? Was he jealous? Most gods were lousy with jealousy. She didn't need a book to tell her that. She had the misfits.

Still wearing the smile James had put on her face, Lexi arrived to find Hades standing at the wet bar, downing a gin and tonic. Far be it for her to judge him for imbibing right after breakfast. Maybe it was later in the underworld.

She'd planned to challenge him to a game of billiards, but she'd barely stepped into the room when she was sideswiped by Sami, the quiet one from Kolkata, who seemed to have tripped his way over to her.

"You look like you're enjoying your party," he said, glancing sidelong at his brother, who was never more than a few feet away.

"It has certainly had its moments."

Hades had noticed Sami's approach and was walking up to Emily . . . Athena. *Damn.* Did Sami know there were gods mingling among them? Was he as clueless as she had been twelve hours ago? Based on his wide-eyed, innocent gaze and the way he held his body taut like he was waiting to get punched, she decided he was still out of the loop. Although his brother was Dion's age, so he'd probably been brought into the secret circle.

Lexi smiled, realizing the opportunity like a frying pan to the head.

"Why don't you and your brother play a game of cutthroat with me? Don't worry, it's not as dangerous as it sounds."

She gave him all the time he needed to breathe deeply and wring his hands as he made his decision.

"Yeah, sure. I'm not much of a player, but Yash plays."

"Great. You go ask him while I get the balls racked up."

She pulled out her phone as she made for the billiard table, queuing up her favorite dance playlist. And just like that, the mood in the room switched from stiff to effervescent. Sami and Yash joined her as she set up the game, and Yash wasted no time, leaning into her ear to speak over the music.

"Go easy on him."

She offered him a thumbs-up and leaned right back. "What about you?"

Yash laughed as he grabbed a cue stick and flourished it like a jousting lance. Lexi couldn't believe her luck. Perhaps she'd found some real competition. Her family was crap at billiards. Yash had also inherited the best features of his family: tall like his dad, with his mother's light-brown eyes. He looked kind of like a god.

Sami managed to keep himself together during the game, but it was clear he didn't have a competitive bone in his body, although Yash insisted on pointing out Sami's other fine qualities, like his interest in archeology and his extensive insect collection, which was currently on display at a Kolkata science museum.

Yash also kept Lexi on her toes as he matched her skill with each opportunity she gave him, and she struggled to keep her edge while subtly interrogating him about his family.

"It's just you and your brother at home?" she asked while he set up for a shot that required a difficult double bank.

"We have a much younger sister. She's twelve."

"Oh. I expect she's already started boarding school, then."

He smiled up from his position over the cue stick, and Lexi had the distinct impression he was onto her. "One of the finest on the continent. She'll be returning home by the time we're back in Kolkata."

She let up long enough for him to make the shot, which he missed, then she started again while Sami took his turn. There were only a few balls left on the table, so she bypassed the subtly and went in for the kill.

"I've heard you already graduated from uni. Software engineer, right?"

"That's right."

"So, what's on your agenda for the future? Working in your field? Or will you take a wife first and start playing house?"

He cocked his head and studied her, his lips pursed like he was suppressing a smirk. Either he was shocked at her boldness or was quickly coming up with a story he could tell her that wouldn't get him into trouble.

"I still have time before the family commitments kick in. I hear you're planning a solo summer trip. That must be nice."

Was he taking a jab at her? "Yeah, if it happens."

"Why wouldn't it happen?" He looked pointedly around the room, which was filled with wealthy friends and the finest furniture money could buy. Yes, he was jabbing her. He thought she was the spare.

"I guess the Maxwells aren't playing by the same rules as your family."

His brows rose, which gave her some satisfaction, and when she glanced at Sami, he was watching them with the same curious expression.

"Uh, it's your turn, Lexi," said Sami.

Lexi leaned over the table, having already found her shot, and spun the ball into the pocket with enough finesse to finish Yash off. The ball landed so hard it almost bounced back out.

"That's game," she said. "Thanks for playing, boys."

While Sami was quick to retreat to the safety of his parents' embrace, Yash hung back, taking his time to replace his cue stick in the rack. Then he stopped to offer some parting words. "I hope the trip works out for you. I've learned to never waste an opportunity."

As he walked away, she tried to decode his message. Was it another jab? Or had he just given her a subtle hint? If he thought she was the spare, did he think she would move to Kolkata if she and Sami synched up? Did they all think that? Hades appeared at her shoulder with an empty lowball glass in his hand.

"That was an impressive display," he said. "I wish I could have been a fly on the wall. Something you said had both of those young men blinking like cats in the sunlight."

"I was trying to get information out of Yash about the ambassador families. I think my plan backfired, but I'm not sure who it backfired on."

"Oh? I'm all ears."

"He got snarky when I mentioned I was taking a solo trip this summer, then he seemed confused when I told him I wasn't sure my family would let me, like he assumed I had all the freedom in the world. But it's more than just Yash's comment. James joked about being the spare child in his family. I guess since my parents couldn't provide a whole litter of kids, I get to fill in while Dion sews his wild oats."

Hades's brows crowded over his eyes, and he glanced across the room to where her godfather reclined on a lounger in front of the bay window, drink in hand, behaving for all the world like a god.

"I'm afraid I don't know what Z's thought processes are with regards to you and your brother. I can tell you what I know about the ambassador families, though. For one thing, they're all more established than your family. They live in estates that were built centuries ago, and they house multiple generations, which means there's always a family member living on the property who can accommodate the gods."

Lexi shook her head, her anger rising as she joined him in staring at the pompous bastard lounging on the chaise. "Sounds like the gods have created a pretty nice setup for themselves, at our expense."

"It's in a god's nature to command and to serve. It's what Gaia intended for us. But any being with free will has the potential for abusing that power."

His explanations always made sense, although that didn't

mean they always comforted. "It sounds like Gaia needs to step in."

Hades offered a soft smile. "It's not that simple."

"Of course, it isn't. Do all of these ambassador kids know their lives are being controlled by gods?" She waved her arm at the trio of boys gathered around a table, cell phones in hand.

"It's likely the older ones do. Perhaps not Sami or the boy from Bruges, due to their age." He grabbed a ball off the billiard table and rolled it between his fingers. "Do you want to try your luck with me? I fancy myself a decent player."

Try her luck? Lexi wasn't so distracted by the conversation that she missed the innuendo. "I have a feeling I'm being suckered, but I can't think of anyone else I'd want to try my luck with."

"All right. But in the spirit of full disclosure, I'm much better on *this* green than I am on the living version."

"In that case, I'll break."

With the bass beating in the background and her focus turned to the game, Lexi managed to sink a ball on her opening shot, but her advantage didn't last long. Hades overcame every obstacle, even when she had him backed into a corner, and he took the win pretty easily. She immediately insisted on a second, and her perseverance paid off, as she beat him with two balls left on the table. Then, for some reason, Dion stepped in to try his luck against her.

"What are you doing, Dion? You hate losing to me."

"I'm just having fun, like everyone else. I'll break." He shrugged his innocence and leaned close to her as he racked up the balls. "What did you think of Sami? He's a nice guy, isn't he?"

What a dirty spy.

"I don't know, he hasn't said more than ten words to me."

"Yeah, he's kind of shy. But James isn't." He wiggled his eyebrows, and that was it for her.

"Stop the act, Dion. You've never cared about my interests in men, so I know what you're doing. Let's just skip the game, and you can tell Mom and Dad that I would sooner marry Jackie O than commit to someone out of convenience."

She threw her cue stick on the table and snatched Hades by the wrist just as a song from her favorite singer started blasting through the sound system. "Let's dance," she said, giving him no choice but to join her. Something told her that he knew his way around a dance floor.

Before she had a chance to prepare, Hades spun her into his chest and back out again, taking on the task without reservation, just like he'd done with every other challenge. Maybe it was the gin flowing through his bloodstream, but she had a feeling it came naturally to him. Their hands parted and Lexi drifted away, whirling across the floor like she didn't have a care in the world. It felt amazing.

"You're an excellent dancer." The words rushed out as she drifted back to Hades and pulled him close, speaking at his ear. "I wonder what else you can do with your body."

His eyebrows rose, and Lexi bit her lip as her adrenaline surged. She'd been aware of her godfather's gaze on them, and she'd been trying not to care whether she was pushing his buttons. But she'd become less certain about a few things over the course of the weekend, like what she really meant to the omnipotent god, and how far he would go to get his way. As these thoughts entered her head, her godfather appeared to lose his patience. Pursing his lips and squaring his shoulders, he stomped across the room to the dance floor.

Seventeen

Lexi expected a lecture when her godfather joined her and Hades on the dance floor, but he'd only wanted to challenge her to a game of billiards. Of course, she knew it was an excuse to keep her away from his brother. History had taught her that there was no way to beat him, and now she knew why, the rotten cheater.

After giving up her second loss to her godfather, she blamed him for having an advantage over her, even when he swore he'd played fair. But she didn't expect him to play fair again, and the more she let herself believe that he was Zeus, the father of all gods, the harder it was to see him as her godfather. This took a toll on her enthusiasm, and she attempted to improve her mood by suggesting they all head down to the swimming pool.

Music followed the party outside, along with the mobile bar cart, and the competition continued with water polo, pitting Lexi, Dionysus, and Hades against Zeus, Apollo, and Mnemosyne. Despite Dionysus's drunken state, Lexi's team managed to squeak out a win, which resulted in an argument between Zeus and Apollo. Apparently, Apollo had formed a crush on Sami's mom, and he'd been distracted by her as she lounged on a chaise.

Towels were dispensed and everyone relaxed poolside to enjoy cocktails. Lexi sat on the edge of Hades's lounger, enjoying his warmth while they talked with Athena. Lexi knew their movements were being monitored, but she couldn't seem to control her fingers as they drifted across his stomach. She didn't even realize that her hand had dipped down to the waistband of his swim shorts until he took hold of her wrist.

"Not that I wouldn't enjoy having you continue what you're doing," he said, "but I suggest we find a more private venue for it."

"That's an excellent idea." Lexi offered him a taunting smile, feeling almost no guilt for breaching their agreement about deference. A moment later, a large, self-important shadow appeared beside them, blocking out the sun.

"Lexi, dinner is being prepared. You should have your guests retire inside to dress." The words choked out of Zeus's mouth like he was being strangled. "Before you join them, however, I would like to have a word with you—in private."

"Happy to."

Good. Lexi was ready to take care of this once and for all.

Zeus's complaints started even before he'd closed the door to the study. "I do not want you cavorting with Hades any longer. I must insist."

The scowl she wore could have rivaled his best. "First of all, I've been told to spend more time with my guests, but only the ones you and my parents deem worthy. That's a double standard if I've ever heard one. Second, Hades has as much right to be here as you do."

"Hades is not just any guest. He is a god, and you'd do well to remember that."

"A god like you and all the other immortals? I'm going to need a stronger argument than that."

He huffed as he paced the room, folding and unfolding his arms like a pouty child. So, nothing new. "You're young and still naive. You have no idea what you're getting into with Hades. He'll use you to satisfy his lust and return home without a second thought for your welfare. Do us both a favor, Lexi. Quit this nonsense and stop throwing yourself at him."

"There's nothing wrong with showing interest in a person who speaks the same language. Do you know how hard it is to find someone like that? I'll tell you. It's hard. Sometimes impossible, especially for people who've been chaperoned their whole lives. And it doesn't mean I'm throwing myself at him."

"There are other young men at this party who are interested in you."

Lexi's face burned with anger as the freight train that was her will opened the throttle. "I'm not playing along with your Stepford wives bullshit. My mom clearly wasn't given a choice in how her life played out, and these boys who were trotted out here to impress me are just cookie-cutter humans, raised to excel and fit the mold created by the gods. You can't fool me anymore. I've seen behind the curtain. Our entire relationship has been based on lies."

A hiccup caught Lexi in the throat, and she realized she was gripping the edge of the wingback like it was the only thing holding her up. Zeus stopped his pacing and looked at her like she had grown a second head.

"Our relationship has not changed. I love you as much *now* as

I did when you were born. Believe it or not, the gods are not in the habit of taking on the mortal role of godparent."

"Fine." Lexi pushed away from the chair and focused on moving her feet and making a good argument. "Then why didn't you choose to be Dion's godfather? He's the firstborn. The prodigal son to take over the ambassador post. What's so special about me?"

She continued her trajectory toward the mahogany desk, not paying Zeus any attention until she heard a snort. When she looked over, his brows were pinched, like her question had rattled him.

"Your mother asked."

When their eyes met, Lexi could almost read the unspoken words behind his gray gaze. She'd grown up smiling up at those eyes, scowling at them, pushing the limits he set for her until they turned stormy. And she always knew when he was hiding something, which was often.

"So, it was guilt then? You knew she'd been fucked over, and this was a way to make amends. Hades told me the gods can't mess with free will."

"Someday you'll understand. Can we just focus on the topic at hand? There are risks when cavorting with gods in the bedroom. You've read the stories."

"Don't lecture me on who I should or shouldn't have sex with. You've had your way with every goddess on record. And the list of humans must be just as long. What's your real point, Zeus?"

His lips hardened into a thin line. Maybe because she wouldn't back down. Or maybe because she was no longer using the name he'd given himself when he became her godfather.

"Do you really want to risk your feelings with Hades? He isn't in a position to cultivate long-term relationships. Besides that, the likelihood of you conceiving from a union with a god is much greater than the mortal average. Do you want that kind of responsibility? You've barely begun to experience life yourself."

"You mean my life as a servant to the gods? Sure, I can hardly wait to get started on that glamorous career." She folded her arms to mimic his stance, which only made him stiffen more.

"You are not a servant! You'll be given freedom to enjoy the pleasures of the world. All we ask is for you to make your home here, with your family. It's not an unusual ask. People do it all the time."

"But you're not asking me, are you? You're telling me. You and my parents have given me an ultimatum. Play by our rules or be excommunicated. I'm being forced to make good on someone else's commitment. Even if that commitment is a life of luxury, it still isn't freedom."

Miraculously, he didn't have a rebuttal. Was it because he felt guilty, or was he completely clueless about the point she was trying to make?

"I've always considered the consequences of my choices," she went on. "I'm probably the most responsible person you know. And I'm not a little girl anymore. I want to experience the world on my own terms. Solo. Which includes romance. And I have the right to choose who I do it with."

"Then choose to do it with a someone who is not a god!"

His shouting made her see red and scarlet and every angry hue of the rainbow, but she knew it would only get worse if she tried to shout over him. So she responded in the calmest voice she could muster.

"I've already made up my mind. I want Hades to be my first."

Zeus threw up his hands and sparks flew from his fingers as

the air sizzled and popped like bacon in a pan. Lexi jumped back to avoid the spray while he rushed around the room, tamping out embers.

"You are the most stubborn child I have ever . . . please, Lexi. I will grant you anything you ask for if you'll just reconsider. You know I don't like being the bad guy."

Did she know that? Sure, he'd eased up on the reins a few times when she'd made a good case for herself, especially when her parents had already given in. But maybe she hadn't been pushing the right buttons. The ones that really mattered.

As Lexi listened to his pleas, her anger subsided. He didn't seem so powerful when he was trying to bargain with her. She waited for him to brush an ash off the couch before giving him a hug around his barrel chest. The contact sent an electric current through her that lifted her momentarily off the ground, but she didn't let go. She wanted to prove she was tougher than he gave her credit for.

"I appreciate your concern for my welfare, and I'm making an effort to believe that's why you're making such a big deal out of this." She stepped back so she could look him in the eyes, those stormy gray eyes. "But this is my life and my choice. Please, try to respect that. And remember, in the mortal world, there are things called condoms."

Z was an unreasonable ass. While Lexi and her guests dressed for dinner, Hades agreed to a conversation with his brother on the beach. He knew Lexi would be the focus, and he had hoped they could discuss the matter like two levelheaded gods. But Zeus wasn't level anything, and his voice boomed like a clap of thunder as he tried to bully Hades.

"Give it up, Hades. Lexi is not worth the risk."

"Spoken like a true godfather," Hades said. "If it was Heracles vying for Lexi's affection, you wouldn't be stomping around like an overgrown satyr."

"I wouldn't have to. Heracles has no need to add to his list of consorts."

"That's because he has a plethora of gods to choose from in Olympus. I have one, and we had to resort to trickery to buy us three months out of the year."

"The human realm is filled with willing mortals. Don't tell me you haven't amassed a plethora of consorts yourself."

"Most mortals don't appreciate being abandoned by their lovers for years, sometimes decades, at a time. Not the best circumstances for nurturing long-term relationships. Of course, we both know nurturing isn't your strong suit."

Hades's temper flared despite his efforts, and he fisted his hands to rein it in. He refused to make the ongoing battle with his brother obvious to anyone who might be watching from the estate.

"I'm just curious," Hades said, his voice low and even. "What kind of ruler waits for the worst to happen before he reacts? Is it vengeance you're seeking? Is Lexi a pawn in a bigger game? She has a strong spirit, and I expect we've only seen a sample of it. When she finds out about her true nature, the damage will be done, and she'll curse you for eternity."

"Listen to yourself, Hades. We're immortals. She'll eventually resign herself to her obligations without complaint."

Hades threw his head back and roared with laughter. Z's lofty position had finally relieved him of his common sense. "If you believe that, then you're a fool. Or maybe you've never taken the time to truly know Lexi. But I've come up with a compromise. I'll back off from her if you tell her she's the daughter of the Titan Mnemosyne. Otherwise, I might have to tell her myself before the worst comes to pass."

"Enough!" Z threw his arms toward the sky, discharging his anger in a bolt of electricity. Twice in one weekend. He was on a roll. "I forbid you to tell Lexi about her parentage! She'll know when it's time for her to know and not a day sooner!"

"You may be able to control when I can and cannot leave the underworld, but you cannot forbid me from doing anything in this realm! We're equals here!" Hades discharged his own anger in the form of a fireball, which hissed as he hurled it into the surf. So much for reining in his temper. "I'll continue to enjoy Lexi's company for as long as she'll have me."

"Ha! When she learns that your service keeps you tied to the underworld, she'll abandon you for a more practical choice. No god in their right mind would give up their rights to Olympus."

Z's face contorted into a mask of exposed teeth and pinched brows. This was usually where their conversations ended, in an explosion of thunder and fire. But they were on the Maxwells' property, and it was possible that they had already attracted an audience.

"Do you remember when your powers were coming in?" Hades said as he shook the pins and needles from his hands. "The nymphs were frightened as hell of you. Nothing and no one in the palace was safe. I recall a particular incident involving an apron catching fire."

"*You* were frightened of me too."

"Of course I was. An untrained god is a danger to everyone. There were a lot of close calls before you had things under control. And *you* had support and guidance."

Z kept quiet, which meant something had been jarred loose in his stubborn brother's head, so Hades went on.

"Immortality tests us. And we must constantly remind ourselves not to become exhausted by the difficulties we face, but to use them as opportunities to better ourselves. If you give nothing else to Lexi, give her the truth as she begins her eternal journey."

The wind had picked up, but no more than what Hades had expected. And no more came from Z apart from a heavy sigh before he walked away up the beach. His brother tucked his arms behind his back, grabbing his wrists—a god deep in thought. How long had it been since they'd managed a disagreement without destroying something?

Of course, he wasn't deluded enough to think the conversation was over, but Z had the sense to wait until the risk of exposure wasn't so high. Hades took his time going back to the estate, hoping to slip inside unnoticed. Perhaps Lexi was still getting ready.

As he approached the patio stairs he noticed someone running across the lawn to the front of the estate. A floodlight flashed on, illuminating the auburn hair of the goddess in question. How much had Lexi overheard?

Eighteen

Lexi's heart galloped as she jumped behind the wheel of her car. She usually avoided driving when she was angry, but she had to get the hell away from the estate, and the garage was closer than the stable.

She fumbled under the car mat for the key as she clicked the garage door opener above her head, ignoring her conscience telling her to consider the consequences. Once she had a clear path, she backed up at full throttle and whipped the car around.

A clean getaway would have been ideal, but as soon as she shifted into Drive someone rounded the east corner of the house. She couldn't see who it was, and she didn't care. She was in no mood to talk. Anyone attempting to pacify her might get a knee to the groin.

Slamming her foot on the gas pedal, she sped toward the gate as she pressed the remote, never slowing down as the wrought-iron hinges creaked open. With tears blurring her vision, she squeezed through the gap with inches to spare and barreled toward the main road.

She needed to get to the gorge; the only place she'd ever found privacy. Was that why she was running away instead of demanding an explanation? Because every person she'd ever called family was a liar, and she couldn't believe anything they told her?

At the main road, she floored it. Fortunately, the sightseers had already gone home. She only needed the road for a mile or so, and while the engine whined, she cursed at the empty passenger seat.

"How could you not tell me I'm a demigod?! What the actual hell?"

Was it true? Was Mnemosyne her birth mother? That would mean her father had had an affair with Nora. And all these years, her mother had been raising the child of that affair. The daughter of a Titan. But why hadn't Mnemosyne raised Lexi in Olympus? Lexi knew the answer to that.

"You needed me to babysit Casa Nova Scotia, didn't you, Zeus? You're a control freak! The humans got that part right."

Emotions burned Lexi's throat as she screamed through her anger, and she wiped her eyes just seconds before the hairpin turn. Her car took it in stride, and she whizzed around the corner like a driver in the Grand Prix. The next curve came on fast, and she leaned into it, enjoying the control. Then she skidded to a stop and made a sharp left off the road.

The Maxwells' property shared the western edge of the gorge, where it butted up to a provincial park. She considered it her personal playground, having unlimited access to the park's utility road. Usually it was her and Jackie O, but her car managed the short, bumpy ride before she nosed into the trees.

It was fully dark when she arrived, but the gibbous moon offered enough light to see the trail that she and Jackie O used for their excursions. Unfortunately, Lexi's three-inch heels were not as practical as horseshoes, and they severely hampered her navigation. After aerating the soil with her ruined stilettos, she arrived at the boulder field next to the river and sat down to pull them off.

Lexi grimaced at their sorry condition, but as she picked dirt from the heels, she realized that a two-hundred-dollar pair of shoes damaged by mud was nothing compared to her current crisis. What happened now that the cat was out of the bag? She had a strong suspicion it had been Hades giving chase across the lawn when she tore out of there. Did he suspect she'd heard everything? Would he tell her if she hadn't?

Leaving her shoes and stockings on the rock, Lexi urged her legs on, navigating the downward slope of boulders leading to the river. Her desire to jump into the freezing water grew stronger with every step. Maybe a little hypothermic shock would take her mind off the crazy. Maybe the shock would never come. She was a god, right? So, what kind of power could she wield?

The auras.

She'd been seeing the yellow glow for a while, but only around animals. Mara treated her like the town fool for it. And there had been times when she thought she'd controlled the water during meets, commanding it out of her way and improving her times. Even the air seemed to stay at her back when she played lacrosse. Had her family been purposefully ignoring the signs?

When Lexi reached the riverbank she almost leaped in without a second thought, but she knew that was a dumb move. The river was nicknamed Bonecrusher for a reason. Even a god would heed that warning.

Behind the river's roar, Lexi heard sticks crunching under heavy footfalls—or heavy paws—and she held her breath to listen. Wild animals made their homes in the gorge. A bear was a definite possibility. She'd crossed paths with three, and once she'd had to play dead. Goddess or not, she wasn't prepared to fight a wild beast in hand-to-paw combat.

Glancing around for a weapon, Lexi spied a thick branch jammed between two rocks at the river's edge. It was big enough to cause damage but small enough to wield without clobbering herself with it. But what if it was a human? Could she clobber a human? Even in self-defense? A loud snort echoed from the tree line, answering her question. Humans didn't usually snort that way.

With renewed purpose, Lexi maneuvered over the boulders to fetch her weapon. When she arrived at the branch, she realized she would have to get wet to reach it. Running from her future was making less sense by the second, but she didn't have time to curse her stupidity. Something moved in her peripheral view, and she hurried to step into the river with her bare feet.

The water felt like an ice bath, numbing her toes almost instantly. No amount of godliness protected her from that. Setting her foot between the rocks, she balanced on one leg and stretched for the branch while the current pushed her from behind.

The rough bark dug into her palm as she wrapped her hand around its thickness. It felt dry, which meant it probably wouldn't fall apart on the first thwack. She just needed to yank it loose. There was another snort, followed by a series of hard cracks, like a metal pole hitting a rock. What the hell was out there?

Panicking slightly, she wiggled and pulled and yanked. Finally, the limb came free, but so did the rocks around it, and the weight from her body forced them into a landslide. Suddenly, she was following them down the embankment into the river, branch in hand.

"Shit!"

Lexi flailed her arms to stay above the surface, her limbs moving like taffy. Really cold, stiff taffy. But she managed to maneuver the branch under her armpits. The fast-moving current was already dragging her downriver, and the bark tore at her cardigan and punctured her skin.

She fought the current as she paddled back to shore, but the rocks beside the riverbank were stacked in precarious piles, looking more like a death trap than salvation. She might have to take her chances finding a better opening farther down.

"Lexi!" A figure appeared, sprinting along the embankment.

So, not a bear. And not a human. It was a god. Dressed in his formal dinner wear, Hades navigated the boulders like an Olympian, shouting loud enough to wake up all the bears in the forest.

"Just hang on to that branch! I'm going to build a dam up ahead!"

As he rushed forward at godlike speed, Lexi managed to cough out a watery reply. "A dam?"

With the river tossing her back and forth, she focused on avoiding the larger rocks jutting up from the riverbed as they came at her like Thor's hammer. She wasn't so cocky to think her swimming skills were a match for Mother Nature, and she kept a firm hold on the branch as water flowed into her mouth and out through her nose. How the hell was Hades going to build a dam before she reached him?

Not long after this thought occurred to her, she saw movement in the distance. It looked like a swarm of birds circling above the river. But as she bobbed nearer, the birds became boulders floating magically across the water and dropping onto each other in a rough heap.

The makeshift dam bridged the gap between the shoreline and a larger rock that broke the water's surface. Loose and uneven, her lifeline was not ideal, but she had to credit Hades for managing it. He did say his power was weaker in the human realm, and as she steered toward the dam, Lexi wondered if the gifts that *she'd* inherited could also be used to save her ass.

With the wall of boulders approaching fast, she had no time to come up with the perfect plan. She abandoned common sense and thought about what a god would do. They'd probably use whatever nature had given them. She quickly ditched the branch and leaned back, using the whitecaps as support. One thing she could credit to years of swimming was understanding the power of water.

With her feet stretched in front of her, she imagined there was a slalom ski attached to them as she focused all her energy on controlling the raging river of death. If adrenaline was the fuel behind a god's power, Lexi had a full tank, but she still couldn't believe it when her body rose with the waves.

Anyone watching would have thought she was speeding toward her doom. But her only audience was a god, and she thought she heard him laughing as the water lifted her up, like a parent might do with a child after they'd fallen. Her feet slammed into the dam with an unforgiving thud, and momentum took over as a cascade of water pushed her forward and surged over her head.

Lexi did her best to tuck and roll toward the shore and not back into the river, and Hades was immediately there, kneeling beside her as soon as her body came to a stop. His hand offered warmth where he rested it on her back.

"Are you hurt, Lexi?"

"Give me a sec." She took her time sitting up and deciding

which sensations were injuries and which were caused by the cold. "It's hard to tell. Most of my body is numb."

"That was quite a stunt. I thought I was watching Poseidon. But he would have been waving at me with a smug grin on his face. I want to say I'm surprised that you came up with such a plan, but you've been surprising me all weekend."

"It was a flimsy plan based on an educated guess."

"Guess or not, it's a credit to your moxie."

"Moxie?"

"Yes. It's the best I can do at the moment. Do you think you can stand?"

He extended an arm, and Lexi used it to slowly push to her feet. As soon as she was upright, Hades pulled her into his chest, surrounding her in the healing effects of his body heat. This was supplemented by the thick scent of musk, powered by his recent workout.

"What the hell happened?"

"I thought you were a bear. I was reaching for a stick and fell in. If you hadn't helped me . . ."

"I only built the dam. The rest was all you."

"You seriously had nothing to do with that wave at my back?"

"A meager amount, perhaps. Water is not my forte."

A snort caused Lexi to lift her head from his chest. "Did you hear that? Maybe there *is* a bear."

"It's not a bear. It's your horse. I had a feeling she would know where to find you."

"Oh. So that *was* you running across the lawn after me. Does anyone else—"

He put his finger to her trembling lips. "I can answer all of your questions later. Right now, I need to dismantle the dam."

The rocks that had kept Lexi from succumbing to a watery death submitted to Hades's waving arms, lifting out of the water one by one and dropping into the boulder field. Could she have actually died? How resilient were the immortals?

"Shit," Lexi whispered as the revelation of living forever hit her like a boulder.

"It's not as impressive as it looks," Hades said as he guided the last rock out of the river and let it fall.

Lexi smiled, letting him think that his godly power had impressed her, because it had. She wasn't ready to talk about everything in her life changing. Another snort erupted from the trees, followed by a sharp crack. Jackie O liked to kick the rocks to let Lexi know she was ready to leave, which gave her the context she needed.

"I think someone is worried about you," Hades said. "We better let her know you're okay before she yanks her hitching post out by the roots."

Jackie O struggled against her ties when she saw Lexi approach. She even whinnied when Lexi threw her arms around her friend's neck.

"I'm so sorry you were worried, Jackie O. I owe you, big-time."

Her horse whinnied again, which meant there was more going on than worry, and a few seconds later three figures burst through the trees. Big surprise, Zeus was leading the charge. Behind him, Dion and her mom, the human one, hurried to keep up.

"It looks like the cavalry has arrived," Hades said, making no attempt to remove his arm where it wrapped protectively around Lexi's waist.

"Lexi! Are you okay? We were so worried." Her mom spoke as she stumbled over the rough terrain. Zeus offered his hand, but she refused his help. She seemed angry with him, and a bit tipsy. Did she still think Lexi didn't know the truth?

"I'm fine, Mom." Lexi continued to soothe Jackie O as the shadowy figures finally became familiar to her anxious mare.

"Why did you run away? Oh my. You're soaking wet. You didn't fall in the river, did you?"

"Unfortunately, yes. But Luke rescued me before I made it to the ocean."

Her mom turned her bloodshot eyes on Hades. "Thank you for saving her. I don't know what I would do if anything—" She threw her arms around his neck in a smothering hug, and it all felt so phony that Lexi nearly burst out laughing.

"Your thanks are appreciated but unnecessary," he said. "To Lexi's credit, I believe she would have saved herself if I hadn't found her."

"Regardless of Lexi's aptitudes, it was very irresponsible of her to run away," Zeus said. "You had us worried, young one. It was Dion who guessed you'd come here. Your vehicle was our only clue."

Lexi glared at Zeus and the air turned sharp with electricity. She couldn't say if it was him or her causing it, but she was happy to claim some of it. "Are you sure you were worried about *me*, or was it the possibility of losing a precious servant?"

For a moment the mighty god appeared taken aback, cocking his head and having the audacity to look insulted.

"Please stop throwing that term at me. I will never see you as a servant. Do you think I have no feelings for my own goddaughter?"

Lexi's laughter crackled like the frigid wind, and Hades tightened his grip on her waist. "Goddaughter, huh? Excuse me if I'm not amused by the irony. I thought the term was demigod? Correct me if I'm wrong."

"What are you talking about, Lexi?" Dion blinked at her, appearing utterly confused, and she realized that he might have been kept out of *that* loop.

"Nothing, Dion. It's a private joke. Let's just go home. I'm freezing."

Hades pulled off his jacket. "I'll give you my shirt to change into. That should help."

"Why don't you let Dion drive your car home?" said her mom. "You can ride with me and Zeus. I don't want to worry about you a second longer."

"Thanks, Mom, but I'd rather stay with Jackie O and Luke. We'll ride back together."

"But you're wet. And you just said you were cold."

"I'll be fine once I change into Luke's shirt. The car key is under the floor mat, Dion. I'll meet everyone at the estate in half an hour."

The trio stared at Lexi like she'd asked them to walk through hot coals, and her mom was the first to relent, offering a sigh that sounded more relieved than reluctant.

"It's against my better judgment, but you're entitled to have things your way," she said.

Lexi escaped behind a bush to change before Zeus could insert himself again. She was ready to give him a fight—she just hoped it wouldn't come to that. Through the shrubbery she watched Zeus and Hades take their conversation out of earshot, leaving Dion with Jackie O. It annoyed her that Zeus held such sway over Hades. Wasn't Hades the older brother?

By some miracle the three intruders left without so much as a threat. She didn't care how Hades had done it; she was just glad they were alone again. Jackie O seemed glad too. She nudged

Hades affectionately, and he returned the gesture with a scratch on her cheek.

"Jackie O likes you," Lexi said. "And she has discriminating taste." She opened the pouch on the saddle and shoved her wadded-up clothes and shoes inside, although everything was ruined.

"We need to get you home and resting in front of a fire. How would you prefer we ride? You might be warmer behind me, and the weight would be better distributed for your horse."

"Jackie O is an Arabian. She can handle your weight if you sit behind the saddle and hold on to my waist for balance. I do have one request, though. Please don't take me with you if you fall. I've done enough of that for one weekend."

He offered his warm, enchanting smile. "I think I can manage that."

Nineteen

Jackie O kept up an urgent pace, jostling Lexi in the saddle as they navigated roots and potholes. Lexi knew her horse hated riding in the dark, so she stifled any complaints. It was the biting wind that annoyed her more, and she shivered even with Hades's godly heat at her back.

"I'm sorry you heard the truth about your parentage this way," he said, bringing his chin to her shoulder. "And I apologize for the role I played. Z is rightfully stubborn when it comes to the offspring gods conceive with mortals. It's his job to make sure the demigods behave themselves."

"Is that why *he* was in charge of telling me about this instead of my own mother?"

"Yes. And on *his* timeline."

Lexi shivered as another revelation hit her. All the times she'd recited her debate speeches to Nora for feedback, or when Nora offered a sympathetic ear while Lexi ranted about some injustice at the hands of her overprotective family, she was actually ranting to her birth mother.

"And what about Dion? Does he know?"

"It seems he doesn't, but I expect he will soon."

"Wow. That's going to blow him away. Even I haven't wrapped my head around it."

"It will take time."

Lexi tried to focus on the questions that bubbled to the surface in a steady stream, but every time Hades spoke at her temple, the warmth of his breath and the brush of his lips on the shell of her ear made her groin clench in the most delicious way.

"Are you really forbidden from leaving the underworld without Zeus's permission?"

He released a sigh, and the muscles in his chest tensed against her back. *Damn.* She should have saved that question for later.

"Maybe I overheard that wrong," she added quickly.

"No, you heard right."

"That's ridiculous."

"It does sound ridiculous. But I've made peace with it."

Lexi had read about the injustices portrayed in the Greek mythos, and it seemed she'd been living some of them herself. She needed answers, but there were a few questions she wasn't anxious to get the answers to. And how was she supposed to think straight when she couldn't get her mind off her crotch?

"Is Persephone the only goddess who lives with you?"

She glanced sideways at him, catching his soft smile. Or was it a sad one? "Yes. December through February, most years."

"So, no other goddesses spend time with you at the palace?"

"No. It's just me and the nymphs. And Cerberus, of course."

"Cerberus is real?"

"As real as you and I."

Lexi didn't want to imagine him with his arms wrapped around another woman, but the gods were a horny bunch. She would have to come to grips with that if she planned to give herself to one. Wasn't she a goddess too?

"Are there any goddesses you visit in Olympus? You know, during your rare visits topside?"

"Unfortunately, I'm forbidden from entering Olympus. And not many gods are interested in visiting the underworld. One has to wade through a lot of horseshit to get anything approved. Let's just say my situation is not ideal for cultivating long-lasting love affairs with goddesses."

As Hades spoke his hand moved across Lexi's hip, dipping lower until his fingers grazed her inner thigh. The shiver that followed was not caused by the cold. Was he trying to distract her from learning too much and dropping her infatuation? Maybe he was showing her that long-lasting commitments weren't everything.

"I want to feel sorry for you, but you're a god, so I'm finding that hard to do."

He chuckled against her face, tickling her ear, but she was more focused on his fingers as they traveled stealthily beneath her skirt. "I don't expect special treatment."

Her sex trembled as his thumb reached her panties, and he began a slow circling maneuver across the fabric. "What are we doing, then?" she asked, although she didn't know why.

"I thought we could take advantage of our seclusion."

Hades pressed his mouth to her neck and butterflies erupted inside her stomach as he stamped her skin with hot kisses. Then he reached for her chin, turning her head to access her lips, and unfiltered desire flooded her body as he possessed her.

Their tongues entwined while his fingers traced the seam of her panties, and she felt herself slicken with anticipation. With an urge that seemed out of her control, Lexi pivoted her hips to welcome him in, and he slid a finger under the seam, making her gasp.

Swaying with Jackie O's cadence and the rotation of Hades's finger, Lexi submitted to the sheer eroticism of it. When the lights of the estate came into view, she desperately wanted to turn back. Why had she let Jackie O hurry them? That thought didn't last long, and she let Hades continue chasing the sweet sensation that had been building since he started his pursuit.

Hades seemed to sense her urgency and sped up his pace, tucking her tighter into him as his talented finger sent her over the edge. The rush was unstoppable, like the moment a firecracker catches and the explosion is inevitable. Lexi squeezed her eyes shut while stars burst behind her eyelids. It felt like rapture, and Hades held on to her like he meant it.

Silence took over during the last one hundred yards. There was nothing more to say. All the questions had flown out of Lexi's head anyway. She just relished the warmth of two bodies entangled together. At the stable, her legs trembled when she climbed out of the saddle, but that didn't stop her from wanting Hades more than her next breath.

Jackie O was ready to call it a night, and her mare waited patiently while Lexi fumbled with the gate like it was her first day on the job. All the while, Hades's mouth was on her neck, and he spoke against it as he dug his arousal into her hip.

"I'm going to walk with a limp the rest of the night."

Lexi locked the gate and turned around, grabbing his hips and fitting their bodies together. "Then we should do something about that before we're no longer alone."

He smiled and backed her into the gate. She'd only seen hints of the wicked smile he offered her now as he leaned in and kissed her. His hands slid down her waist in a luxuriously slow crawl, then he slipped them beneath her shirt, seizing her bare skin. She nudged them upward, giving him permission to continue exploring.

"What have you done to me?" Hades whispered at her ear as his fingers brushed the curve of her breasts.

Although he appeared eager to take things all the way, his movements seemed tentative as he continued around the weighty flesh, warming her where he traced the perimeter of her nipples. Lexi writhed under his teasing touch, considering the rewards over the risks of throwing him into the hay stall and having at it right there.

What did it matter anyway? Her life was currently fucked, and she hadn't had a chance to figure out what to do about it. So why was she suddenly thinking about the risks Hades would face and the punishment Zeus would inflict on him if they continued their pursuit of pleasure? Did Hades believe the rewards were worth it?

Hades must have felt her apprehension—maybe her body had tensed—because his hands fell away, and he stepped back to look at her.

"What's on your mind, Lexi?"

"I'm sorry. I don't want you to stop what you're doing. I just, I feel like I'm being selfish. I don't care about the consequences. Not anymore. And I don't want that to influence the choices you make."

She lowered her eyes, kicking a clump of wet straw with her toe. Hades lifted her chin with his fingers and drew her into his amber gaze.

"You excite me, Lexi. That's a rare thing when you've been a god as long as I have. You remind me of my human nature. You have me damning the risks. And I always consider the consequences."

Lexi wanted to believe that she could be special to a god, even as she reminded herself that she was one too. "What are the risks for you? Will Zeus keep you in the underworld for a century? Will he forbid Persephone from visiting?"

She didn't know why she'd included Persephone. She'd been imagining the goddess losing her memory and forgetting she'd ever been in love with Hades.

"Zeus can't keep Persephone from visiting the underworld. She holds more sway over the gods than any of them care to admit. But he can deny my requests to leave for as long as his anger and resentment last."

"That sounds like an ego problem to me."

He chuckled as he adjusted the crotch of his pants. The mood had definitely taken a turn. "You're wise beyond your years."

"Is that a trait among gods?"

"Not at all. Poseidon has a son who spends more time in jail than out of it."

"So, this son is a demigod?"

"Yes, but that doesn't mean his power is any less destructive. The question is, what do you plan to do with yours? And, for what it's worth, I'm at your service, whatever you decide."

She didn't really know what to do with her powers. She didn't even know what they were. But one thing was still certain—she had every intention of giving Hades access to her secret places, and now that she had more information, now that her conscience was clear, she wanted to have the experience somewhere other than the stable, where the smells were better.

"Let's rejoin the party and see what kind of fight I'm up against."

Twenty

Hades watched Lexi talk with Z and Mnemosyne in a private corner of the living room. She'd changed into a simple ivory dress that struggled to cover her lap. Since their interlude in the stable, he'd been occupying his mind with mundane thoughts, like the souls waiting for his return and the inevitable argument with Charon about hoarding the coins offered by relatives of the deceased. He couldn't afford to dwell on the taste of Lexi's mouth or her lemon-scented skin, which beckoned him like spring flowers.

"What do you suppose they're talking about?" Lilith came up beside him, loosely cradling a glass of merlot and smelling strongly of spirits. Reaching only to his shoulder, she was a woman of delicate features, akin to a nymph, with pale-blue eyes and wheat-brown hair that framed her face in loose waves. Through the lines of age and worry, he saw a youth who had once been hopeful. Another mortal life sacrificed for the gods' pleasure.

"Based on Z's scowl, I'd say Lexi is making some good arguments." It didn't take much effort to notice the resentment behind Lilith's tight smile, despite her attempt to mask it. "What do *you* hope they're talking about?"

She glanced up, an unhappy resolve etched behind her glassy gaze. "Lexi's freedom. And Dion's. It's all I've ever wanted, apart from my own. But it's too late for me."

Hades nodded, appreciating her insight and willingness to share her plight. "I feel as though I should apologize, perhaps in the way mortals feel responsible for the deeds of other mortals. Zeus can behave like a tyrant, but I'll be the first to say that I don't envy the demands of his position."

"It isn't healthy for one immortal to hold such power, especially when it comes to the welfare of mortals. Power only insulates the powerful from the lives they control. I had this argument with Charles when I first learned the truth. Of course, it happened after he'd already made the oath."

"I'm sure it took a long time for you to come to terms with that. I also expect it's been difficult raising the daughter of a Titan. You must have felt pressured to meet certain expectations."

"Not from Mnemosyne. Oh, no. She's the shining example of a benevolent goddess, leaving me to raise Lexi however I wished."

Lilith didn't hide her sneer as she lifted her glass in a mock toast. "She seduced my husband as an act of vengeance against your brother, in case you didn't know. As punishment, Zeus kept Lexi out of Olympus. If you ask my opinion, Mnemosyne is the only one who avoided punishment."

She took a large swallow from her glass and continued on as if she hadn't stopped. "It's been Zeus piling on the expectations. Keeping Lexi under constant surveillance. Grooming her to be an ambassador, separate from the gods. She's going to be horrified when she learns about the nymphs."

"Lexi has had a lot to process this weekend. Let's save the nymphs for later." He proffered a smile that he hoped would calm her, and she rewarded him with a laugh. It was probably due more to the liberal amount of alcohol in her body than amusement, but it was laughter all the same. "What about Lexi's powers? Have you seen any signs that they're strengthening, apart from the incident during the race on the beach?"

"Nothing too concerning. She's caused a couple of minor accidents that she didn't realize were her fault. And she arrived this weekend claiming that we'd painted the house, although I'm not sure if godly powers had anything to do with that. Zeus assured Charles and me that her gifts could lie dormant for thirty years, as long as she didn't know about them."

Hades suppressed a scoff, knowing it would only have her probing him. Despite her knowledge of the gods, Lilith was clearly not considering the potentially dangerous powers of a Titan's direct descendant. Instead, he watched her scan the room and locate her husband.

"I'm afraid I've been punishing Charles ever since that night," she said. "And he swears he'll never abandon me. He supported me when we learned that I could die if I carried another child after Dion. And he never backed down when Zeus ordered us to find another way."

"A mate who supports you through the worst of times is a rare thing. Rarer than any god. I'm glad you have that in each other. Perhaps it's time for you to forgive and let go of what no longer serves you. I suppose I could say the same to Lexi."

Lilith rested her mouth on the edge of her glass, wetting the rim before taking a sip. "I know you care for Lexi. I've seen the way you look at her. There's emotion in your eyes, which is different from simple attraction. Contrary to what Zeus believes about your motives, there's more going on between you two, isn't there?"

Although Hades would not have characterized his attraction to Lexi as simple, it wouldn't have been appropriate to point that out. "Lexi has an unquenchable passion for life. I've seen this in her actions and in the stories she tells. She speaks her mind without reservation, but she also brings out the best in those around her. All very desirable qualities."

"I'd expect no less from a goddess."

A smile swiftly claimed her lips, almost wistful, and Hades raised his flute of champagne in a salute. She left him with an eyebrow lift that she barely pulled off, then she traveled across the marble tiles in shiny black heels, doing a grand job of balancing, something he figured she'd had plenty of practice with.

Lexi twisted the hem of her dress as she listened to Zeus explain why she should embrace her role as an ambassador with godly gifts, while Mnemosyne sat beside him being uncharacteristically quiet.

"When were you planning to tell me?" Lexi asked.

"When it was time for you to know," he said.

"You're not even trying." Lexi clenched her teeth, forcing her body to stay put and not do something she'd regret . . . again.

Zeus pursed his lips, doing a less subtle job of hiding his emotions, and Mnemosyne gave him a nudge on the arm to prompt him. "Just imagine the attention you'll command now that you know such power is at your disposal," he said. "Success will come easy."

"When have you known me to do things because they're easy?

I'm sorry, but you need to do a better job of convincing me to keep house for you at the expense of my freedom."

"Don't use that freedom horseshit on me again. You're free to go anywhere you wish. Do whatever you wish. The only boundaries are the ones you impose on yourself. I've been telling Lilith this for years."

Lexi frowned and her gaze flicked to her mother standing on the other side of the room talking to Hades. "I wouldn't expect you to understand. You've never known what it's like to be human."

Mnemosyne lifted her hand, and it looked like she wanted to reach for Lexi, but she just lowered it back to her lap. Was she worried Lexi would bite her head off too? "It might help if you didn't think of these things in terms of freedom," Mnemosyne offered, her voice soft and patient. "How much freedom does anyone really have—mortal or immortal? There are always rules guiding us and defining us in our pursuits. Whether it be for prosperity, safety, or love. But these rules don't keep us from having choices."

"And mortals have the certainty of death to relieve them from their burdens," Zeus added. "Immortals have an eternity to live by those rules. How much freedom do you think I have, Lexi?"

"I wouldn't know because you've kept me in the dark."

"Well, now you know. And I'll tell you that it's not as much as you might think. In fact, most gods have duties that direct their choices. But here, you can embrace your power as you live a life of leisure among family and friends."

"What about the family I've never met? The ones in Olympus? What if I wanted to pay them a visit and embrace my power there?"

Mnemosyne tucked her chin into her collar and pretended to be interested in the stitching. Zeus never flinched.

"It's not that simple. It takes years for a demigod to assimilate to Olympus after leaving the human realm. Especially an untrained one."

"Again, not my fault."

She held Zeus's stare, remembering that he'd been her uncle Z just twenty-four hours ago. A man she battled with often, but who still supported her wins and laughed at her jokes. Had he ever really cared, or was it all a performance? And what about Mnemosyne? Did she think about Lexi when she was in Olympus?

"How do you feel about me staying here, Mnemosyne?" she asked. "Now that the truth is out."

"As opposed to where? Olympus?" She glanced at Zeus, and Lexi knew she was choking down the words she couldn't say. "I would love to have you living close to me. But it would be selfish to ask you to give up your mortal family."

"What do you mean? How long would it take me to assimilate? Maybe if I practiced every day—"

"A century, Lexi," said Zeus plainly. "You will swear an oath to stay in Olympus for a century if you choose to leave the mortal realm."

"What? Everyone I know would be dead."

"And you would still be at the genesis of your existence," Mnemosyne said. "There will always be time for you to choose Olympus."

"So, that's it, then? You all get your way. You had that tied up in a neat little bow didn't you, Zeus?"

"Honestly, young one, it's not as terrible as your stubborn will wants to believe. You don't have to marry a boy from one of these families. Choose someone else. Someone you love. Of course, he or she would have to be worthy of our trust, but the gods are not unreasonable."

"What if I didn't want to get married? That's not something most gods do, right? They just screw each other. No commitments. No hurt feelings."

She didn't mean to look at Mnemosyne but it happened anyway, and the Titan met her gaze without reproach. She'd been at the game a long time and knew exactly how it was played. Zeus just scratched his beard, looking confused, like he hadn't expected Lexi to have a viewpoint that didn't match his own.

"There are plenty of unorthodox partnerships happening in the human realm these days," he said. "Who am I to interfere with your choices?"

Since when?

She wanted to laugh. Instead, she located her brother, who stood with her dad and the family from Belgium. Would Dion be moving his future wife into the estate to help him produce baby Maxwells? Of course he would. He was the heir to the throne. So why did Lexi have to stick around? *Ugh.* How could she even consider dropping everything on Dion and his innocent future wife? She sounded like a selfish god already.

"Lexi, please. Can we call it a night?" Zeus said, his voice coming out softly, almost sad. "Let's just pretend that things haven't changed until the party is over. I'll answer all your questions about Olympus and the gods tomorrow."

Her godfather had always found ways to make her feel guilty for being angry with him, even when he deserved it. This time, she wasn't giving him a pass.

"If only it was that easy. Trust has been broken. No, it's been obliterated. And not just with you. With everyone. It'll be a long time before I believe anything this family tells me. And now that I know how much time I have, I don't recommend you hold your breath."

Zeus's jaw stiffened, and she prepared for another excuse, but his gaze dropped to the floor, as if her words had actually stung him. She let him have his pity party and glanced over at Hades. Dressed in a white button-down shirt and heather-gray pleated pants, the tone of his muscles clearly defined beneath them, he looked like a god in human clothing.

Her mom had left him standing near the bar nursing a flute of champagne, and since then, he hadn't taken his eyes off Lexi. When they'd returned from the gorge dinner had already been served, along with a plethora of lies, and the other families appeared reluctant to even look her way now. As far as they knew, she was a spoiled human girl who had thrown a tantrum and run off. Zeus was going to keep her secret locked up tight.

"I need some privacy. I'm going to my room." Lexi stood and straightened the hem of her dress. "Mnemosyne, will you reassure Hades that I haven't retired for the night? I know he's been worried about me since my swim in the river."

"Of course, Lexi."

Ignoring Zeus for all she was worth, Lexi took the stairs up to her bedroom and closed the door. She stretched for her phone on the nightstand as she dropped onto her bed, desperate for a bit of normalcy. The text icon was lit. James had sent her a message, and it read like a cruel joke.

I hope you're having a brilliant day!

Impulsive Lexi wanted to throw her phone across the room, but levelheaded Lexi took three deep breaths and sent a reply—a censored one.

Thanks. It's been a strange day indeed. Details at five. LOL

Lexi hit Send and shoved the phone under her pillow. Chatting with James about the drama unfolding at Maxwell Manor was not her idea of normal. What she needed was some fresh air.

The temperature had dropped, and she wrapped her arms around her chest as she stepped onto the balcony. The cold made her painfully aware of how much her body ached. Not just her muscles, but her brain felt wrung out too. She crawled onto the chaise, which gave her a partial reprieve from the wind, and squeezed her eyes shut.

As far back as Lexi could remember, her brain had operated at full speed. It commanded her to anticipate potential outcomes for every decision and develop solutions for every problem. Was this an attribute of the gods? If Zeus was any gauge, she'd guess *no*. But Hades had a more human outlook. Even the other misfit gods showed some consideration for future events. Had eternity warped Zeus's idea of what a life was truly meant for?

A deep voice lilted below her, speaking her name as if it was part of a lyric. She knew exactly who owned those sultry vocal cords, and a thrill rushed through her as she sat up to acknowledge Hades. He stood in the courtyard below her, wearing a sheepish grin, hands clasped behind his back.

"Can't anyone get a little peace and quiet around here?" She offered him a weary smile, which almost turned into a yawn.

"I apologize. Would you like me to come back later?"

"No. The damage is done. I'll probably be awake all night trying to figure out what to do with all the information that's been dropped in my lap."

"Is there anything I can do to help? I've been told I'm quite good at psychoanalysis."

"I'm not sure. I need honest answers. Are you in a position to provide those?"

"All I have are honest answers. It's been my job for years." Hades stared up at her, his eyes clear and intense even in the dark. She climbed off the chaise and yanked the boat ladder out from underneath. Regardless of her aches and exhaustion, she wasn't about to pass on some private time with Hades.

"Climb aboard."

Twenty-one

Lexi had a god in her bedroom. On top of that, she was one too. What were the odds of that happening? Given what she knew now, better than anyone might have guessed.

"How are you feeling?" Hades asked. "We may be immortals, but we still feel pain."

"I'm pretty sore, but I'm dealing with more pressing problems than a few body aches."

"Do you want to talk about it?" Hades had taken a seat on her blue velvet sofa, which sat below a sofa-sized mirror. He patted the spot next to him and she relaxed into the cushions.

"I feel like I'm going insane. I keep telling myself that this is real, but somehow my mind won't believe me."

"I need more specifics."

"For one, I'm a goddess. But I don't feel like one."

"Really? That demonstration in the river didn't convince you?"

"I was raised to think I was human. Even with proof, humans are skeptics."

"Would it help if you had more proof?"

"How would we do that?"

"Well, it's clear you have control over the element of water, although I don't think we should experiment with that in your bedroom. I also have a hunch that you're manipulating air. If your power is as potent as I think it is, you should be able to command that element easily with the right focus. Try it out on a throw pillow."

He pointed to the pink flower-shaped pillow resting at her elbow, and she picked it up. "Do I throw it in the air and try to shoot it down like a clay pigeon?"

"Not exactly, but you can think of your hand as the shotgun. It's your source of power. Sometimes it helps to imagine a beam of light extending from it. Intention and belief is essential when controlling nature. You'll want to focus your will on keeping the pillow off the ground using that beam of light. The element should rise to serve you."

"Okay. Test one commencing."

Lexi held the pillow in front of her and took aim with the other hand, giving it the same focus she'd given the river when she was trying to save her ass. Electricity tingled inside her palm as she tossed the pillow up, and the damned thing stayed there, hovering a good six feet above the floor as she gaped at it.

"See. There's your proof." Hades waved his hand at the pillow, and it shot out of her beam of invisible light. "Now, try to get it back from me."

She laughed and flicked her wrist hard at the pink target. It zoomed across the room and hit the French door, where it wavered and started to fall. But she doubled her effort and sent it flying upward into the ceiling fan.

With a gasp, she jumped off the couch as the pillow was batted into the canopy draped over her bed. The energy flowed easily now, causing a slight tremor in her arm, but she wanted to keep the pillow from hitting the ground. To her horror, instead of zooming back up it started to smoke as it landed on her comforter, and she shook her hand to break the spell.

"Shit!" She pounced on it to smother a tiny flame that had already scorched one of the seams, while Hades, still sitting on the couch, covered his mouth to stifle his laughter.

"I guess we can add fire to that list," he said.

"I could have set the whole place on fire." She clutched the burnt pillow to her chest as she walked back to the sofa, already thinking of places to hide it.

"Not with all the gods downstairs. But now that you know what you're capable of, you'll need to treat that power with respect. A poorly timed action could have catastrophic consequences."

"You mean like all of Zeus's poorly timed actions that brought me to my catastrophe? I'm just so glad you could be part of that." She breathed out a sigh, still trembling from her adrenaline rush. "To be honest, if you weren't here, Jackie O and I might be miles away by now."

"Possibly leaving a trail of destruction behind you." Hades tucked her under his arm and pressed a kiss to her temple. "I'm glad I was guided here."

"You think you were guided here? Do you believe in fate?"

"I believe in *the Fates*. They call me to the Elysian Fields now and then, usually with bad news. But sometimes I'm pleasantly surprised."

"Where do you spend most of your time when you're at home? At the gates?"

"Yes. I perform my duties ahead of anything else. But I'll admit that my heart isn't always in it. That's when I visit the other regions of the underworld. The Asphodel Meadows is a favorite of mine, where the Lethe is most serene. When I'm in the mood for adventure I'll head to the less explored places, where the creatures prefer to be left in peace. It's important to remind them that they're not alone."

Lexi shivered, but it wasn't from fear. It was curiosity, even without knowing what these creatures were. Or it could have been his fingers tracing lazy circles on her shoulder.

"What are the rules for visiting the underworld? Would a demigod, for example, have to take an oath to stay for a century and assimilate? Like they have to do in Olympus?"

"Did Z quote a century?" He shook his head. "He treats centuries like they're decades. The timing is different for every demigod." Then he blinked at her as if he'd just heard the question. "This is for educational purposes only, right? The underworld isn't under real consideration."

Lexi knew the trouble Hades would get into if she was that hasty, so she didn't let his veto dash her hopes. "Of course. I'm nothing if not a thorough investigator."

As they smiled at each other, Lexi noticed that his hand had begun an upward trajectory across her thigh, and she was reminded that they were alone, and that time was of the essence. But time meant something different to the gods. Once her party guests said their goodbyes, it could be a century before she saw him again. Goddess or not, that felt like forever. Hades was leaning into her lips when she finally found her voice.

"When will I see you again?"

She quickly kissed him back, letting the question hang there while her stomach lurched at the thought, interfering with the pleasure of his warmth sliding across her skin. He felt like summer. An endless summer that kept her bathed in sunlight and pleasure. And Hades didn't seem anxious to end it, either, as he spoke against her mouth.

"Will knowing that affect how much you enjoy today?"

"Maybe."

He broke the kiss to look carefully at her, giving her full access to the god behind the amber. "A century feels like a long time to a mortal. But you are not a mortal, Lexi. You'll stop aging in a few years and never feel older than that. When life has an infinite timeline, very few things will feel urgent."

"That's poetic and all, but it doesn't make me feel any better now."

"I can only say that I'm sorry for that. It may take you a century to come to grips with it, possibly when you're saying goodbye to your mortal family. But you'll eventually live with a new concept of time. And we'll see each other, if that's what we both want."

"Is that what *you* want?"

He brushed her chin with his fingers, taking it gently and tugging her toward him until their foreheads touched. "*The maiden's beauty was more than he could bear. / Skin softer than a dove's wing. / Lips redder than a pomegranate. / Hair like silk spun of mahogany.* / He wanted to possess her, to drink her in, to love her until the stars held no meaning—I want to see you now and any time in the future that you'll have me."

Lexi's breath was silenced by his kiss at the same time his fingers reached the hem of her dress. His touch was like a burn she looked forward to, scorching her as his passion flared. Or was that his power? She brought her hand to his chest, working a button loose from his shirt as he peppered a trail of kisses to her throat, nibbling and sucking her earlobe into his mouth.

"I want to taste my way across your skin," he whispered. "From your lemon verbena–scented neck to the sweetness between your thighs."

Her body responded with a clench so tight that a moan escaped, and she yanked on the button until it pulled loose. Then she spread his collar open and slipped her hand inside. She couldn't decide which sensation felt better, his rippled abs beneath her fingers or his fingers grazing the seam of her panties.

She writhed against his hand, already racing toward a climax when he slipped a finger underneath the fabric. She could have fallen over then, as he touched her right where she needed it, but he only lingered for a few exquisite moments before he took his fingers back.

As he slid off the couch and sank to his knees between her legs, her pulse jumped. "You have the reins. Pull on them if I go too fast."

Hades took hold of her hips and eased her forward. Then he hooked his fingers around the seam of her panties, and she let him pull them off her legs. The anticipation was nearly as erotic as the rush she felt when his mouth finally reached her. Then the warmth came. Then his tongue. Her sex vibrated, and she wondered if he could feel it.

She stopped wondering when his finger joined the party, taking her out of her head and up to a place she'd never been. A place where everything was perfect and all she felt was pleasure. She could have come ten times over but she reined it in, accepting everything he gave her. She deserved this.

When she finally let go, she found herself grasping his hair, and held his head with both hands as she ground against his mouth like something wild. He seemed just as enthusiastic, keeping her on that high until her body jerked off the cushions.

When the sensations ebbed she eased onto the floor, and they slouched into each other, panting. She was about to comment on the cold tiles when a knock on the door startled them both.

"Lexi, this is Mnemosyne. Zeus is asking after Hades. If you know where he is, you may want to send him back to the party."

Mnemosyne's footsteps retreated down the hall, as if she didn't need to stay to make sure Lexi was in her room. She'd probably heard the grand finale. Somehow it wouldn't have bothered Lexi if she had. Mnemosyne wasn't the typical mom. She'd been the only one encouraging Lexi's interest in Hades.

"I suppose that's my cue." Hades pushed off the floor and helped Lexi to stand, which wasn't as easy as it should have been.

"Wow, my legs don't want to function," she said, using the sofa for support.

Hades smiled like he'd just received first place in something. "You've had an eventful day. I'm sure everyone would understand if you called it a night."

He was right. After that incredible orgasm, her body was completely spent. And the thought of relaxing and enjoying the aftermath sounded a lot better than making conversation with a bunch of busybodies. "I wish you could stay."

"So do I. Why don't we reconvene after you've rested, when the guests have gone to sleep. Let's say three o'clock under the balcony?"

"We'll synchronize our watches." She smiled as she pretended to tap an invisible watch on her wrist.

He left her with a tender kiss on the cheek, escaping down the boat ladder. Then Lexi waved down one of the staff and asked them to relay the message that she was retiring for the night. There wasn't much happening besides the same overindulgences anyway. But rest didn't come easy, not with the image of Hades's head between her legs playing over and over in her mind. After a few fitful hours of sleep, she woke up at two thirty and noticed another text had arrived from James.

Sounds like a story that's better shared in a call. Let me know a good time to do that

Based on the time stamp, he was probably getting ready for class. Did she want to start a conversation with a guy across the ocean? Hell, no. Not while she had a god within her reach. As she waited for the time to tick closer to three, she listened to the house. Not for the sounds of the staff but for heavier footfalls, the ones belonging to someone who didn't know the meaning of stealth. Something about the quiet made her wary that Zeus was roaming the halls.

Lexi finally climbed out of bed at 2:50 a.m. and padded across the floor to the bathroom. Despite the body aches and lack of sleep, the prospect of sneaking off with Hades to finish what they'd started thrilled her like nothing else, including that time she'd ditched Mara to corner Seth Baker in his dorm room. Lexi didn't care if Zeus found out, but she prayed he wouldn't.

She assessed her reflection in the mirror, debating whether to change out of the dress she'd slept in. She opted to keep the dress on but slipped out of her bra and panties. There was no sense adding extra obstacles, although Hades didn't seem to have trouble with them.

Before heading to the balcony, Lexi grabbed her riding jacket just in case they ended up back at the stable. It was the only place she could think of where they might find privacy.

Bracing against the wind, which had been tormenting her all weekend, she rehung the boat ladder and peered over the side to the shrubbery below, tensing when she saw a shadow that didn't belong. She could only hope it was Hades and not the king of everything.

Her stomach clenched in anticipation as she climbed down, and she startled when a pair of strong hands gripped her waist and lowered her gently to the ground. It was Hades, and the desire to kiss him flooded her like a tidal wave. But he didn't give her a chance before he hustled her around the corner of the estate.

"Is something wrong?" she asked.

"Z is walking the perimeter. I just saw him head down to the stable."

"Damn. I was going to suggest we go there."

Their movements led them to the side entrance of the garage, and when a floodlight flicked on, they ducked beneath it. Lexi sucked on her lip as her brain did a mental scan of the property. The beach was out. Not enough cover. And the outcropping of rocks would be too uncomfortable. Same with the trail. Not to mention the wildlife that might happen upon them.

Lexi realized she had closed her eyes when she felt Hades's breath against her face. Then he was kissing her. The lethal blend of his cologne, if that's really what it was, made her lightheaded, and his tongue tasted sweet, like he'd been eating pomegranate seeds.

His hand moved to her thigh then slipped under her dress. When he realized she was naked, his progress stopped and he stepped back.

"I've been worried I was being too bold, but—"

"Ditto."

She smiled and kissed him again as her head spun and her body tingled. Then a thought occurred to her that was so perfect, so brilliantly simple, that she laughed when she said it.

"The limo."

Twenty-two

The floodlight followed them into the garage, disappearing as the door closed. A dim glow still shone through the door's frosted window, turning all the objects into silhouettes, but Lexi didn't need the light. She knew her way around because Ham was meticulous about his garage. With a sure grip on Hades's hand, she strode to the limo and opened the door, triggering the dome light. Then she slid across the back seat and Hades followed her in.

Under the limo's spotlight, Lexi peeled off her coat and shimmied out of her dress while Hades watched with an amused smile. Was he surprised by her lack of modesty? Or was he just appreciating the view? The light blinked off, and he hadn't moved.

"Are you just going to sit there admiring me in the dark?" she said. "At least let me share in the experience."

"I'd love to admire you much longer, but I know we don't have the luxury of time."

Lexi thought she heard uncertainly in his tone as he relieved himself of clothes. Or was it disappointment? It pissed her off that they didn't have the luxury of time. They were just getting started, and she wanted to see how far their connection took them. She suspected that wouldn't matter to an immortal goddess, but it was mattering to her more and more.

Hades stripped, and it was like watching a present being unwrapped: a gorgeous, golden-skinned, amber-eyed present. When his task was done, Lexi kissed him, wrapping her arms around his neck and draping her legs over his hips to bring their bodies as close as the back seat would allow.

It had never been like this for her, flesh against flesh in such an unrestricted, vulnerable way, and she enjoyed the delicate shiver that traveled from her scalp to her groin. When she felt his erection against her inner thigh, more shivers erupted. Then she rallied her courage and snaked her arm between their bodies to take him in hand. His tongue responded to her touch, lashing the inside of her mouth as her fingers explored him, both plush and firm. She circled the tip with her thumb, enjoying the control she had of his pleasure.

With his hand at her back, Hades lowered Lexi to the seat, and she tugged him down with her legs until his hardness rested against her belly. Their mouths drew apart, and she kept her eyes trained on his face as he trailed his fingers across her cheek. He was watching her, too, his needy respirations telling her he was all in.

"Hades, I'm handing the reins to you."

She felt his pulse race behind his chest as he reached to the floor of the limo to grope for his pants. "Will you excuse me a moment? I have to fetch something from my pocket."

"I have no other plans."

Hades had come prepared with a condom, and her body idled beneath him as he made the necessary modification. Then he bent over her mouth again and brushed a kiss across it.

"You are miraculous. And I'm the most fortunate god on earth."

He lowered to her entrance, circling and coating himself with her eagerness. It felt like a tsunami to her, which she was grateful for as he pressed the thick tip inside. The sensation brought on feelings that Lexi wasn't prepared for, like surrender and the awareness that there was no turning back. But Hades approached the task with incredible tenderness, as if he was using the practice of zen despite their time constraints. He filled her slowly, almost too slowly, until she felt something give way.

"How does that feel?" he asked, a gentleman even when he was acting like a rogue.

"Like freedom. Please, don't stop."

She lifted her body so her breasts grazed his chest, and he surged forward with a controlled drive, then gradually retreated. Her body hummed in response, like a musician being given center stage after years of playing backup. And he kept at this for a while, speeding up the tempo then slowing it down again, as if he wanted her to enjoy the whole performance.

All the while her climax lingered in the background, elusive and frustratingly out of reach. Not that she wasn't enjoying everything about the experience, but she didn't feel in control of it. Then Hades slipped his hand between her legs, and her body reacted with a powerful jerk. There it was.

With her head tilted back, Hades pressed his lips to her throat, his breathing erratic at her ear, his fingers bringing her closer to release. She found herself counting as she tried to extend the moment, and she'd only reached five before she exploded around him in a strangled cry. Hades reacted seconds later with a fierce tremble that echoed through her body in exquisite waves. The world melted away, and Lexi let herself get carried off by the tide.

When Hades lowered his body to gently rest on hers, she remembered her own body, and draped her arms over his shoulders, staring at his handsome silhouette. His eyes had warmed to a golden glow, reminding her that he was a god and that she was a goddess. It felt like a dream.

"How did I do, my lady?"

She brought her mouth to his lips, speaking against them. "When do we leave for Asia?"

He chuckled. "Let's take one risk at a time, shall we?"

Lexi smiled, but the longer she lay there beneath him, with his strength inside her, the more she felt like she had lost herself. At least a part of herself. But she didn't need that part anymore. In fact, she'd never felt more whole. While Hades cradled her head in his hands and offered her his lips, she focused on the rhythmic cadence of their breathing and the slowly retreating throb in her groin.

Could he tell the fabric of her world had been torn? Her perception of life changed forever? Was that the seduction of sex? Unrestrained carnal release and to hell with everything else?

"Are you okay?" he whispered into the darkness.

"Never better." She trailed her fingers along the grooves of his arms, admiring the musculature.

"Do you want to talk about it?"

"Should we? Is that normal?"

"It's your first time, if I'm not mistaken. I want you to know it's an option."

Lexi bit her lip, feeling braver than she probably should have. "Can we skip the sex talk and just do it again?"

Hades swooped down to claim her mouth, slipping his hand

underneath her and forcing their bodies closer. She gasped at the fullness.

"I'd like nothing more than to make love to you until the sun rises," he said. "But we have a manic god stomping around the estate. I think we should take what we've been granted and leave with our skins intact."

She wanted to argue with him. To complain about that manic god treating them both like children. But being caught with their pants down wouldn't be ideal, so they gathered their clothes and climbed out of the limo to dress. Even as she quivered in the aftermath of their encounter and her muscles ached from her eventful weekend, she wanted to feel him inside her again.

Once dressed, Hades opened the garage door a crack and peered outside. "Everything looks clear from here." As he reached his hand out to Lexi, his eyes twinkled like the northern lights. "You are amazing. I can't remember the last time I felt this way."

They walked hand in hand to the balcony. And although Lexi's legs were a bit wobbly and her head dazed, she truly had never felt better. When the boat ladder came into view, hanging from her balcony like an escape hatch, she thought about hauling Hades down the beach path with no plans of returning.

But it was not to be, because they were not alone. A figure stood in the courtyard beneath her balcony, looking like a manic god with an enormous scowl.

"Oh shit." The exclamation was out of her mouth before she could stop it, and Zeus rolled out of the shadows like a dark cloud.

"If you mean *Oh shit, I have some explaining to do*, then your sentiment fits the situation perfectly." His moustache bristled, but Lexi was ready for the challenge. She would not let him bully her.

"I don't have to explain anything to you. I already made myself perfectly clear."

"So did I." His lips curved into a smile, like he, too, was ready for the challenge.

"Why are you being such a prick? Let me live my life, then I might consider sticking around to make yours less of a hassle."

The grip Hades had on her hand tightened, and she read it as a signal to tread carefully. Was that for him or for her?

"Let me take this moment to remind you who I am," Zeus said. "I'm the ruler of all gods. In matters of import, I have the final say."

"Okay. I'll let you know when something of import comes up."

Zeus stared pointedly at Lexi and Hades, their fingers entwined in solidarity. "Hades, you have flouted my position since the day my fate was handed to me. Why do you continue this folly? Is it so difficult for you to enjoy the company of a simple mortal and not be tempted by someone who is out of your reach?"

"Do you mean not be tempted to build a relationship with someone who isn't dead before I can schedule a second date? You always seem to forget that I'm forbidden from entering my birthplace and fostering relationships there. You forget because you never visit the underworld. None of the gods do. Out of sight, out of mind. Isn't that the saying?"

Zeus growled under his beard but didn't seem to have an immediate rebuttal. Which was fine, because it was Lexi's turn.

"I think that's all bullshit. And, for the record, I'm interested in building a relationship with Hades." She turned to Hades and repeated the words he'd said to her just hours before. "Now, and any time in the future that he'll have me."

"Even if that future is a century from now?" Zeus said.

Lexi glared at him. "Is that threat aimed at me or Hades?"

"At both of you. If you want to live the life of a demigod among mortals, Lexi, you will answer to me. You can travel and work and cavort with anyone you wish. But your status as a god requires that your activities continue to be monitored by nymphs. That's just how it's done."

She blinked, hoping she had misunderstood him. "What nymphs?"

"The estate staff and your friends at school."

She blinked again as the weight of his words sunk in. "You mean Mara?"

"Yes, Mara. And the other one you don't speak to anymore."

Heat spread through Lexi's chest as her anger spiked. "You are an egomaniac, you know that?!" She let go of Hades and raised both hands at Zeus, her skin prickling as she forced as much intention at him as she could manage. A wall of air came back and hit her so hard it sent her tumbling into the grass. She lost her breath but was already scrambling to her feet when Hades offered his hand.

"Lexi, let it go," he said softly.

"I'll let it go when *he* lets it go."

Zeus wore the face of a judge when Lexi rounded on him again. This time she didn't try to use her godly power, just the power of her words.

"I will never submit to you or your spies. You'll be cleaning up after my messes for eternity!"

"Unless I decide to keep you confined to the estate! And if you continue to threaten me, that can be easily arranged."

Zeus waved an arm at the wall of the estate and the white stone and marble rippled away like mist, revealing an immense structure of gold underneath. It reached all the way to the third floor, and she gaped at the rows of thick columns shimmering magically beneath the manor's facade.

She hadn't been imagining things when she'd questioned her parents about the house paint, when she tried to convince herself it was the sunlight. She was seeing through the gods' glamour. It had been placed there to hide what it truly was—a prison of gold.

"If you think you have no freedom now," Zeus said evenly, "keep testing me and you'll spend your first century as a goddess here."

"I think we all need a break from this topic," Hades said. "Threats rarely lead to compromise. Lexi, please."

He looked at her through pale eyes, their usual glow subdued by emotion, and maybe fear. It would be stupid to think of Zeus as her uncle Z anymore. She needed to admit defeat on this one.

"Fine. I'm going up to my room. We can talk about this tomorrow." She took Hades's hand in hers, despite the trembling. She didn't care if Hades thought she was afraid; she just didn't want Zeus to know. "Good night, Hades. I had an unforgettable evening. Will I see you tomorrow?"

He smiled, although she had no trouble reading the sadness behind it. "I'll make it so, assuming I'm not struck by lightning before then."

Twenty-three

Z didn't strike Hades with lightning after Lexi disappeared inside. In fact, he nudged Hades onto the beach path without a hint of brutality. Although Z might have been planning to smite him down there and kick his body into the sea.

"Hades, this is a problem that cannot be fixed easily. I'll admit that we're both to blame here. So, it makes sense that we put our feuding aside and come up with a solution together."

Hades chuckled, although he shouldn't have. Z only gritted his teeth.

"I know I don't ask for your assistance often, but you seem to have earned Lexi's trust," Z went on. "Surely, you can convince her that she'll have as much freedom as any demigod living away from Olympus. The nymphs are here to assure the safety of mortals."

"I know that. Maybe you should tell her tomorrow when you have your talk."

"She's more likely to listen to you. I'm afraid I've made it to the top of her shit list."

"Well, you don't exactly have a gentle approach."

"Hence my request."

"Or you could work on improving your approach. For instance, rather than threatening her with a century, why not give her ten years in Olympus. Her parents and brother can certainly manage the estate while she embraces her godly powers in the proper environment."

Z pursed his lips. Hades didn't really expect his first suggestion to be well received. "She's Mnemosyne's daughter. A direct descendant of a Titan. We both know it will take longer than a decade. Although I'm beginning to see your type. It wasn't so long ago that another of Mnemosyne's unplanned offspring caught your eye."

Hades ignored Z's jab at his failed love life and continued to offer suggestions as the path opened to the beach. "How about twenty years? Her parents will still be around. I assume they've been drinking ambrosia like the other mortal ambassadors. That should preserve their bodies for at least another forty years."

Z paced the sand, snatching at the seagrass as he walked away from Hades. "I would have to go back on my word to Lexi's family. I've made promises to them, and I don't like breaking promises."

"I take it these were promises you didn't have full control over? Promises that depended on Lexi not finding out she's an immortal? At least, not until the nymphs reported she was flying her horse on the beach."

"Yes." Z huffed as he pivoted and walked back.

"I don't think it would have been much longer."

"Clearly!"

Hades was beginning to wonder what his brother and Mnemosyne had talked about during their earlier conversation with Lexi. "What does Mnemosyne want for her? Have you asked?"

"She wants Lexi to find happiness. Whatever that means."

"It means Lexi should be allowed to pursue the things that bring her happiness. Even if it upends the plans of others. It seems to me that she has spent most of her life following paths that aren't her own. She wants to travel solo. So let her do that."

"But the dangers of an inexperienced goddess gallivanting around the human realm are too great. She would need at least two nymphs to travel with her. It's something even the council will not budge on."

"Then teach her."

"That's not my job."

"Then make it someone's job. Lexi isn't the first demigod to be born. Give her the tools so she can pursue her happiness without blowing things up."

Z shook his head, but apparently it was not to disagree with Hades. "I suppose that's a reasonable place to start. I'll enlist Athena's help. I'm going to bed. I expect you'll be leaving for Asia tomorrow?"

"I won't overstay my welcome."

With a twisted look that Hades decided was frustration, his brother left him standing on the beach and entered the path that would take him back. The doors to Lexi's balcony were closed and the curtains pulled. He hoped she would sleep well into the morning.

He turned his back on the estate and faced the sea, watching the waves roll in to slap the sand. The uneven pattern of the surf combined with the certainty that it would always come ashore was a perfect metaphor for his life. What had started as a detour on his way to the Asian islands had turned into a seduction on the part of a clever, untried goddess. If he hadn't arrived with his heart in tatters, already battling a changing tide, he might have had a fighting chance.

Instead, he found himself wishing he could stay. He wanted to lie under the stars with Lexi and talk about his home. To make love to her in the surf. To help her embrace her role as a goddess. Would Z allow him to extend his visit and provide her with a few lessons? *Ha!* He must have been exhausted to entertain such an idea.

But why had Z softened after Lexi went to bed? Why had he changed his supreme ruler stance and asked Hades for help? Although his brother was not incapable of reason, Hades didn't fully believe that Z's request was a god simply using manipulation to get his way. It went deeper than that, but he couldn't guess why.

Regardless of the reasons, there wasn't much he could do but hope Lexi felt the same about him in a century.

Lexi couldn't sleep. She was too freaked out. All she could do was sit on her bedroom floor and stare at the walls. The glamour no longer worked on her. Now that she knew what was underneath, she could only see the gold bars of a prison. And she was terrified of being trapped inside.

So she did the only thing that made sense. She played with her power. After flooding her bathroom with water she decided to focus on air, and succeeded in keeping two throw pillows floating without much effort or triggering the smoke alarm. She'd even rearranged some things in her room. But how well could she defend herself with that skill? It had fully backfired with Zeus.

Her mind had also been wandering to unhelpful places, specifically to the Titan who had given her the power. Apart from her ability to recite every poem written since the dawn of time, Mnemosyne was able to remove and return the memories of anyone at will. The more Lexi dwelled on this, the more worried she became. What if Zeus forced Mnemosyne to remove Lexi's memories so she wouldn't know she was a god? So she wouldn't know she was a prisoner?

Was it so wrong to want freedom on *her* terms? Did anyone even care whether she found happiness? Her parents had their flaws, but their advice about life had motivated her to be the person she was today. And one mantra they used ad nauseum was taking responsibility for her own success. Apart from the obvious irony in that advice, it felt like a good motivator for these circumstances.

Without much of a plan, Lexi grabbed her backpack and shoved some items into it: clothes, her cell phone and charger, an empty journal, her credit cards, and all the cash she had on hand. If she was going to be on the run for a while, she would need snacks too.

She hurried down the staircase almost haphazardly, her frantic desire to escape outweighing caution, but she made it to the kitchen without being followed. The fruit bowl offered excellent choices, and she loaded up on granola bars. As she stood at the fridge filling a water bottle, she became aware of the walls again—glowing, smothering.

Her heart gave a panicked thud and she bolted out of the kitchen and down the hallway almost at a run, water sloshing from the bottle as she tried to tighten the lid. She blew past the guest rooms on tiptoe as she made for the laundry room and the closest door leading to freedom. With a twist and a *click* she slipped outside, her feet cushioned by the manicured lawn and the estate wall at her back. She'd escaped the golden prison, and Zeus would have to catch her to make good on his threat.

But Lexi still didn't know where she was running to. The hedgerow maze loomed in front of her, an ominous contortion of nature. It had been modeled after Daedalus's labyrinth, the Hellenistic interpretation, and she had lost many hours inside it. She'd even found hideouts over the years—natural alcoves in the shrubs where a body could be tucked away. It would have to do for now.

She walked toward it in measured, determined strides, hoping nobody was watching from the upper-floor windows as she disappeared through the curved trellis. Tendrils of fragrant honeysuckle caressed her shoulders as she entered, and she felt the weight of the estate fall away. With the stars and her memory to guide her, she trekked to the center of the maze. The sun was due to rise in less than an hour, so she needed to come up with a better plan than hiding out in her own backyard. The maze was probably the first place her family would look for her, besides the stable.

Lexi arrived at one of three alcoves and hunkered down with her backpack, digging out a banana. Then she dropped her head back to stare up at the sky. Most of the stars were hidden by the approaching dawn, and she traced the ones that were left with her finger. Cassiopeia had always been her favorite, a constant in the north. It was steadfast and reliable, unlike her family.

She tensed at the sound of footfalls. She wasn't alone. *Damn.* Someone must have seen her enter the maze. Was it one of the staff? A nymph who'd spotted her from their bedroom window? Was it Zeus? Did the arrogant god ever sleep? She stowed the banana in her backpack, preparing to make a quick exit, as a figure rounded the corner and stopped to look at her.

"Lexi."

"Hades. How did you find me?"

Her heart pounded with adrenaline and relief as he walked over and took a seat beside her. "I heard someone in the kitchen. Why are you out here and not in bed resting?"

"Because I no longer trust my godfather. And I don't want to be a prisoner in that place."

Hades let go of a sigh as he slipped his hand around hers. "Z tends to threaten first and negotiate later."

"Actually, I've experienced that firsthand, so thanks for reminding me. But it doesn't mean I'm setting foot inside that godly monstrosity again."

"Understandable." He captured her in his gaze, where all his emotions seemed to live. "You don't have to make any big decisions now. Take the summer to absorb everything, wherever you decide to do that."

"There's a lot to absorb."

"I was raised in Olympus, and it was decades before my siblings and I found our stride."

"How long did you live in Olympus before you were banished?"

Hades cringed, as if she had cursed him. "Not long enough."

With their fingers entwined, they sat in the shadow of the hedgerow, listening to the birdsong as the sky lightened, erasing the stars. Lexi appreciated the comfort he gave her without the obligation of conversation. More and more she realized how similar their stories were. And despite them being strangers just days ago, Hades was the only one who understood her. More importantly, he was the only one who didn't want to control her.

Unfortunately, it wasn't long before voices echoed from the patio as breakfast was being set up.

"If you want to stay here a while longer, I'll go entertain your family," he said. "They're probably expecting you to sleep late."

"Thanks. I need more time to think."

He left her with a kiss and a wry smile that said he wouldn't be surprised if she disappeared after he was gone. But rather than run, which was what every nerve in her body wanted her to do, she tucked into her knees and let herself cry.

The noise level had picked up on the patio when Lexi realized she'd dozed off. In fact, as she stretched the kinks out of her neck, she heard her parents' voices on the path inside the labyrinth. She shouldered her backpack and stood, shaking the exhaustion from her brain. Did she want to talk to them? Give them a piece of her mind? Or did she want to run for the exit?

She decided to take her chances and just focus on getting to the opposite side of the maze. As the Fates would have it, she didn't make it far before their paths crossed. No surprise that her dad was looking impatiently at his watch as he rounded the corner.

"There you are. Your godfather told us you two had a disagreement last night. He thought you might try to run away." He glanced at the backpack, scrunching his brows. "Really, Lexi?"

"I'm still here, aren't I?" Her anger was the first to show up, and their false shock was textbook. Did they really not expect her to be mad? "And it wasn't just a disagreement. He threatened to imprison me inside the estate. I've seen what's hiding under all that marble."

"He wouldn't do that," said her mom, although the uncertainty in her tone suggested she didn't believe her own words.

"Honey, let's look at this through a bigger lens," her dad said, his chin lifting as he slipped into CEO mode. "You're a demigod.

You have incredible power and an eternity to use it. What human wouldn't say yes to an opportunity like that?"

"All I'm hearing is *What's wrong with you? Why can't you be grateful for this thing that everyone thinks is so perfect?*"

"You're missing my point. I'm saying that you have all the time you need to focus on your pursuits. Mortal humans don't have that luxury. Your mom and me, and your brother, we only have a short time to enjoy the fruits of this world."

"I'm sorry. I must have misunderstood. Are you saying *Hey Lexi, even though we never told you that you're a demigod and we spied on you and controlled every aspect of your life, we need you to behave like a good little god and keep doing it until we die?*"

She forced her brows up, daring them to deny it, but her father hadn't achieved his success by backing down. "All your mother and I are asking is for you to give us a break once in a while. Go on your trips. Find yourself. But live here with your family while our bodies hold out. What's a few decades to an immortal?"

"Clearly, we have differing opinions on what *family* means. My idea of family is someone I can trust to support me and my pursuit of happiness even if they don't agree with me. Or if it screws with their plans. We're all responsible for our own success. Isn't that what you've parroted at me? Honestly, the way I'm feeling right now, I would choose a stranger to have my back over my family."

"Lexi, you don't mean that," her mom said miserably. But Lexi didn't have to see her expression to hear the apathy.

Somehow, the judgment behind that simple statement fueled the adrenaline simmering under Lexi's skin, causing her fingers to tingle and her chest to expand. She was just a tool to them. An asset to achieve their own versions of happiness. They were too far gone to see it any other way.

"I do mean it! I'm done with all the lies and fake bullshit! Get Dion to babysit!"

Lexi balled her fists, letting the anger fill her, then she jerked them hard at the ground. The earth rumbled, causing dirt and leaves to bounce at her feet. Then a crack zigzagged through the packed soil, making its way from one side of the hedgerow to the other. Lexi jumped back, her arms flailing, and suddenly one of the eight-foot shrubs creaked and groaned as the roots were sucked upward out of their home. How had she done that? How was she supposed to stop it?

Her pulse roared in her ears like a raging waterfall as she watched the mighty hedgerow follow the downward movements of her hands, crashing to the ground in a cacophony of crunching branches and filling the space between them. As they all stared at each other over the fallen tree, voices filled the maze. One of those voices belonged to the last god she wanted to talk to, especially with the evidence of her mess lying at her feet.

Lexi did the only thing that made sense. She ran.

Twenty-four

Lexi ran like her life depended on it, taking corners so fast that her knees hit the dirt twice. At least she wasn't uprooting hedges anymore; she just focused on the heavy footfalls giving chase behind her. Then she heard his voice, except he wasn't talking to her.

"This is why I asked for your help, Mnemosyne. Do it now. For everyone's well-being."

Lexi knew exactly what he wanted Mnemosyne to do. Erase her memories. Make her forget who she was and what she cared about. She couldn't let that happen, and her feet barely touched the ground as she raced like the wind. Neither god had caught up to her when she finally bolted through the exit like lightning.

From there, it was a familiar hurtle to the stable. Jackie O was her only hope. She wasn't sure how she was going to outrun her life on a horse, but she felt like she had no other choice. She slid through the stable entrance at a gallop, slipping on the hay as she hurried to the mare's stall.

"C'mon, girl. We're going for a ride. No time to saddle up."

Being the true friend that she was, Jackie O didn't resist as Lexi fitted her with a harness and reins. As Lexi guided her horse out of the stable, Mnemosyne and Zeus were just leaving the path. Zeus was red faced and annoyed, while Mnemosyne followed at a graceful pace behind him. Serene as always.

"Lexi! Don't you dare get on that horse!" Zeus shouted his command, but she was already climbing onto Jackie O's back and spurring her into motion.

"Leave me alone! I need time to think!" she screamed as her horse bolted away from the gods, kicking sand into the air and snorting her excitement. Jackie O always knew what Lexi needed, and right now she needed to get as far away from the estate as her friend was willing to take her.

The wind blew Lexi's hair into her face, but she didn't need her vision. She knew the beach would take her three miles before the rocks forced them into the sea. It wasn't nearly far enough, but it was her only option. She kept Jackie O at a gallop, not bothering to look back. She was never going to look back. Only forward. Her future was just as important as anyone else's.

Jackie O whinnied, and Lexi looked down to find her horse's legs kicking wildly as the ground retreated away from them, like a runway when an airplane makes its initial ascent into the air. Jackie O's hooves were no longer pounding the sand. She was flying!

"It's okay, girl," she said, only because it was the first thing that came to mind. It absolutely wasn't okay, and she was pretty sure Jackie O wasn't the one causing their sudden departure from terra firma.

Lexi's objective to escape evaporated like smoke in the wind, and all she cared about now was landing Jackie O back on the ground. They had leveled off at around eight feet above the sand, and she risked a glance behind her, finding a small crowd forming on the beach.

"We're going to fix this, Jackie O. I'm going to get you down safely."

Lexi knew how far the sand bar stretched from the shoreline. If she was going to have any hope of saving her horse, they would need to land in the water. Jackie O would hate that, but at least she knew how to swim.

"Let's turn around, okay? We need to go home, girl."

Lexi tugged on the reins, nudging Jackie O toward the sea, and the muscles in her horse's neck tensed as she fought against Lexi's guidance.

"Please. We'll only be in the water for a few seconds. We can't land you on the beach. You might break something. Please, Jackie O."

Tears brewed beneath Lexi's line of sight, lasting only seconds before the wind swept them away. Her horse whinnied again, and Lexi focused all her energy on turning Jackie O around before they reached the outcropping. If she didn't act fast, neither of them would make it. Slowly but surely Jackie O followed Lexi's lead, making a wide left turn in the air and flying over the ocean like a freaking Pegasus.

Lexi breathed a prayer of thanks when she finally glimpsed the stable ahead of them. Now came the hard part. She would have to land her horse in the water. It had taken Jackie O nearly two years to accept the ocean, and she still hated to go in it. Fortunately, to keep the mare's phobia in check, Lexi had been forcing Jackie O to get her hooves wet whenever they walked on the beach.

The crowd had started to run toward them, with Lexi's burly godfather leading the pack. She didn't even dwell on what the repercussions of this catastrophic situation would be once it was all over. Her number one priority was keeping her horse alive.

"There's the stable, Jackie O. There's home. We need to land in the water to do this safely. Then we'll just swim to shore. The waves are nice and calm, and I'll be with you the whole way."

Jackie O snorted, but that was just her way of cursing Lexi. Which was fine. Her horse knew that instructions were coming, and Lexi leaned her weight on Jackie O's neck as she attempted to bring them closer to the water. Again, her horse resisted, jerking upward and taking them higher. A seagull appeared suddenly, squawking as it blew past their starboard side. Jackie O snorted again, and Lexi was able to use the distraction to urge them lower.

Lexi figured a trained god would know how to bring a flying horse in for a safe landing, but she wasn't a trained god. And Jackie O was no flying horse.

"After this is all over, I'm blaming Zeus," she growled, as they drew closer to the estate.

The water was just inches from Jackie O's hooves now, and they were still flying too fast. How was Lexi supposed to slow them down? Did her spiking adrenaline have something to do with their speed? If that was the case, they were screwed. Her heart was beating faster than they were flying.

Lost in her thoughts, she barely noticed that they'd drifted toward the beach. Then a strong pull to the port side slowed them down, like a train conductor yanking on the brakes, and they were dragged toward a crowd of raised arms. As far as she could tell, the gods were working together to bring Lexi and her horse back to safety.

With the stable just ten yards away, Jackie O touched down at a canter, and they slowly came to a stop on the sand. Lexi collapsed onto her horse's neck, breathing in the scent of her windblown mane and the sweat that soaked the mare's skin. She didn't care about the voices echoing around her. She had stopped running. And she would not leave Jackie O until her friend had recovered.

"Lexi, are you okay?"

The voice belonged the only god she didn't want to punch, and she pulled her hair back from her eyes to look at Hades.

"Physically? Yes."

"And Jackie O?"

"She seems okay, but I need to get her into the stable to check for sure."

"Please, let me escort you both."

With a firm hand on the reins, Hades guided them through the stable doors. It didn't escape Lexi's notice that they weren't being followed.

"Where is everyone?" she asked. "Why isn't Zeus here cursing me for eternity and telling Mnemosyne to erase my memories?"

"Who told you she was going to erase your memories?" His brows arched as he hesitated at the door to Jackie O's stall. "Did Zeus threaten that as punishment?"

"Not exactly. When they were chasing me through the maze, I heard him tell her to do something 'for everyone's well-being.' I figured, since Mnemosyne's gift is to remove memories, he would use that against me when he reached his limit."

Hades pursed his lips and blew air through them. "I can see Z pulling that card, but Mnemosyne would never agree to it. Your memories are safe, Lexi. Although if that's what he was asking of her, it doesn't bode well for him at the next council meeting, if I'm forced to bring it up."

His hand came to rest on her arm as he looked up at her. "I've been granted thirty minutes with you before Z has his say. Are you up for that? We can talk while we inspect your horse for injuries."

"Sure."

He helped her dismount, and she spent the next minute centering herself on solid ground. Jackie O seemed happy to be back home, and headed for her water trough. She even allowed Hades to feed her a carrot from the treat bag.

"I didn't mean for that to happen," Lexi said. "I guess my powers are triggered when my emotions are high."

"That's when they usually make themselves known. Remind me to tell you about Poseidon and his first race with an Andalusian."

"I blame Zeus for keeping so many secrets from me. What if none of you had been there to help us? I had no idea if my plan was going to work."

"You mean landing you both in the ocean? I think it had a good chance."

"I appreciate the vote of confidence. Do you think I'm overreacting?" She rubbed Jackie O's hips to check for spasms.

"Absolutely not. The stories I could tell you would curl your hair."

She chuckled. "That's reassuring. Because I don't mind telling you that scared the shit out of me. And Jackie O will probably be grinding her teeth for days."

"Whatever your reasons, they must have been significant for your power to manifest that way. Not every god can control the flight of horses."

"Well, I didn't feel in control today. Do you think Zeus will punish me? Will he lock me in that stupid golden palace?"

"Not as long as I have a say in the matter. And I do, whether he likes it or not. He isn't as omnipotent as he thinks. But he does know how to put up a fight."

Lexi sagged against the stall. Her inspection of Jackie O hadn't turned up anything of concern. Her biggest issue would be getting her horse to accept the ocean again.

"I'm just so angry," she said. "And it's not just this weekend. I need to find a safe place where I can think without being lectured or watched. I thought that part of my life was past me when I turned eighteen. But here I am still wishing they'd just give me some fucking space. I feel like I'm suffocating."

Hades rested his shoulder on the stall beside her, his gaze unfocused and pointed at the opposite wall. "There are more things beyond the horizon that you've grown up with than you can imagine. I know you'll find what you're looking for, and even a few things you didn't know you were looking for. You have an eternity to do it."

"But what about now? I need something I can control now or I'm going to lose my mind."

"Okay. Tell me something right now that you believe will bring you happiness."

Lexi thought it would be easy to come up with an answer, but all she could do was recount the "friendly" suggestions her parents had made over the years, pushing her in the direction that had the most promise or the best potential for success. She'd never seriously thought about her own happiness, and she didn't know whether to be angry at her parents or herself for not seeing it sooner.

She turned to Hades, if for nothing else than a reassuring smile. And the one he offered came as easily to him as breathing. This was when the answer arrived, like a secret message transferred from one like-minded soul to another.

"Friendship. Real, true friendship. It would make me happy to know I had someone I could trust. Someone to love and who loves me back, even when they don't agree with me or they don't understand why I'm acting like a lunatic. Someone who cares enough to ask what's wrong and keep me company. I don't want to feel alone anymore. Or worse, surrounded by people who don't really care."

His arm came around her shoulder and she leaned into his embrace, shuddering through a sob and trying not to spill tears on his shirt. How often had she cried with no one else but her pillow to offer comfort?

"You already have that, Lexi, in me. I know our paths have only just crossed, but if I were to guess, our fates are more closely tied than most of the other gods'. I've felt the pain you feel. The hurt of not being heard. Not being seen. To have your life determined for you. I feel it more often than I care to admit."

Lexi stepped back to stare at him as something shifted inside her. The moment didn't last long, but it felt significant. Like the Fates had slapped her to wake her up.

"I'm sorry that's been your life. And I'd like nothing more than to give us both what we need to be happy. But how? We don't even live in the same world. And you need permission to leave your home. Hell, that might be *my* fate too. How would we keep in touch? How often could we see each other?"

Hades offered a shrug that almost looked like defeat. "We could pass messages through our mutual friends. But as far as seeing each other, I'm afraid even a decade between visits won't offer enough time to cultivate something as meaningful as what you're suggesting."

"Unless—"

Hades shook his head. "I know what you're thinking, and I would never ask you to abandon everything and everyone to join me in the underworld. I can't guarantee that Z wouldn't punish us both for that."

"What am I giving up? A life according to the gods? I'll have that anywhere, won't I? At least with you I'd have one true friend. And if you pissed me off I'd have the whole underworld to throw my tantrums in."

Hades didn't have an immediate argument for that, but his silence was still an answer, and she appreciated him for it.

"How firm are your plans for Asia?" she said. "We could hide out somewhere until this all blows over."

He chuckled. "If we left the estate together, we couldn't hide for long. Trust me when I say that nymphs know everything."

She nodded. She'd been there. "Well, one thing's for sure, I'm not going back into that house of lies. So whatever plans are made, they'll have to happen in here."

"Should I relay that message to your godfather?" His smirk was playful, making her feel less like a lunatic.

"Actually, I'd like to talk to Mnemosyne first."

Twenty-five

Lexi was eager to have a serious mother-daughter talk. Deep down, she trusted Mnemosyne. At least, she trusted Nora. But her nerves twitched when the Titan entered the stable's tack room. Lexi had set up temporary housing there, staying hydrated with bottled water and eating apples meant for the horses.

"Hello, Lexi. I'm glad to hear that you and your horse didn't sustain any injuries. We were all quite worried." As Mnemosyne spoke she maintained her usual cheerful smile, glancing around at the saddle racks and grooming supplies crowding the space. It probably looked nothing like the stables in Olympus.

"I was worried too. Not so much for me, but for Jackie O. Thank you for doing your part to save her."

"It's been a long time since I've found myself involved in such an invigorating group effort. We can get along when the situation requires it." She noticed the chair Lexi had pulled out for her and swept her peacock-blue maxi dress out of the way as she lowered into it gracefully. "Hades tells me you have some questions. I'll try to answer them as honestly as I can."

"I'm not surprised Zeus has a gag order on everyone. Typical."

"I promise not to lie to you. I'll simply tell you if I cannot answer."

"Okay. I was thinking we could start with some backstory," Lexi said as she took the seat across from her mother. "Were you and my dad in love when I was conceived? I'm just wondering if it had been a long affair."

The smile Mnemosyne had arrived with softened. "I've never known you to avoid the hard questions. No, we weren't in love. It happened spontaneously. Zeus and I had been at odds for a long time prior to our visit to your family's estate. He hoped we could get things sorted during a relaxing weekend. This plan backfired spectacularly, and I allowed my emotions to interfere with my judgment when he abandoned me at the estate. To spite him, I seduced Charles."

Lexi wasn't sure if the answer made her feel better or worse. It sure fueled her growing anger at Zeus. "When you learned you were pregnant did you want to raise me in Olympus?"

"It would have been my pleasure to raise you. But my actions that night were in direct conflict with council rules, which were set up to keep the gods and ambassador families safe from such pairings. The council decided that you would be raised among the mortals, forcing me to watch you grow up at a distance. Demigods can be difficult to manage at the best of times, so I was granted permission to visit often."

Lexi didn't like her explanation. Obviously, this was Zeus punishing Mnemosyne. But it also sounded like he wanted to keep Lexi in her mortal prison so he wouldn't lose a precious ambassador. "And I just proved them right, didn't I?"

"We already knew you were coming into your power. Zeus and I have had several difficult conversations about it, but—"

"He didn't want to tell me yet because he's a stubborn jackass."

Mnemosyne's tinkling laugh made Lexi's cheeks flush with heat. "He's had a long time to perfect that, I'm afraid."

"Okay. Enough about Zeus. I'd like to ask you about Hades. You two seem to know each other pretty well. What's your history together?"

Mnemosyne leaned back in her seat, blinking up at the ceiling rafters as if she needed a moment to recall the memories. "Hades is a complicated god, more so than the others. Before he took up his post I'd been tending to the mortal souls of the deceased, removing and restoring memories to help ease their transition out of life. When Hades was ready to perform his duties, I helped him with his own transition from an Olympian to the ruler of the underworld."

"Wow. He never mentioned that. He *did* say he's not allowed to enter Olympus, though. Why?"

"A prophecy from Gaia demanded it. And, being gods, we heed every prophecy that comes from Gaia. But I often wonder if the prophecy might have been misinterpreted, possibly even intentionally. Perhaps to serve one or more gods. I don't believe it has served Hades well to be denied the camaraderie of his peers."

"I agree, it sucks. But maybe it helped him in some ways. Hades seems like the most grounded god of the bunch. No offense."

"None taken. My experience with Hades has shown me a kind, passionate god who has embraced his duties with focus and resolve. Although, if you spend enough time with him, you'll see that he has moments of doubt and has been known to brood for days, which I cannot blame him for. You two seem to have forged an alliance." Her brows rose as she steepled her fingers in front of her mouth. "I'm almost tempted to say that he's met a fine match in you, Lexi. You both provide something that the other needs."

"I think you're right. I've never met anyone like him. He listens. I feel like I could tell him anything and not worry about being lectured or judged. And I don't want to wait a century before I see him again."

Lexi lowered her head and realized she was clenching her fists in her lap. Her stomach was also cramping, which might have been due to a lack of breakfast.

"I doubt it will be a century. But let me ask you this: What do you imagine for yourself in the next century? I know you haven't had much time to dwell on your immortality, but just because we have an eternity doesn't mean we shouldn't cultivate a purpose."

"You mean a purpose outside of homemaker?" Lexi hadn't meant for her words to come out so harshly. She wasn't blaming Mnemosyne for her situation. In fact, she wanted to hug her for asking the question. "Now that I know I'm no mere mortal, I don't think any of the things on my to-do list will thrill me. What demigod wants to work for the man? But shouldn't I wait until I know what my gifts are before I choose my purpose? When did you know yours?"

Mnemosyne chuckled, and Lexi knew it was because of her nervous rambling. She had plenty of excuses for being anxious, like the fact that her birth mother was a Titan of Olympus.

"The gods come into their power around the quarter century mark. This usually starts as small feats of supernatural manipulation, like what you showed us today. Our specific gifts, the ones that are unique to each god, can take longer to cultivate. Although not always. I was writing and reciting epic ballads at the age of eighteen. Of course, I am a direct descendant of Gaia."

She offered a shrug that was neither modest nor arrogant.

"I'm not trying to pressure you to find your purpose before you're compelled by your gifts, I just want you to consider your immortality as you make choices. Unlike mortals, when a god makes a poor choice, the consequences can stay with them for many mortal lifetimes."

They had segued into a topic that Lexi was very interested in, and she thought hard about the next question she wanted to ask. Once she revealed her intentions to Mnemosyne, there would be no taking them back. "What if my choice is to join Hades in the underworld and find my purpose there?"

Mnemosyne pursed her lips, but Lexi was certain she saw a smile trying to sneak onto them. "I'm not surprised you're asking me that question. Your circumstances have put you in a position to make choices you may not otherwise consider. Based on what I know about Zeus, I doubt he'll be in support of such a choice. In fact, you'll likely have a fight on your hands. That is, if you decide to tell him ahead of time."

The Titan allowed a smile to break through, but it didn't linger. "However, that may not be the only battle you'd need to prepare for. Certainly you're aware that Persephone shares winters with Hades. Their relationship has been ongoing for many centuries, and their bond has rarely been tested, even though both have taken consorts. I won't break Hades's trust by saying any more on the matter, but I'll tell you that he, too, is in a vulnerable state. Have you spoken to him about your interest in the underworld?"

"I've asked him questions, but I haven't told him that I'm seriously considering it."

"Well, I suggest you do that before he leaves the estate, or you may lose this opportunity."

Lexi felt relieved that Mnemosyne wasn't trying to talk her

out of it. And to hell with Zeus. She was more concerned about Hades. Would *he* try to talk her out of it? Or would he jump for joy? Her stomach growled, and she pressed her hand against it.

"Why don't I bring you back some breakfast?" Mnemosyne said. "You must be hungry after your eventful morning. Or I could have Hades bring you something."

"Actually, will you send Zeus in? I know he's still out there waiting to have his say. I can feel the vibration of his boots as he paces."

"Very well. I'll leave you to make your peace with him, or not. Either way, I'll be here to support you." She stood and headed for the door.

"Oh, Mnemosyne. Why don't you have Zeus fetch me something to eat before he comes in to read me my last rites. It will be my final act of rebellion before our relationship implodes."

"Let's hope it doesn't come to that."

Mnemosyne left the room, and Lexi rested her head on the table, folding her arms under her cheek and giving her body a chance to recharge. She'd narrowed down the options she would choose for herself and her future happiness, and she knew that Zeus wasn't going to be happy about any of them.

Twenty-six

Zeus walked into the tack room with a smug grin and a plate of eggs and toast. No doubt, he knew what an act of rebellion looked like. She also suspected he thought he was getting his way. It was the cocky ones who were the most clueless.

"Here's your breakfast, Lexi," he said as he slid the plate across the table. "I hope the eggs aren't too cold. The wind is really picking up outside."

He dropped into the chair across from her without preamble and watched her dig in. "So, where shall we start?"

"Why don't you start while I work on this." Lexi glanced up from her plate, praying that all he could see in her eyes was confidence.

"All right. I think we can both agree that you're in dire need of training. Had I known you were so close to wielding your power, I wouldn't have pushed so hard."

Bullshit. "Go on."

"I've spoken with Athena, and she has agreed to stay three more days to help you practice a few skills."

Of course he'd choose Athena. She was a hard-ass. Lexi acknowledged him with a nod and continued eating.

"I concede that this situation has had me flummoxed. Not only are you a demigod, but you're the daughter of an ambassador. It's a wholly unique situation that I hadn't fully prepared for. And I apologize for my neglect in this regard."

She nearly choked on her toast but managed to swallow before that happened. "Who told you to say that? Mnemosyne? I'll bet it was her."

"I don't need to be told when I've miscalculated. A good ruler knows when to put themselves in check."

She didn't respond even as he sat silently watching her eat. Did he expect her to congratulate him on being such a good ruler? She finally set down her fork and gave him her undivided attention.

"Fine. I acknowledge everything you just said. But I'm not stepping foot in that estate until you leave the property. I told you that you've broken my trust, regardless of your epiphanies and apologies. I'll sleep with Jackie O if I need to."

He snorted and looked ready to argue, but she locked him down with a gaze so fierce nobody could mistake it for anything but a challenge. "I will acquiesce to your request, but I'll not leave as long as Hades is here."

"Really? That's the hill you're dying on? Whether or not I sleep with your brother? How old are you again?"

His brows rose. "I understand that you're upset, but I don't appreciate your tone. You do not have the full picture of a god's life yet. You don't know the sort of consequences you could face from your choices."

"Then let me live my life and find out for myself. Why do you feel the need to direct every action I take? What is so fucking important about me? I'm just some random demigod. I'm sure there are hundreds of us roaming around. Is it the estate that's so precious to you? Are we sitting on all the gold that's owned by the gods?"

"Certainly not. We would never keep everything in a single location. I'll admit, there's a lot invested in this estate and I'd like to keep a trusted family here to protect it. Some of that gold belongs to you, young one. But that's not my point when I talk of consequences as a god."

"I don't care about gold."

"You would if it all went away. You've never been without means, and I think you would change your tone if you experienced poverty for yourself. That's a true loss of freedom."

Lexi couldn't dispute his point, although, having the powers of a god would always give her an advantage. She could help herself and others. Wasn't that the point of being a god? They were supposed to use their power for the good of humankind. At least, that was how humankind saw it.

Zeus stood from his chair. Apparently, he was done. "Why don't you leave the stable with me and come say goodbye to your guests on the patio. Some of them have suspended their departure to wait for you. I also suggest you apologize to the parents of Sami and Roderick. Neither boy was aware of our true nature yet, and both have been in shock since your stunt on the beach."

Lexi had too much on her mind to worry about her party guests and the carefully made plans she'd fucked up for them. But rather than start another argument, she planted a fake smile on her face, grabbed her empty plate, and left the stable with Zeus.

Their walk up the path took place in silence, and the closer they came to the estate, the harder it became for Lexi to breathe.

Was he playing a trick on her? Was he planning to throw her over his shoulder and carry her inside? She should have made him take an oath not to.

When she saw Hades and Mnemosyne relaxed and chatting in patio chairs, this helped a little. Surely they wouldn't let Zeus get away with such a dirty trick. Were they talking about her? Would the Titan be able to keep their secret? She loved to tell stories.

"I'm glad you decided to see us off, signorina Lexi." Aphrodite offered a sparkling smile as she swept up to Lexi in a sheer lace gown, revealing the gifts she'd been blessed with. "You gave us all a fright this morning. But it looked like you would have managed things without our help."

"I'm glad you were there. Jackie O hates to swim."

"One day I'll introduce you to Poseidon's horses. They're all excellent swimmers."

Lexi was reminded of the stories of Aphrodite and Poseidon, and wondered how many were true. But there would be time for those conversations later. Sir Henry leaned in with a peck to her cheek and a whispered comment.

"You really showed Zeus a thing or two this weekend. My best to you, Lexi." His tanned cheeks grew even darker as he tapped his walking stick to his forehead.

Apollo and Artemis had already left, and so had Dionysus, but Athena hung out poolside, fully dressed and clad in leather boots, like she was preparing to charge into battle after catching some rays. When those pleasantries were managed, Lexi followed her parents to the front of the estate where Rod's and Sami's families prepared to leave, and she made her apologies with as much sincerity as she was capable of. She wished she could get the boys alone to tell them to grab as much cash as they could and run for their lives.

During the awkward conversation Lexi watched Ham organize two loads of luggage into the limo's trunk like a Jenga puzzle. Could he guess what had happened in the back seat? How many secrets did he know?

After the fake farewells, Lexi retreated to the front of the estate. Incredibly, everyone left her alone, and she sat on the steps for a while, tracing the swirls in the marble and trying to detect a glamour. A few memories surfaced, but none of them triggered any melancholy. Apart from the horses, she wouldn't care if she never returned to the place again.

"Hey, brat." Dion's usual saunter looked more like a limp as he walked up, like he'd been riding an unbroken horse bareback. "What are you doing out here?"

"Staying out of prison." She smirked, and he pursed his lips.

"Strangely, I don't need to ask why you're being so cryptic. But I do need to tell you something important, and it needs to happen now, before anyone finds us."

She turned and saw he was frowning. "What's going on, Dion?"

He exhaled a long stream of air, and her heart started beating faster. Dion wasn't the type to get serious, but when he did, it was seriously serious.

"I just overheard a conversation that could get *me* thrown in prison if it ever gets out that I was privy."

"A conversation between who?"

"Zeus and Mnemosyne. I was passing by their bedroom. Normally I ignore the noises coming out of there. But you know how Zeus's voice booms. I heard your name, and my feet just stopped moving. The longer I stood there, the more crazy shit I learned, and the more crazy shit I learned, the riskier it was for me to stand there. So, I left to find you."

"What were they saying about me?" She blinked at him as her insides twisted into knots. After everything that had happened over the weekend, she honestly didn't know if her brain could handle another bombshell.

"Did you miss the part about me getting thrown in prison for repeating what I heard?"

"If it's about me, I should be the *only* person you tell. This family keeps more damned secrets than the dead."

"I love you, Lexi. And it's because I love you that I'm even telling you that I overheard something crazy about the father of all gods. Something he would do anything to keep under wraps, even threaten Mnemosyne with eternal damnation if she talked."

Lexi responded with an open mouth. She couldn't begin to imagine what eternal damnation might look like for a god, and she wasn't in the state of mind to try to figure it out as Dion continued his censored confession.

"The point is, Zeus is a lousy, selfish, conniving bastard, and none of us can trust him. Especially you. Whatever he has promised you will only last as long as you obey him completely. If you step one toe out of line, there's no doubt in my mind that he'll make you a prisoner. Not just of the estate, but of the mortal world. The story of Prometheus comes to mind."

Oh, hell. That was a very believable and visually disturbing definition of eternal damnation. Spending forever trapped in a home by the sea was a luxury compared to having her liver eaten by an eagle day after bloody day. She preferred to avoid both.

"So, where do we go from here?" she asked. "Do you have a plan for how I can avoid this life of forced obedience? Everyone else seems to think I have no right to complain. That as long as I have access to unlimited wealth, I should be happy, even if I have to live by someone else's rules and marry someone I'm not in love with. For eternity, I might add. How many husbands will I outlive?"

"You hit the nail on the head, Lexi. You're immortal. Something I didn't know until this weekend. It's bullshit to sentence an immortal to a life of forced obedience. To never be able to choose your own path. If you ask me, that's worse than prison."

"It's bullshit to sentence a *mortal* to a life like that. A mortal like you. And like Mom. *Your* mom."

"I came to terms with my fate years ago," he said to his fingernails, which were buffed to a glossy sheen. "I've been pushing my luck with it too. Asking for more time to find a girl to marry. Making myself indispensable at the company. I'm afraid I was hoping you'd fill the gap I was leaving, at least for a while longer. I was hoping that once you got the traveling bug out of your system and met somebody nice, you'd stick around and keep my future wife company."

"That's pretty shitty, Dion."

"I'm not proud of it. It's a shitty situation. And I'm not saying I wouldn't feel shitty for doing it even if I didn't know you were a demigod. But learning *that* changed things for me. And Zeus is being completely unfair about it. So when I overheard him with Mnemosyne, there was no question in my mind that I wouldn't tell you what I'd heard, or at least an abbreviated version of it. I want you to have the freedom that everyone deserves, mortal or immortal."

Lexi sat with Dion's revelation for a few seconds, while he craned his neck to check for silhouettes in the estate windows. He'd make a terrible criminal.

"Listen, Dion. I want you to know that I plan to petition the council of the gods to have them stop this practice of binding ambassador families with unbreakable oaths. It sounds dangerously close to interfering with free will."

"If anyone can do it, I'd put my money on you."

She smiled. "How long have you known the secret about our friends, the gods?"

"Three years. When I graduated college. That's when I learned that my life was already scripted for me. I guess they like to keep us clueless and carefree for as long as possible."

"So none of the other boys visiting this weekend knew the truth?"

"Maybe. Maybe not. We're told not to discuss it."

"Of course you are."

"I do hope you can get them to loosen their grip. Each generation should have a choice." His eyes widened and he jumped up like he'd been zapped by a cattle prod. "I should go. Whatever you decide, I support you."

She watched him bolt around the western edge of the estate, and that's when she noticed a figure emerging from the trees. She knew it was Hades by his stride, always poised and untroubled despite the weight of responsibilities he carried. He'd accepted his purpose and perfected it. Being around him gave her hope that a purpose was possible. That happiness was possible. There was so much she could learn from him. Too bad fate seemed to be against them.

But why was she so ready to let her life be directed by some outside force? She was her own force. A godly force. As she watched him approach, with his eyes on her face and a simple smile on his lips, she came to a conclusion. For the first time in her life, she knew what she wanted. And it felt like freedom.

Hades was good at reading emotions. If pressed, he would even admit that he'd perfected the art. So he knew, as he walked toward Lexi, that something was going on behind those ocean-blue eyes. Something deep. Was it an idea? Resolve? Was she just happy to see him? Hopefully, she'd be willing to share.

"I hope I'm not interrupting something important," he said. "I won't be offended if you send me away."

"You're just the god I wanted to see." She patted the marble beside her, and he took his seat.

His last guess appeared to be the correct one, and he gave her hand a squeeze to let her know he felt the same. "How may I be of service?"

"I've got some ideas I'm bouncing around, and I'd like to run them by you."

Ah, so his first *and* last guesses were correct.

"The reason I wanted to talk to Mnemosyne was to get her side of the story about my conception. I asked her what happened between her and my dad. Turns out they hadn't been involved in a long-term affair, which kind of reassured me. Then we talked about Zeus. Then we talked about you. You didn't tell me she helped you find your feet in the underworld."

Hades knew Mnemosyne was holding back when he'd asked about her conversation with Lexi. She had taunted him with that secret smile she liked to wear when she was sitting on something interesting.

"She made several sacrifices to stay and help me settle into the role. I wouldn't have adjusted so well without her guidance. I didn't mention it before because I was worried you might have thought we were somehow colluding, which was not the case."

"Okay, so we can both attest that my mother is one of the good gods. I hate to say it, but the gods I've met are not getting off to a great start. They lied to keep me in service to them. Even the nymphs have been lying to me. Do you know the story with Ham? Is he in the loop?"

"I don't know Ham's story, but I suspect he's a mortal in service to the gods as penance for breaking an oath. And I apologize for the poor impression you have of the gods. Most of them don't visit the human realm as much as you've been accustomed to. The few you know well are here because of your demigod status and their desire to know you better."

She pursed her lips as she stared at the marble. "I'll take that into consideration and decide if it lets them off the hook or not. I know Zeus has them all under a gag order. I also think I understand the logic behind these ambassador family estates. But that doesn't take away the fact that the gods are exploiting the ignorance and greed of mortals who can't see further than a century, if that much. The oaths they take condemn generations of innocents."

"Perhaps you should do something about it."

"Maybe I will. As soon as I'm living among the gods, I'm going to bring it up."

Hades wanted to kiss her in that moment. To show her how much he believed in her. Lexi was beginning to stretch her wings, and he didn't doubt she would soar as high as any god before her. She turned to face him, as if she'd heard his thoughts.

"I'm also giving the underworld serious consideration. What do you think about that?"

As she held him under an unwavering gaze, an odd sensation

overtook him. He was pretty sure it was hope. It seemed he'd been right on all accounts. There had been resolve in her face. Did he dare hope a goddess would be willing to follow him home? Did he dare think of the consequences of such a choice? For both of them? What else had Mnemosyne said to her in the stable?

"Why?"

It was the only rational question he had. Hades needed to know if she knew *why* before he could entertain her suggestion. While his heart galloped, he tried not to see uncertainty in the way her eyes glistened and her mouth moved around the words as she spoke.

"I've just been granted immunity from death. As long as I don't fall on any swords, I have an eternity of choices to make. Of course, I know there are consequences, so you can save that speech. But if I'm going to do right by myself and live authentically, I'll be the one making those choices, for better or worse. Why the underworld? Because I can see a potential future there. I can see purpose, and friendship, and maybe even true love."

Every argument Hades might have used was driven out of his head by her admission, as well as some of his doubt.

"I'll take your stunned silence as a good thing and continue," she said. "I realize there aren't many gods in the underworld, but since Zeus doesn't seem keen on having me join him in Olympus, I feel like the underworld will give me more opportunities to practice my skills than if I stayed here. And just so we're clear, the fact that you're banned from Olympus factors heavily in my decision. I'd much rather be where *you* are than where my controlling godfather is. Can I even call him that anymore?"

Hades blinked when he realized she'd asked him a question. Although perhaps it was rhetorical. "I wouldn't."

"Good. Then all we need to do is figure out how to blow this joint without letting the blowhard find out."

She stood and paced the steps, crossing in front of him and mumbling plans as his head spun. It had been centuries since a goddess had chosen to follow him to the underworld. He wanted to jump up and kick his heels. He wanted to sweep her into a dance and spin their bodies until they were dizzy and laughing. He was sure he could make her happy. He would certainly try his damnedest.

"Could we just take a walk and never come back?" she said. "How do we get to the underworld?"

Lexi stopped in front of him, her brows raised as she posed her question, and Hades had to bring his thoughts back from hand-holding along the river Styx and bouncing children on his knee.

"We would need my chariot," he said.

"A chariot? You're kidding me, right?"

"Chariots have served the gods since the beginning of our existence. We have no need to modernize like mortals. Z ascends through the clouds to reach Olympus, while I descend through the earth, usually by way of a canyon or a gorge."

"Like the gorge in our backyard?"

"Yes. But Lexi—" He grabbed her hand and held on to it as he stood. Then he pressed her palm to his chest, hoping she could feel his resolve. "I would love nothing more than to spend the next century with you, perhaps beyond that. But are you truly prepared to face the punishment of a century in the underworld? I'd like to say that Z will be overruled by the council, but if he's angry enough, this could be *your* fate for a long time."

Lexi's gaze dropped again, and Hades hoped she wouldn't misconstrue his question for indifference. It would be like a dagger to the heart if she saw him the way she saw the other gods she hated. "And your fate, too, right?" she asked.

"I won't be spared his wrath. However, I know the meaning of a century. I've been confined to my home for longer than that."

She squeezed his hand as her focus returned to his face, sending his pulse racing. "As far as I'm concerned, the gods can have their fancy estates made of gold. If that's what I'd see in Olympus, gated communities with a bunch of preppy clods throwing their powers around, I'd be better off anywhere else. Although I wouldn't say no to a trip to Asia first."

He chuckled, although he wanted to laugh out loud. There was so much more behind her words than levity. "I may have mentioned this before, but there's no hiding from the nymphs. If your destination is the underworld, it needs to be the first stop on our itinerary."

She offered him a beautifully devious grin. "All right, then. Since you're my second, I'm putting you in charge of getting us there."

Twenty-seven

Lunch consisted of leftovers, and the few remaining guests lounged by the pool enjoying the spring sunshine. Since she was still boycotting the estate, Lexi relaxed on a chaise in her clothes. Hades had excused himself inside to pack for his trip to Asia, and Zeus was holding court under a large umbrella, although the only thing keeping him company was a goblet.

When Hades appeared again, he was dressed in the suit he'd arrived in, and Lexi's stomach did a somersault as she hopped off her lounger to meet him.

"I don't want you to go," she said, gripping both of his hands tightly. "If Zeus doesn't agree to my terms, please say you'll stay a little longer."

"What's this about Zeus agreeing to terms?" Zeus left the shade of his umbrella, casting his own shadow on the deck as he invited himself into the conversation, just as she'd suspected he would. And Lexi faced him head-on. If there was ever a time in her life that she needed to be brave, it was now.

"I want to be able to see Hades again before I turn thirty. It's a promise I want you to make in exchange for my compliance."

Zeus scrunched his brows, and Lexi tried not to hold her breath. Under any other circumstances she would have expected him to give her request careful consideration, but this weekend had tested everyone's tolerance. He could have been contemplating any number of things—a promise from *her* in return, a punishment for Hades for the part he played, immediate imprisonment in the house of gold.

Finally, the hard lines softened as he let go of a strangled sigh. "I'd like to leave this place with a clear conscience so I can return with one. It's one of the reasons I enjoy coming here. If Hades petitions for a visit to the estate in seven years, I promise to make certain it's granted."

"Thank you." Lexi threw her arms around his chest and squeezed. He may have been the ruler of the gods, with more authority than even the Titans, but he'd been her uncle Z all her life, and she was glad that the last words they might speak to each other were civil ones.

When she stepped back she did her best to keep the mask of courage on her face. "I'm going to walk Hades to the path now. I assume I'll see you and Mnemosyne when I get back."

"Of course. We'll wait here for you."

Although Zeus watched Lexi and Hades with a wary eye as they headed for the beach, he didn't attempt to follow them. Hades planned to take their private trail to the gorge where he would summon his chariot. She hadn't asked for more details than that, especially when there were more important things to focus on, like Hades's lips as they said goodbye.

"Promise you'll be there," she said against his mouth. She couldn't imagine waiting even one week to kiss him again.

"I promise, I'll be there."

They held each other for a long time, letting the waves and the seagulls serenade them. When they finally broke apart Hades was wearing a smile, much like the other smiles he'd offered her. But this one didn't quite reach his eyes, making her think he didn't believe *she* would be there.

Lexi returned to the estate with an awful foreboding feeling, but she did her best to ignore it as she bid Zeus and Mnemosyne farewell. The Titan seemed eager to return to Olympus for their annual flower-judging contest. She'd helped Demeter with the tulip garden and wanted to support her friend, but Lexi's gut told her there was something else behind the urgency. Maybe a request from Hades to get Zeus the hell out of there.

Eventually, Lexi was left alone on the pool deck. Her mortal mom had retired to her room to sleep off a headache, and her father and Dion were in the study catching up on work. There was only one more loose end to tie up—Athena. She found the warrior goddess boxing an invisible foe down on the beach, and Athena jutted her determined chin in greeting.

"I don't suppose you're interested in starting your lessons right now?" The goddess continued to punch the air, her long ponytail snapping back and forth with the movement.

"That's a hard pass. I think my body has spent its reserves. I'm just down here to check on Jackie O."

"It'll take time getting used to your new powers. I'm sure you're already tired of hearing that. Well, since you don't need me, I'll do some laps in the ocean and see where the waves take me. We can meet back here at sunrise."

She flashed Lexi a toothy smile that might have said *Buckle up, buttercup*. Or she may have just given Lexi a free pass for the next fifteen hours. Lexi made for the stable and took a moment to leave a note for the nymphs, letting them know where to find Jackie O when they came out after dinner to lock up. Although Lexi wasn't counting on more than an hour before a search party was formed.

Unfortunately, she hadn't considered Jackie O's reluctance to leave her stall when she went to fetch her. The mare turned her back and snorted her displeasure as Lexi tried to point her toward the exit.

"C'mon, Jackie O. I promise we're not going anywhere near the ocean. We're just taking a walk on our favorite trail."

She grabbed an apple from the feedbag and tempted her horse with it, but the attempt failed. As a last resort Lexi aimed her palms at the straw covering the stall floor and whipped up a small cyclone. Jackie O jerked her head and rotated away from the whirlwind as it followed her stomping hooves, and Lexi finally coaxed her horse through the door.

"That's it, girl. I just need your help with one more thing, then you can rest for as long as your little heart desires."

Lexi ignored the ball of guilt welling up as she fitted her horse with a halter and grabbed a length of rope. If Jackie O had to spend a couple of hours waiting to be rescued, Lexi didn't want her burdened with the extra weight of a saddle.

Once outside, she glanced at the estate, saying a quick goodbye to the people she'd known for the first twenty-two years of her life. Compared to eternity, that was a drop in the bucket, and she reminded herself of this as she and Jackie O made the trek to the gorge.

On the way, she reminisced with her friend. "Do you remember that competition in Lawrencetown? You brought home a ribbon in every event. And that was before we'd started flying together. It was all on you."

She laughed despite the anxious knot growing in her stomach. "What about that time we were caught in a downpour at the gorge and you refused to leave until it was over. Mom and Dad were basket cases when we got back."

When they arrived at the abandoned ranger station twenty minutes later, and Lexi secured Jackie O to her usual spot beside a patch of wild sage, reality really hit her. She might never see her horse again.

Tears welled in her eyes, and she didn't try to stop them as she threw her arms around Jackie O's neck and blubbered. The guilt came on full force when her horse nickered her version of comfort, and Lexi barely heard the leaves crunching before Hades appeared in the clearing. He had made good on his promise, and his smile told her that he was glad she had too.

Then his expression turned sober as he joined them, and Lexi wiped her face with her sleeve. "I wish Jackie O could come with us," he said, giving her horse an affectionate pat on the shoulder. "But she doesn't carry the right DNA to survive a trip to the underworld. I'm sorry."

Lexi lifted her head, hoping she didn't look like a gross mess. "Is it terrible of me to have the most trouble saying goodbye to my horse and not the people who raised me?"

"Not at all. She's someone you were able to confide in, which is something of great value."

"I hope she doesn't hate me for leaving."

"That's the difference between animals and those of us who identify as human. Animals have a greater capacity for compassion. I expect she senses your emotions and only wants you to be happy."

"I wish that too."

Hades pressed his hand to Lexi's cheek, and she appreciated the gesture. She was feeling unsure for the first time since making the choice to leave.

"I'll admit that my job has made me overly sentimental," he said. "But I think you'll find that emotions are often our best compass. No single decision can bring about all the solutions or cause all the heartaches. They simply make up the parts of life."

He leaned in and kissed her, and she allowed his touch to ease her worries and remind her why she'd put her trust in him. He'd offered her more in the span of a weekend than anyone had offered in her lifetime, including two things she never felt she had—honesty and friendship.

She inhaled against his lips, feeling her resolve click back into place. "I believe you."

After a tearful farewell with Jackie O, Lexi's worries assaulted her again as they traveled the path to the gorge. In a matter of minutes she would climb into a chariot with the god of the underworld and dive headfirst into the depths of the earth, staying there for perhaps a century.

Actually, she had no idea how far down they'd be going. She was flying blind, trusting the words and deeds of someone who had been a stranger to her just four short days ago. She wanted to blame her libido for that. It hadn't been tested. But neither had her heart.

Navigating the landscape on autopilot, she led them to a fifteen-foot rock wall. The only way up was on foot, and it was a fitting obstacle, but nothing she hadn't tackled a hundred times before. Nobody could have convinced her she'd be climbing it with Hades one day.

"How are you with heights?" she said, mostly for levity, and Hades's smirk said he'd caught on.

"Would you like me to name all the mountain peaks I've stood on? I don't think we have the time."

"Okay, smartass. Just try to keep up."

Lexi planted a swift kiss on his mouth before starting her ascent. The incline wasn't too steep, and she could tell by Hades's determined grunts that he didn't need a coach. She arrived at the top in no time, and once Hades pulled up next to her, they looked down into the gorge at the river below.

"Truly breathtaking," he whispered. There was something about his reverence for the scenery that gave her hope. Despite the many views he must have seen, he hadn't lost his sense of wonder.

"Now what?" she said.

"Now we ride."

He pressed his fingers between his lips and filled the canyon with an ear-piercing whistle. Then he held her hand as they stared at the horizon. She didn't know what to expect. Currently, the sun was hiding behind a rather ominous embankment of clouds. Would a team of winged horses burst through them? Would some mysterious underworld beast be pulling the chariot?

A silhouette soon appeared as if by magic, surging upward from below the clouds and dispersing gray tendrils into the sky. A team of horses, four abreast, controlled the chariot. Their iridescent black coats shimmered like scarab beetles. She guessed they were Friesian, given their dark coats and strong musculature, and she noticed they didn't have wings. Their hooves pounded the air instead of pounding the road, just like Jackie O's had. Clearly, these horses carried the right DNA to fly without the help of a god.

Fighting the impulse to deny the magic, Lexi gawked as the team approached, and her eyes barely registered the flash of lightning that pulsed inside the clouds, chalking it up to Mother Nature. Or maybe it was part of the show. Then a clap of thunder boomed so loudly it made her jump, and the horses had the same reaction. One of them reared up, sending the chariot careening sideways and putting it on a crash course with their cliff.

Hades groaned and cursed at the sky. "Damn it, Zeus!"

Twenty-eight

Lexi dropped to her knees and seconds later the wheels of Hades's chariot skidded across the cliff just shy of their heads. The front wheel wedged itself into a gap in the rocks, stopping the team with a sudden jolt, and the horses whinnied as they fought against their leads. No doubt they were eager to escape the fury of a pissed-off god.

"Are you sure it's Zeus?" she said. "I don't see anything up there besides clouds."

"I know my brother's handiwork. We need to hurry or we'll never make it." Hades hauled her up by the waist, and together they ran for the chariot.

When they reached the horses, an auburn-haired mare tossed her head like she was battling a swarm of bees.

"Settle down, Misty. I won't let anything harm you." Hades spoke in a composed, sedate tone, as if his voice held its own brand of magic. "Misty hates leaving the underworld, but she's my fastest horse, which keeps the others motivated."

Lexi offered the horse a sympathetic but unflinching stare. "I know how you feel, Misty. I'm scared too."

This seemed to work, and they regarded each other for a few intense seconds. Then another thunderous crack had Misty snorting. Lexi turned to stare at the clouds, shielding her eyes as the sun tried to break through and searching for signs of the reckless god she used to call *uncle*. A shiny silhouette could be seen, approaching at the speed of a small aircraft, but she knew better. Moments later, the distinctive shape of a chariot led by a team of ivory horses became all too clear.

Hades detached Misty's lead, and she immediately stretched toward Lexi, sniffing and snuffling around her head. "Misty will take you from here, Lexi."

"Wait. Are you suggesting I fly on her back over the gorge with only a harness?"

"I've seen you do it before. Remember, you have the powers of a goddess. And it's probably your best chance to reach the underworld. I'll distract Z while you make your escape."

"I'm going to the underworld without you?"

"I'll be right behind you. Oh, and you'll need to recite a password before you can gain access—*fterá pagonioú*. It translates to *peacock feathers*. Let me hear you say it."

With confusion and adrenaline battling for supremacy, Lexi repeated the words until Hades was satisfied with the inflection. Sadly, by then, Zeus and his team had reached their cliff and were making a wide circle over their heads.

"I knew you two were up to something!" he shouted. "You blame the gods for their dishonesty, Lexi, but you are a liar and a hypocrite."

"It takes one to know one!" she screamed at the sky, fighting dizziness as she looked up at the legs of four galloping horses.

"Your poor choices this weekend have forced my hand! You

will come with me to Olympus and receive the appropriate training under *my* supervision."

"I have no intention of spending the next century with a bunch of gods like you. It's just more of the same controlling bullshit!"

Lexi took hold of Misty's withers and hoisted herself onto the mare's back. The horse tensed beneath her, and Lexi bent forward, caressing Misty's neck as she slid the reins into her hand. She already felt a kinship with the animal, probably because they were both scared out of their wits.

"Okay, Misty. It's just you and me. I'm trusting you to know the way home."

Zeus had piloted his chariot close enough that she had a bird's-eye view of the tempest brewing in his eyes. She didn't see how an escape was possible, at least not without injury, but she was going to give it her best shot.

She glanced at Hades, and his smile gave her hope, something she really needed at that moment. "We'll meet again on the other side," he said. Then he slapped Misty on the rump and the horse bolted into the air without so much as a running start.

Lexi tucked in behind Misty's head, holding on for dear life as they soared above the gorge. The river weaved and twinkled far below, and she had to remind herself that she wasn't afraid of heights. But this was no ski lift in Switzerland, and she had a god with an ego complex shouting at her.

"What makes you think your life will be any better in the underworld?!"

"Because Hades knows the importance of listening! He treats others like they matter! And, most of all, he has learned humility!"

Lexi shouted into the wind, not really caring if Zeus could hear her. A moment later he pulled up beside her. The desperation behind his stormy eyes and ruddy cheeks smothered her anger for a second.

"Come with me, Lexi. We'll work out an arrangement. It doesn't have to be a century."

"I don't believe you. I don't think I ever will."

He roared and it sounded like thunder. "If you go with Hades, you'll be there so long you'll forget what freedom feels like!"

Hades had his team in the air now and was gaining on them as Lexi continued her argument with Zeus two hundred feet above the gorge.

"Why does it bother you so much that I want to be with Hades?"

Hades had an answer for that. "Because he can't control you in the underworld. He can't oversee your training and decide how he wants to suppress your power."

"But why would he want to suppress my power?"

"That's a very good question, Lexi," Hades said. "And we can address it after you're safe."

He gestured to a land bridge stretching between two canyon walls, his eyes sparking like wildfire. She knew it was now or never, and she spurred Misty lower, while Hades guided his team toward Zeus's chariot, forcing them both to change course.

"Lexi! Land that horse immediately or you'll feel my wrath!"

Zeus's threat made her think of a corny movie script, but the force behind his words felt very real. What would he do to punish her? Would he keep her in the underworld forever? Would he throw her in Tartarus? What about Hades? How would he suffer for her choices?

Misty wasn't sticking around for more arguments. They dipped away from the iron-fisted god and headed for the bridge.

But Lexi knew the gorge like she knew her own backyard, and the only thing beyond the bridge was a wall of solid rock. Once she realized this, her body froze.

"Are you sure we're headed in the right direction, Misty?"

Of course, Misty didn't respond. She just kept flying toward the mountain like a bat out of hell. Lexi squinted at the rock wall through watery eyes, although she wasn't sure what she was looking for. A portal? A hidden door that opened at the commend of magical horses? All she could see was a crack traversing the mountainside, jagged and much too narrow.

Were they supposed to squeeze through that little gap? They were going to die. Was that how someone entered the underworld? Through death? Lexi's idea to find her freedom seemed to be taking her further away from it. What was that password again?

"Try not to be afraid, Lexi. Just hold on tight!" Hades's reassurance arrived a little late as he pulled his chariot beside her, the wind tousling his chestnut hair and his eyes shining like stars. "I won't be far behind you. *Fterá pagonioú!*"

"Hades! You will regret this for the rest of your days!" Zeus's shout echoed inside the canyon ahead of a loud *crack*! The flash of light that followed blinded Lexi and startled Misty, causing them to veer off course.

Oh gods! Zeus was going to be the cause of her death. Lexi stroked Misty's head, trying to calm them both.

"It's okay, girl. Ignore the mean god and just take us home."

Putting her faith in the horse, Lexi fought the image of smashing headfirst into the rocks as she pressed her head into Misty's neck and let her eyes flutter closed. She didn't need her sight to feel the canyon wall coming at her, and she kept repeating the password out loud, wondering if they would be the last words she uttered.

An arctic wind suddenly enveloped her, and all sound abruptly stopped. Only the breathing of the horse and her own erratic panting filled the void. Lexi slowly lifted her head and peeked at her surroundings. There was nothing to see, only pitch blackness, and the air felt moist and glacial. Her skin crawled at the cold nothingness.

Was she dead? Was this dark, empty place her new home? Where were the fields? The rivers? Where was Hades? Had he been forced to fight Zeus for her freedom? What if he lost? Guilt and doubt washed over Lexi like a tsunami, causing her to feel very alone and very foolish. But there was nothing she could do except hold on tight and trust in her magical guide.

"This time you have gone too far, Hades!"

Z's obstinate bellow echoed across the gorge, and Hades had to duck his head to avoid the lightning strike by inches. His brother seemed determined to behave like a royal pain in the ass, and while Hades wanted to point this out, he knew he'd have to choose his words more carefully, for both his and Lexi's sakes.

He swung his team around, plotting a course alongside Z's chariot to have a few words with the fatheaded lout. "Don't you think it might be *you* who has gone too far this time? You're going to an awful lot of trouble for a demigod. What are you so desperate to protect?"

"If you'd stop thinking with your dick for once, you'd understand why I'm doing it!"

Hades bit back a curse. If anyone thought with his dick, it

was Z. "Are you telling me I don't know how it feels to lose control of something precious? To feel disrespected and abandoned when someone I care about is ripped from my grasp?"

His rebuttal appeared to dampen Z's anger, and Hades watched the menacing gleam fade from his brother's eyes as they maneuvered their chariots in a circle. "I don't want Lexi becoming feral in the underworld. We know the consequences of an improperly trained demigod."

"If you bothered to spend a modicum of time in the underworld, you would know that not everything there is feral. And I'm quite capable of making sure Lexi realizes her full potential. I'm sure Hecate will have something to do with that as well."

Z snorted, mimicking the horses as they carried them from one side of the gorge to the other. "Demigods are different, unpredictable. They must be carefully monitored. Plans must be made and followed. That's *my* job!"

Was it just his imagination, or was his brother scrambling for a sound thesis for his argument? Something that didn't paint him as a tyrant? Hades glanced at the rock where Lexi had vanished. She was in his domain, and her safety was all the assurance he needed.

"Is it also your job to erase the memories of those who threaten your careful planning?" he said, hoping he wasn't making matters worse.

"Do not claim to know my plans! Lexi doesn't know them either. She's conjuring up excuses to justify her poor behavior."

"Lexi's decision to enter the underworld was her own. And she made the choice because you couldn't find a compromise *she* was happy with. By her own admission she's been controlled by others all her life. I believe she saw this as her only way to escape the strong will of a god who doesn't understand her."

There was more Hades wanted to say, but he dared not leave Lexi alone at the gates with Thanatos, so he made a final pass by Z's chariot and delivered his ending oration.

"Lexi is aware of your threats, and she still made this choice. I promised my allegiance to her, knowing what the consequences could be for me as well. I expect she and I will manage the consequences together. Should you wish to discuss them with her, you're always welcome to visit."

Z's face settled into a marble pose, like a heavy stone fighting against the pressure of an earthquake. It was an expression Hades knew too well, and he snapped the reins, causing a spark to pass between himself and his horses. This was all they needed to shoot ahead, blazing a fiery trail toward the gap in the mountain.

"You'll regret this, Hades! In your wildest dreams, you cannot imagine the pain I can inflict."

Actually, Hades *could* imagine it. He felt it every spring and any time his hopeful requests went unanswered. He was used to the pain. Numb to it. But perhaps this time his brother would learn a long overdue lesson in humility. A sarcastic smile crossed his face when a streak of lightning blasted the mountain ahead of him, blackening the rocks as he slipped into the darkness.

Twenty-nine

"I'm not dead!"

Lexi tried to explain her situation to the angel of death standing at the iron gates. She'd given him this title based on his scowl and dismal attitude, although he'd introduced himself as Thanatos. She knew him to be a minor god of the underworld, but the guy didn't appear minor at all.

Muscles bulged beneath the simple gray toga he covered himself with, and he flaunted a large pair of black feathery wings. His face was handsome but his dark, haunting eyes and chilly vibe gave her the creeps. So did all the spooky souls floating around and the drop-to-your-death cliff at her back. This place put *Tales from the Crypt* to shame. She rallied her courage as she continued to plead her case.

"I'm a goddess. My name is Alexandra Maxwell, daughter of Mnemosyne. Can't you tell the difference between me and the rest of these mortals? I'm not transparent."

"No one gets past the gates without payment, or without Hades." His flat tone had a finality to it that would have discouraged anyone, but she refused to be bullied. She was a goddess, for fuck's sake.

"But this is Hades's horse. Don't you recognize her?" Lexi stroked Misty's neck, grateful she had at least one friend. Where the hell was Hades? Had Misty taken a wrong turn somewhere?

Thanatos glanced at Misty with disinterest. "She looks like any horse. If you *are* a guest of Hades, where is he? My lord always tells me when he's expecting visitors. And he rarely gets visitors." He raised his brows with a skeptical air, but Lexi ignored his attitude and gestured at the darkness behind her.

"He should be here any minute. He had me fly ahead on his fastest horse. We had to escape from—"

"Then I suggest you wait for him over there." Thanatos jutted his chin toward the milling throng of ghouls, and Lexi pursed her lips as she eyeballed the rude gatekeeper.

Hades had mentioned some of his fellow gods didn't have the best skills for guiding souls to their final resting place, but he seriously needed to think about replacing this guy. Once again, she was reminded that good looks didn't excuse a shitty attitude.

As Misty led Lexi away from the gates, Lexi whispered into her new friend's ear. "I'm no expert, but I think that guy needs to get laid."

Misty bobbed her head as if she agreed wholeheartedly, and they stopped to wait for Hades near a glowing torch. Apparently, her arrival was something of a novelty, and several curious souls drifted up to her as if blown by an undetectable wind.

Despite their wispy forms, Lexi could see their lips moving, and their words came to her in vague whispers, as if they spoke in some kind of ghost language. She couldn't understand a single thing they said but they seemed to be pleading with her, their faces twisted into tortured expressions. Did they think she could help them?

A heavy feeling of grief overcame her as she listened to them lament, triggering a parade of depressing images—experiences she'd had during her life that didn't end well. She felt as if a blanket of chain mail had been thrown onto her back, and she dropped her head into her hands to cry. It was a loud, sniveling, messy cry, and Misty bent over her shoulder, snorting hot air onto her cheek. But Lexi was too overwhelmed with emotion to acknowledge the horse's kind gesture.

"What the hell is going on here?!" Hades's angry shout cut through Lexi's wailing as his team of horses slid to a stop in front of the gates. "Have you lost all your senses, Thanatos? Why did you let her stay out here?"

Hades hopped off his chariot and sprinted toward Lexi. The moment his arms wrapped around her, she cowered into them like an injured bird. "I'm sorry, Lexi. This is no way to be welcomed home. Please, forgive me."

Hades's apology comforted her more than she thought it would, and the heartache left her like a vanquished demon. She offered him a pathetic nod, and, swifter than a team of magical flying horses, he lifted her into his arms and walked to the entrance. The gates opened of their own accord and Thanatos stepped aside, bowing his head as a respectful guard should.

"We will talk later about your recurring lapses in good judgment," Hades said to him. "See that my chariot and horses are taken care of. Come, Misty."

The growl of Hades's commands vibrated against Lexi's head. She hadn't seen him truly angry before, but she wasn't so naive as to think he didn't have a temper befitting a god.

They entered a forest, and the darkness swiftly gave way to light. It was the kind of light that came with daybreak, and the pastel tones of purple, pink, and salmon made everything look enchanted. Lexi blinked at the landscape as recognition dawned. Her favorite trees grew here—plums and dogwoods and red maples, all decorated for spring.

Misty was already trotting ahead, leading the way down a path lined with thick ivy. Beside them a stream dotted with ferns and mossy rocks bubbled along happily, while the music of birdsong lilted overhead. It might have been Hades's proximity, but Lexi felt her heart lighten the farther they walked, and she lifted her chin to take in the unexpected view.

Hades smiled down at her. "What do you see, Lexi?"

This seemed like a strange question to ask. Couldn't he see for himself? "I see plum and dogwood trees, like at home. They're covered in spring blooms. Even the sky has color, like the day is just beginning here. I feel like I'm in an enchanted forest. I hate to admit it, but part of me doubted you."

His eyes twinkled like sunshine glinting off gold, which added to the magic. "You can thank yourself for all of that. You're seeing aspects of earth that brought you joy when you were experiencing your former life."

"Former life?" Lexi's traumatized brain tried to decipher his meaning as it slipped to the dark side. "I'm not dead, am I?"

"No. What I mean is, every soul who takes this path sees it differently, depending on what they've carried with them from life. I designed the supernatural elements myself, after much trial and error. Death is merely a transition from one experience to another, and I wanted the path to offer familiarity so the souls could embrace their transition with comfort and peace."

Lexi definitely felt comforted in the cocoon of Hades's arms, but she couldn't help thinking about the tortured souls they'd left behind. "What about those souls waiting outside the gates? They looked like they could use some peace."

Hades's pace slowed, and Lexi immediately regretted her comment. It *had* come across accusatory. *Damn.*

"They'll be taken care of as soon as I get you settled. I expect Hecate will be along shortly."

Lexi reached around Hades's head and pulled his face toward her, planting a kiss on his lips. He looked pleasantly surprised.

"What was that for?"

"You deserve so much more than you receive. And I plan to do something about that."

"Well, Alexandra—daughter of Mnemosyne—abductor of my heart—goddess of powers yet to be explored, you, too, deserve more. And I'll endeavor to do something about that."

Lexi kissed him again, savoring the sweet, musky scent of his skin. Her body suddenly ached to have him—all of him—and she broke away to whisper in his ear. "How soon can we start exploring?"

The path of souls looked different this time. The trees were fuller, the scents sweeter, and Hades's favorite birdsong filled the air, which he hummed under his breath as he carried Lexi down the path. He knew why the forest had decided to show off for him today. He was holding a beautiful goddess in his arms, a goddess who accepted him despite his grim title and ominous reputation.

His thoughts buoyed his spirits, putting a skip in his step, and Lexi smiled up at him as if she'd noticed this too. "While I *do* love being in your arms, you can put me down now. If I'm going to be living here for the next century, I'll need to get my bearings sometime."

"As you wish." Hades set Lexi on the path, and she immediately craned her neck back to peer up into the tree branches.

"I've never heard that birdsong before. What kind of birds are those? I can't see them. Oh, right. Maybe I'm the only one who can hear them."

It took a moment for Lexi's words to register. Was she hearing *his* birds? "What does the song sound like?"

Lexi whistled the tune, mimicking his birds perfectly, and he stared at her like a bewildered soul. How had she tapped into his joy so quickly? It had taken Persephone many seasons to do it. Perhaps he and Lexi shared a gift in kind.

"I've been seeing these auras, especially around birds," she explained. "Maybe it'll be the same here."

"You won't see the birds. You'll only hear them. They're a manifestation of my own making, birds I enjoyed as a youth in Olympus. Apart from our chariot horses, earthbound animals don't exist in the underworld, but that doesn't mean you won't find plenty of life here. It just won't come in the forms you're expecting."

Hades took her hand and squeezed it, braving a tidal wave of emotion that crashed through him like the Hawaiian surf. Lexi brought out feelings in him that cut like razors, feelings he rarely dared to grant himself. He could easily get lost in her.

As they neared the end of the path, the waters of the Lethe came into view, and Hades could hardly contain his excitement. There was so much to show her, so much he loved about his home, and with Misty to escort them, they might avoid a sermon from

Charon, who could talk a buzzard off a fresh kill. But it was not Charon who arrived to delay their exploration.

Hecate bustled up the path, her fiery orange cloak billowing and her sapphire eyes blazing. Hades knew she wouldn't be pleased that he'd failed to give her notice he was returning with a guest, but Lexi's situation had taken him by surprise. He prepared himself with a cleansing breath.

"Here you are, Hades. What is this I hear about you bringing a goddess to the underworld?" Hecate's scrutinizing gaze was on Lexi as she voiced her complaint.

"How did you find out so quickly?" Hades asked, although he knew Z was behind it.

"Don't play naive. It doesn't suit the ruler of the underworld."

Hades surrendered to the accusatory quirk of Hecate's pale brows, and he argued no further. "Hecate, I would like to introduce Alexandra, daughter of Mnemosyne and Charles Maxwell. Her family calls her Lexi. Lexi, this is Hecate, goddess of many wondrous things, but her specialties are herbalism and sorcery of every variety."

Hecate waved off Hades's flowery introduction and continued her appraisal of Lexi, who stood like a marble pillar next to him. "And what skills does Lexi bring with her? How will her presence benefit our efforts here?"

Knowing Hecate the way he did, Hades should have warned Lexi in advance. While he'd long counted on Hecate's counsel and friendship, her pointed and often unfiltered opinions rivaled those of any god in Olympus.

"I've just come into my powers," Lexi said, startling Hades with her ready answer, although it shouldn't have. "So far, I've been able to manipulate all the elements, but I've learned that's pretty standard for gods. I took my horse for a flight on the beach today, which I'll admit happened by accident. As far as human skills, I co-captained the lacrosse team two years in a row and led the senior debate team. I'm not sure how useful those skills will be here. Maybe I could help at the gates once I learn how to read lips."

While Hades schooled a grin, Hecate regarded Lexi keenly. The intuitive sorceress could read others with swift ferocity, often seeing things they themselves could not.

"You speak confidently and without reservation. A worthy trait for both gods and mortals. And your posture is sure and straight, allowing energy to flow through you unhindered. I have no doubt you are competent in many activities. Tell me, Lexi, why have you chosen the underworld rather than Mount Olympus? Is there some special interest that attracted you here?"

Lexi glanced sidelong at Hades, offering him a quick smile. "A number of circumstances led to the decision. First, it seemed insane, and incredibly rude, that I be asked to serve the gods when I'm a god myself. Zeus didn't agree, and the option of Olympus was used only as a threat. Hades, on the other hand, behaved like a rational god at a time when I was realizing my family wasn't capable of rationality. That's the condensed version of the story. We'll need wine for the longer version."

Hecate cocked her head, a sign she was fully intrigued by Lexi's answer, and likely surprised by it.

"I also consider Hades to be a friend," Lexi went on. "He's honest, humble, compassionate. And he plays a mean game of croquet. It's hard to find those qualities regardless of someone's mortality."

The corners of Hecate's lips lifted and she eyed Hades carefully. She was the only goddess who could make him feel both strong and weak at the same time. "When you said you were taking a detour before visiting Asia, I never anticipated you'd find a goddess. And certainly not one who was willing to follow you home. It would be wise for you to discuss certain details with Lexi before the winter months are upon us, to avoid any awkward situations or damaged feelings."

Hades felt Lexi stiffen again, and he didn't blame her. Hecate tended to leave subtlety out of conversations.

"I hope you find peace here, Lexi. Please, come see me as soon as you have a free moment. I expect Hades has a lot of work to catch up on."

Hecate gathered a handful of her cloak and swept between them, her dauntless bearing carrying her toward the gates. Hades knew they had escaped the encounter mostly unscathed, and it would be wise to leave the path before Melinoe found them and had her say.

"Misty will fly us to your new home." He tugged on Lexi's hand, and she allowed him to guide her to the stream where Misty was enjoying a drink. When they arrived, she absently stroked the horse's mane as she stared at the water tumbling over the rocks.

She hadn't said a word since Hecate's departure, and the longer the silence grew, the more Hades's pulse quickened. What worries clouded her mind? Was she thinking about Persephone? Did he dare put voice to the words he'd been refusing to speak?

"I've been so focused on myself, I didn't think about the impact my presence would have on the gods here," she said softly. "I should have asked more questions."

Hades heaved out a sigh, which he hoped she wouldn't misinterpret. "Please try not to torture yourself with regrets. You were attempting to escape a situation you didn't want to be in, and you listened to your heart, which can be a very useful gauge. If we don't learn to trust our own feelings, it's easier for outside influences to control us."

He watched Lexi continue her study of the water, clearly lost in thought. If only he knew her better—knew the worries and doubts that plagued her—he could soothe her like a friend might. Like the friend she claimed he was. But they were at the genesis of their relationship. A pair of untried lovers eloping on a whim. He'd have to wing it.

"Despite what you may think, I haven't asked many goddesses to join me here. It's certainly something I'd never do if my feelings weren't genuine. Or if I doubted the tenacity of the goddess's spirit. I believe the confidence you have in yourself will help you succeed in your new position here."

She turned away from the stream to look at him. "What *is* my position here? Will I follow your direction or Hecate's? Where will I live?"

He reached for her hand, cradling it in his and sending her warmth. Lexi's passion for understanding the world around her assured him there would be challenges ahead, but it also gave him hope. She didn't do things in half measure.

"You'll live with me in the palace. And once we arrive, I'll answer all your questions ad infinitum."

She relaxed into a smile, giving Hades a much-needed boost, like that first buzz of alcohol. He intended to give Lexi everything she asked for, and his godly compass told him she'd do the same in return. Theirs was a match born of fire and rebellion, a fitting combination for two gods fulfilling destinies that were written for them. And, with the grace of Gaia, they would find their happily-ever-after despite it.

Thirty

Hades had told the truth. The Elysian Field was real, and it was huge, extending so far to the south that Lexi couldn't see the end of it, even from the back of a flying horse. A range of mountains bordered the west, with forests filling in the gaps. And there was light, too, but not in the form of a sun—more like watercolor brushstrokes, reflecting orange and pink against a canvas of purple and blue.

Misty had no problem carrying them both. In fact, the horse's mood improved significantly once Hades said they were heading home. But who wouldn't be soothed by rolling hills of lush grass, sparkling rivers, and flowers that pushed the boundaries of the color spectrum?

"How eager are you to get to the palace?" Hades spoke at her ear as her hair thrashed his face. "The Asphodel Meadows are stunning in May, and there's a particularly large growth of buttercups this year. They're beautiful but poisonous, so I suspect Melinoe is behind it."

Again, Lexi felt a pang of regret for not having done her homework on the place she'd chosen to fling herself into. But there was no turning back now. "Isn't that where the souls wander?"

"Some, but not all. Many choose the Lethe. If you're not keen to meet any souls, I'll set that intention when we arrive, and they'll leave us alone. Although the souls you'll find there are no longer lamenting. That's only at the gates."

"So it's spring here too? Is that just coincidence, or am I still projecting what I want to see?"

"We're fortunate to have all the seasons here, with a climate similar to the Mediterranean. But our seasons can look different from the ones on earth because they reflect the moods and intentions set by the gods who live here."

With winter only six months away, Lexi wondered what kind of weather the underworld would see come December. "What about Tartarus? Can we see it from up here?"

"No. Tartarus is tucked inside the mountains. That's where some of those creatures live that I mentioned. There are many species who take advantage of the realm: minotaurs, centaurs, satyrs. Most of them get along fine with the gods."

Lexi's mind was having a field day with all the questions she wanted to ask, but her limbs were a bit numb from exhaustion. "If it's all the same to you, I'd like to skip the meadows and just head to the palace. Do you have chamomile tea? I could really go for something to settle my nerves."

"The nymphs have every sort of tea you can imagine. The cellar is always full despite the infrequent visitors. I know they'll be excited to see a new face, so I apologize in advance." He pressed a kiss to her cheek, warming the skin where the wind had cooled it. "If you look to your left, your new home is just coming into view."

Lexi followed his pointing finger toward a multi-tiered structure growing on the horizon, reaching higher than even the mountains. It had been built on a plateau rising out of a huge chasm that cut through the landscape. From her vantage point, it looked like the plateau was hovering in midair, with only a single bridge to access it.

The palace didn't hold the classic lines of a fortified castle, like the ones she'd seen in Europe. Instead, multiple dome-shaped towers rose up at different heights, with arched porticos covering open-air balconies, reminding her of the architecture she'd seen in India and the Middle East. Rather than pale stone, the towers were formed out of reddish-orange clay, like terra-cotta, and she wondered if it had been mined right there in the underworld.

Like a centerpiece on an elaborate wedding cake, the middle tower rose above the others, surrounded by fluffy pink clouds. The dome was made of glass and reflected light like a silver sun, with spires jutting up around the perimeter, each one topped with angels, their wings outstretched and their heads tilted toward the sky. Lexi hadn't anticipated seeing angels in the underworld, but it made sense.

"I've never seen anything like it," she said. "And I've visited my share of cathedrals."

"I'll relay your compliment to Hestia. She designed my home. My sister is an accomplished architect."

"Does she visit you here?" Lexi glanced back at him, prepared to apologize if her question had triggered a bad memory. His smile told her it hadn't.

"She'll visit on rare occasions, usually holidays. But we prefer to meet at more exotic locales. She's partial to Mount Pelée."

As their destination grew larger, Misty snorted excitedly and started her descent. Lexi was finally able to confirm that the palace really did hover magically inside a huge ravine, which appeared to also serve as a moat. The dark waters of a river coursed below, dotted with foam. It reminded her of the gorge back home, a home she might never see again.

As they came in for a landing, Lexi tensed in the saddle. But they touched down just as smoothly as Jackie O had when the gods had helped them land on her beach. Hades swiftly dismounted, making it look like gravity didn't affect him.

"You stay put, my lady. I'll escort you to the door."

He patted Misty's hindquarters to urge her across the bridge, then walked alongside them, smiling up at Lexi like a child eager to show off a new toy. No doubt he was proud of the entrance doors, which were made of copper and scored in a spiral pattern. The windows stretched up several stories along either side, each pane cut into diamond shapes, and the cylindrical pillars supporting the portico were covered in colorful tiles of aquamarine, magenta, and orange. Topiaries carved into various forms stood in alcoves, and the soothing lull of wind chimes blew in from an unknown location.

"It isn't what you expected, is it?" he said.

"Nothing has been, so far."

Lexi looked down at Hades as her mind spun like a top. He'd been unfailingly polite and respectful. And everything he told her was turning out to be true. She felt like a princess riding up to a castle with her prince charming. But she didn't believe in fairy tales. How many dark secrets were lurking beneath the beauty that stretched before her? Could she and Hades find long-term happiness together? Would she regret her choice come winter?

"What I don't understand," she hurried on, "is why any goddess would turn down a life with you? You're the total package: compassionate, witty, supereasy on the eyes. And you own the nicest house on the block. I keep waiting for a fire-breathing dragon to rise up and spoil everything."

Hades filled the gorge with laughter. Was it just her imagination, or did his voice sound more formidable in the underworld? "You won't find any dragons here. But, in the interest of fairness, Olympus outshines the underworld in gold and splendor. The light emanating from the palace of the gods puts the sun to shame. As you've already discovered, the gods are fond of their precious metals. They're like dragons in that respect."

"Well, you don't have to impress me with gold. I'm already thoroughly impressed with you."

Lexi considered telling Hades he'd impressed her with certain parts of his anatomy, but her attention was drawn to a petite woman who had slipped through the front doors and was sprinting toward them. Behind her an enormous black dog lumbered to catch up. It resembled a Labrador, one of Lexi's favorite breeds, but this one sported three heads.

"Who are they?" she asked, although she had already made a guess about the dog.

"That would be Blythe. She's one of the forest nymphs who runs the show here. I'd be lost without her and her sisters. Behind her is Cerberus, who appears to have just woken up."

Hades lowered to one knee and greeted Blythe with a hug as she bounced excitedly on her toes. The nymph was absolutely precious, with yellow hair, rosy cheeks, and perky breasts that jostled under her gauze dress.

When Cerberus finally reached them, he plopped heavily next to Hades, although only two heads looked expectantly at his master. The third scrutinized Lexi, coming almost to her knee where she sat on Misty's back.

"Welcome home, Lord Hades," Blythe chirped. "We all missed you very much. It's never the same here without you. I see you've brought a friend to the palace. She's lovely." Blythe's voice made Lexi think of a lark, making it impossible not to be immediately smitten with her.

"This is Lexi, daughter of Mnemosyne. She'll be staying with us for as long as I can keep her happy. I want you to extend her every courtesy, beginning with a cup of chamomile tea."

Hades stood and offered his hand to Lexi, helping her off the horse, and his luminous eyes twinkled mischievously. But Lexi wasn't so dazed by his sex appeal not to notice Blythe straining to keep her mouth shut, probably holding back questions like *What will Persephone say when she finds someone else warming your bed, Lord Hades?*

"It's a pleasure to meet you, Blythe," Lexi said. "You have the most radiant hair. It reminds me of sunshine."

Blythe's face turned scarlet, and she giggled into her hand like a child. Based on what Lexi knew of nymphs, they could live for centuries, so she was probably not that young. Cerberus, who had been waiting patiently, nudged Hades in the groin, and he finally received an affectionate scratch behind a set of ears.

"I hope you've been behaving yourself, old friend. I've brought you a new playmate. This is Lexi."

Playmate?

Lexi might have chosen another word. She couldn't picture herself wrestling with a giant three-headed dog. He stood nearly eye to eye with her now that she was off the horse.

"Hello, Cerberus. It's nice to meet you. I love dogs, although I've never had one. My dad has allergies."

Cerberus cocked all three heads and surveyed Lexi with six shiny black eyes. After a few moments, in which Lexi held her breath, two heads leaned into her hands and licked them, while the third observed the scene as if he thought licking anything was beneath him.

Hades chuckled, giving Cerberus another hard scratch. "He doesn't know whether he's a lapdog or snooty royalty. But don't worry, he'll be following you around in no time looking for handouts. Blythe, please make sure Misty is returned to the stable and see that she gets anything she wants. I'll let Fiona know about the tea. Oh, and I need the north tower prepared for Lexi."

"Eep," Blythe squeaked and slapped a hand over her mouth much too late. Her eyes had also gone very round. "The north tower, my lord? The one you closed off after—"

"Yes. That one."

Hades's voice lowered a full octave as he responded, reminding Lexi of another god whose iron will she'd recently escaped. Although she never felt anything but kindness from Hades, she wasn't so foolish as to think he was a passive god. He *did* rule the underworld.

"If I may suggest one of the east towers, your lordship. There are many finely appointed rooms to accommodate the daughter of a Titan."

"The guest wing? Why would you suggest that? The north tower has the best view of the meadows."

Blythe's face blushed a deeper shade as she dropped her chin slightly. "I agree the meadows are in lovely form this year, but perhaps the young goddess would not be so interested in poppies."

"Poppies? But we have no poppies in the—" Hades's speech slowed, and the air suddenly felt heavy as Lexi watched realization dawn on his face in the form of an eyebrow lift, followed by a sober head shake. "Blythe, what would I do without your pristine memory? The east wing is the perfect solution, and it would only be temporary until Lexi has time to choose something more fitting. Let's give her the astronomy room."

Blythe's blinding smile improved the mood so completely that Lexi found herself smiling too. "Oh yes! That's a fine suggestion, Your Grace. I'll see that the room is prepared."

Blythe offered Lexi a curtsy before hopping deftly onto Misty's back and getting the horse airborne with a click of her tongue. Hades snaked his arms around Lexi's waist and spun her into him.

"I have a powerful thirst to show you how it feels to be the sole desire of a god."

"That sounds like something I could get behind," she said. "Is there time for a question, first?"

"Of course."

"I know I'm a stranger here, and it will take time for everyone to get acclimated, but I don't think I can stand living in a home full of secrets. I just left a home like that. So, will you tell me why Blythe talked you out of the north tower?"

His hands loosened around her waist and his expression grew sober. She suspected her question would throw a wrench into the mood, but it had to be done if they were going to start with a clean slate.

"The north tower is where Clary spent much of her time. She's the daughter of Mnemosyne, and the only other goddess who has shared the palace with me apart from Persephone."

"You were involved with another daughter of Mnemosyne? How long ago was that?"

"Many centuries ago. And I assure you that I have not pursued any of Mnemosyne's other daughters, just to quell any unhelpful thoughts you might have. I suppose I chose the tower because of its exceptional views of the Asphodel Meadows."

Lexi took hold of one of his hands and threaded her fingers through it. "I'm a sucker for an exceptional view. And the poppies?"

"They're Clary's favorite flower. She kept her bedroom decorated in the motif. I apologize for not being more forthcoming. I can't remember the last time I lost my head over a goddess. I'm not starting out on the right foot, am I?"

His gaze lost focus and he looked past her, or perhaps through her, like a little lost child. She was shocked by his vulnerability, but more so that he'd allowed her to witness it.

"Well, you listened to Blythe and let her persuade you to make a different choice. Your brother never would have done that. I'd say your footing is just fine."

He blinked at her, as if she'd yanked him out of the dark and into the light. Then he pulled her into him and kissed her in a long, luxurious possession. His hands slid down to cup her rear, and he dipped her head back to extend the kiss as he hardened against her thigh. Without any effort, Lexi's body surrendered to him with a breathy moan. Would it always be this way? One kiss, one touch, and they were ready to ride each other like a pair of unbroken horses.

A flash of movement caught Lexi's eye, and she realized they were being watched by more than just a three-headed dog. A dark-haired woman stood between the doors of the palace—another nymph, as thin as a reed. Hades released Lexi from his passionate embrace to acknowledge her with a wave.

"Damn these distractions. Let's go meet Fiona. Then I'm having my way with you. With your permission, of course."

They walked hand in hand to the palace entrance, where Lexi noticed that the nymph was holding a tray of puff pastry hors d'oeuvres. As Hades prepared to speak, she popped one into his open mouth.

"We picked the spinach from Hecate's garden just this morning," she explained. "And the mascarpone cheese came from Hermes's visit to Milan, remember? I've been saving it."

"There are no words in my repertoire to describe the deliciousness of this pastry," Hades said as he chewed.

Fiona waved away his comment as if she'd heard all the words in his repertoire. "You don't have to show off for me. Would *you* like one?"

Fiona turned to Lexi with a curious smile, or maybe it was judgment behind her searching gaze.

"Thank you, I would. I'm a big fan of cheese."

"Make a note of that, Fiona," Hades said as he watched Lexi enjoy her puff, which burst with flavors that seemed almost otherworldly. "And before you fill our mouths with more culinary wonders, please allow me to introduce Alexandra Maxwell, daughter of Mnemosyne. She'll be staying with us for the foreseeable future. Lexi, this is Fiona, our head chef."

"A Titan's daughter. Well, it's a pleasure to have you. We will do everything within our means to accommodate you." Fiona bowed her head, and Lexi thought she saw her suppressing a grin.

"Fiona, please have a pot of chamomile tea and a bottle of Château Pétrus brought to my chambers," said Hades. "And the stemware from Hestia's collection."

"Your chambers, my lord?"

"Yes. My chambers." Hades cocked his head, his brows pinching in confusion. "Am I speaking in riddles today?"

"Not at all. I'll take care of everything myself." Fiona bustled away, leaving an awkward silence in her wake. Hades didn't seem to notice as he grabbed Lexi's hand and whisked her up a staircase that appeared to be made of pressed sand.

"I hope you don't mind if we put off the grand tour until I have ravaged you properly," he said through measured breaths. "I didn't realize how much your presence here would affect me. It seems to be affecting the staff as well."

Lexi allowed herself to be hauled past beautiful tapestries and pieces of art, some of which resembled the works of the Masters. She knew there would be plenty of time to take it all in later. Before she knew it, they'd reached the end of a corridor where an impressive set of hand-carved doors promised grand things beyond it.

The image etched into the wood depicted a man and a woman lounging on a chaise and feeding each other grapes. Lexi knew perfectly well who the couple was. And the passion that had propelled her forward came to a screeching halt.

But why? There were many reasons she'd used in her decision to come to the underworld. Freedom. Autonomy. The promise of something she'd never experienced before. Most of all, she'd made a choice that was wholly her own. Yet that didn't stop the pain she felt in her heart as she stared at the door. Could Hades ever feel for her what he felt for Persephone? Did she believe she could find true love with Hades? Did that really matter to her? She was a goddess. She could have her pick of anyone, immortal or not.

It had probably only been a couple of seconds before she noticed Hades frowning. He looked like he was in pain, and there was a sheen to his eyes. But he said nothing, quickly pushing the doors open and nudging her toward the threshold.

The room stretched as wide as a ballroom, but it was less than half that in depth, giving the feeling of expanse without forgetting the intimacy. The roundness of the outer wall added to that sense of welcome, as if the room was ready with a hug for everyone who entered.

Flames already crackled inside the hearth of a fireplace, which was set against a warm terra-cotta backdrop and surrounded by a mosaic of tiles in earthy tones. They extended to the ceiling and stretched out like limbs of a tree or tributaries of a river. An elegant canopy bed strewn with colorful fabrics commanded the foreground, plush and inviting.

On every surface something green and living grew, curling around frames and mirrors, with accents of copper or bronze adding to the luxury. Strands of floral garlands dressed the crown molding, and the fragrance that permeated the air had Lexi believing she was in a garden.

Hades took her by the hips and turned her so she could see the reach of his gaze. It went deeper than she cared to explore now. "Please, try to understand, Lexi, I hadn't expected to return with a beautiful goddess on my arm. I'm sure this is difficult for you."

Lexi sucked in a steadying breath. Of course it was difficult. Who waltzed into the underworld of their own free will and committed adultery with Hades? If that was even a thing for the gods. It was something a crazy person would do. Or was that just something her parents would tell her?

This had been *her* choice. And if Hades was right, the Fates might have had a hand in it. If time flowed like water for the gods, Lexi wanted to ride the waves for a while.

"It's a lot to take in. Just give me a minute."

And that's when she saw it, staring at her from the opposite wall—a life-sized portrait of Hades and Persephone. The artist had done an excellent job of capturing their emotions. They looked very much in love.

She choked on her next breath, and Hades pulled away to follow her gaze. Then he let out a guttural moan that convinced her he truly *was* in pain.

"Oh, Lexi. I'm such a fool."

Thirty-one

He'd been thinking with his dick. It was the only explanation for allowing such a contemptible act to happen. He'd become so numb to his surroundings that he'd forgotten what it looked like. What it all meant to him.

He could have taken Lexi anywhere else in the palace. Anywhere but the very place he shared a bed with Persephone. If he couldn't trust his own mind, how could he earn Lexi's loyalty? But more urgently, how could he earn her forgiveness?

Dropping heavily to his knees, Hades gathered her hands together and gazed into her liquid blue eyes, shimmering with unshed tears.

"My careless error is inexcusable. I wouldn't blame you if you refused me and left the palace as punishment. I assure you that no one would feel more pain than me. It was the excitement of having you to myself. There's so much I want to share with you."

Lexi put her finger to his lips, stopping his desperate rant. "I don't blame you. Everything is happening so fast, we're bound to have lapses. This room is very nice. Welcoming, even. But is there somewhere else we can go for refreshments?"

With guilt weighing him down like a slab of marble, Hades stood and tucked Lexi into his arms, loving her more with every kind gesture she showed him. He'd behaved selfishly, and she'd forgiven him without judgment. Even the wisest gods could learn from her compassion.

"You're a merciful angel and a goddess of the highest caliber."

"You might rescind that statement when I beat you at croquet again."

He chuckled into her hair then inhaled deeply, imagining where they might plant an extra patch of lemon verbena. Could he convince her never to bathe?

"I'll have the refreshments sent to the astronomy room. In the meantime, you deserve an explanation."

Fiona appeared, clearing her throat as she walked toward them balancing a full tray. "Is everything all right, Your Graces?"

"If you wouldn't mind, Fiona, could you please deliver the tray to the astronomy room. I've already sent Blythe ahead to ready it. Lexi and I will explore the palace to give you and your sisters more time."

"As you wish. That room *does* have a lovely view of the gorge." Fiona bowed her head to hide an expression of relief as her eyes flitted to Lexi. His nymphs had always been more astute than he could ever hope to be.

"You said you don't want any secrets in your home. Well, I'm going to tell you a secret." Hades smiled at Lexi to cover his emotions. They'd been simmering dangerously close to the surface since her arrival. He was certain she'd noticed the moisture building in his eyes, and perhaps even the thrumming in his chest.

How could he explain that each time he saw an image of Persephone his guts twisted into knots, and he told himself a lie.

It was the only way he knew how to cope with a truth that he didn't want to believe.

But if there was ever a time to face his fears and speak the words he'd been smothering for more than a century, this was it. Lexi gave him hope, and she deserved the truth. With his pulse in his throat, he led her away from the painful reminder that she was not the first goddess to steal his heart.

"I'm a liar, Lexi. Not to you. To myself."

She looked at him, her soft gaze offering only solace, and his mind tried to convince him he was just imagining it.

"Persephone's duties in Olympus keep her away from her home here, from me, for much longer periods than the stories relate. Prior to her visit last winter, she didn't come home for three winters. Before that, it was only December. Sometimes only January. She's never been fond of the mortal realm, which means our only time together is spent here. And our correspondence is just as rare. Well, her correspondence with me is rare. I write her every month, even when I know it's an exercise in futility."

They had reached the staircase, but instead of taking it down, they walked up, treading a familiar path that led to his study.

"I'm telling you this not to gain your sympathy. The last thing I want is for you to feel obliged to repair my broken heart. Pity is not a good foundation to build a relationship on. You wanted the truth. And you deserve the truth. I'm just as flawed as anyone you might meet on the street. Moreso when it comes to love. I hope you'll forgive me if you feel like I've led you astray."

A smile slipped onto her face as easily as paint flows over canvas. "I never believed you didn't have flaws. If I thought you were perfect, I wouldn't have followed you here. It would have been too intimidating. I'd be spending all my time trying to measure up to some kind of lofty standard. Also, for what it's worth, I've heard that it's nearly impossible to maintain healthy long-distance relationships."

He stopped their progress on the worn wool rug so he could stare at her. She didn't bat an eyelash, meeting his gaze just as steadily. "I know you didn't choose to come here solely because of me. And I support whatever decisions you make for yourself, even if they take you away from the underworld someday. There's no gauge we use to measure success here, although Hecate will make if feel that way sometimes. As far as I'm concerned, you have the freedom to choose who you want to be, with no expectations."

The chime of his seventeenth-century floor clock struck the ninth evening hour, and she glanced past his head at it. "That's a beautiful clock, although it seems strange to keep time when you have eternity."

"I thought the same thing too. But it was a gift from a mortal, and after installing it, I came to enjoy the reminder that the mortal world still exists outside of my immortal life here."

Her attention swung back to him, and she pressed a tender kiss to his lips. "When you say things like that, it makes me want you even more."

"I'm glad to hear you say that. The feeling is mutual. Why don't we continue the tour and let the anticipation build?"

"If we must." She wrapped her arm around his, wearing a smile he knew was just for him. It felt almost blasphemous not to cater to her desires, but he'd been too reckless and had made mistakes. So, he started the tour.

"The palace was built by the Titans before the war. There were fewer gods back then, and the process was long."

"But everyone in Olympus has supernatural powers, right? Didn't that speed things up?"

"Not every gift is useful for building. Some are better for tearing down."

"So you didn't ask for Zeus's help, I take it?" Lexi pantomimed an explosion with her hands, which made him laugh.

"He has spent very little time in the underworld since the war. When he decided to release Cronus from Tartarus, he gave the order to me, and I carried it out."

He escorted her to the central tower, pointing out the pieces he'd collected on his travels. Her eyes lit up whenever she discovered they'd been to the same places.

"This looks like a relic of the Roman Empire," she said of an archaic bronze bowl perched on a pedestal.

"Athens, actually. I was there when Poseidon and Athena competed for the city's patronage. We all know who won *that* fight. As my obstinate brother sent the floods, I managed to secure this piece before it floated away."

"Wow. It must be incredibly old."

He lifted his brows, and his lips followed suit. "I'd take offense at that remark but there will come a day when you stop looking at the calendar, for your own peace of mind."

She leaned in and kissed him. "It's hard to imagine you being around that long. You have the best of both worlds—a youthful body and the wisdom of experience." Before he could respond, she turned to glance up a spiral staircase, the steps eroded from centuries of use. "Where does this go?

"That leads to the dome room. I'm usually the only one who goes up there . . . when I need time alone."

She smirked but stayed pointedly silent. He had to ask.

"What have you heard?"

"Only that you can get broody, according to Mnemosyne. I'll remember never to disturb you up there."

He took her hand. "You're welcome anywhere in the palace, including the central tower. I just can't promise I won't be cranky if you find me there."

The sky had darkened to indigo by the time they reached the astronomy room, and Hades cringed when he noticed the nymphs had used a twelfth-century Chinese vase as a door stopper. Inside, Blythe and her sister nymphs scuttled about, sweeping dust off the floor and covering the mattress with fresh linens. Fiona was the first to greet them.

"We're nearly through with preparations. Does the young goddess wish to take in the fragrant waters of a bath? We have oils of rose, lilac, juniper . . ."

"No, thank you," Hades said. "I prefer Lexi to smell exactly the way she does right now. However, I'd be grateful if you had access to lemon verbena oil." His gaze flicked to Lexi, hoping he wouldn't see disappointment on her face. There would be plenty of time for baths and all manner of luxuries. She reassured him with a smile.

"How lovely, your lordship. I'll personally see to it." Fiona's eyes twinkled with purpose as she flitted away, reminding Hades why he loved his housemates. They were more like family than staff, and although the gods regularly consorted with nymphs, Hades found their minds too flighty for something as consequential as intimacy.

Sella was next to bustle over, her green eyes lit like Tiffany glass. She pointed at the bed, recently refurbished in ivory sheets.

"I laid out a nightgown for the young goddess," Sella said. "I hope it's to your liking." She offered Lexi a cherubic smile, which Lexi returned without pause.

"Thank you. The room is beautiful. And everyone has been very kind. Excuse me if I seem a little dazed."

Sella gestured to the teapot sitting on the table. "A cup of strong chamomile will set you right. And if that doesn't work, Lord Hades has excellent taste in wine. Let me know if I can assist you in any way. My name is Sella."

She skipped out of the room, which left only Blythe, who walked up to them and folded into a deep curtsy. Being a transplant from the palace of the gods, Blythe had never lost the ingrained formalities of Olympus, despite Hades's insistence that her unyielding cheerfulness was all he required.

"I'm very glad you're here, Lady Lexi. It's been many springs since I've seen our lord look so happy. I hope you'll be happy here too."

Hades watched with some trepidation as Blythe waltzed over to the priceless vase and dragged it into the hallway, allowing the door to shut. When he turned to Lexi, she was taking in her surroundings with an open mouth, no doubt struggling with the enormity of her decision. Or perhaps it was the gadgetry that winked and spun from various locations in the room—an astrolabe that moved with the rhythm of the cosmos, a twirling mobile of planets, carved crystals set on glowing stands. He'd hoped she would be enchanted by it all and not overwhelmed.

He left her to explore and crossed the room to inspect the wine. The vintage was just as he'd requested, and the bottle had been uncorked, allowing the contents to breathe. He filled a teacup for her with steaming chamomile and poured a glass of wine for himself, smiling at his good fortune. The nymphs with their constant fussing were sure to make Lexi feel at home whenever his duties called him away.

He rejoined his dazzled goddess and handed her the cup. "Try this. You'll find the potency rivals any vintage in the human realm."

Lexi appeared to return to herself as she took his offering, and she tapped his glass in a toast. "Here's to new vintages and choices that make us grateful for their potency."

Hades chuckled then drank deeply, keeping his gaze on her face. He'd been in the same position before, looking into the eyes of a desirable female and wanting to possess her. But it felt different with Lexi. There was more at stake than a satisfying sexual experience. There was the potential for love. Perhaps, though he scarcely dared to hope, they'd build something potent enough to carry them through eternity.

Thirty-two

After Lexi finished her tea she switched to wine, and both seemed to hit her with equal force. As soon as she admitted to feeling lightheaded, Hades swung the balcony doors open and escorted her outside for a breath of fresh air, although standing on a tower floating magically over a gorge didn't produce the most calming effect.

The sky had gone completely dark. The kind of dark she'd never seen before because there was no moon or stars to give it light. But an ethereal glow that undulated like snakes moving through the grass hovered close to the ground.

"What causes the ground to glow like that?"

"It's one of the wonders of the underworld." Hades's voice tickled Lexi's ear as he stood behind her, his arms wrapped around her waist and his chin resting on her shoulder. "To be more specific, you're seeing the essence of the souls who have chosen to remain here rather than take the Lethe. Does it bother you to know that?"

Did it bother her? She'd only experienced the tortured souls waiting at the gates. "It would only bother me if they were unhappy."

"They're not unhappy. But I wouldn't say they're happy either. They're simply content. How are you feeling now? Still lightheaded?"

As he spoke, he peppered his lips across her neck. She knew he was eager to make good on his promise to ravage her, and she felt the same need to be close to him. So why was she stalling? Was she just feeling overwhelmed? The enchanted bedroom was a little much, but she wouldn't dare bring it up.

Hades and his perky staff of nymphs had made her feel welcome despite the short notice and the many reminders of who he was. And Lexi had made this choice knowing she would be exploring a world that was unknown to her. Wasn't that exactly what she'd been complaining about since she'd turned eighteen?

"I'm good now, thank you."

"I need you like the horizon needs the sun. But I sense your reluctance to submit."

His whispered plea floated across her skin, making her heart skip a few beats. He was everything she'd imagined in a man. And this one was a god. She couldn't be turning chicken now. She'd always had plenty of courage, but her heart had never been involved before. Was this what it felt like to fall in love? When the thought of losing it sounded like the worst pain in the world? She wasn't that far gone yet, although it felt like she was heading there.

She turned in his arms, speaking to his eyes where she could see the answers. "I would be lying if I didn't say my heart is doing funny things to my head, and I doubt it's the wine or that strong cup of tea."

He took her hand and lifted it to his lips. "It's been a long time since a goddess has stirred me like you do, but if you need more time, I can wait to claim you here, in my domain. *When a flower buds, the fortunate witness the splendor. / But when it opens, only the privileged bask in its beauty.*"

Lexi felt certain she would swoon. She didn't even care if the words were his or something he'd read. Despite his position as the ruler of the underworld, Hades had no qualms about wearing his emotions on his sleeve. If there was any love involved, she loved this about him.

"I've never been more ready to be claimed by you," she said.

"Your surrender is my salvation." Hades's lips twitched, as if he could taste her already, and Lexi clenched, feeling his need between her thighs.

His arms came under her and he easily swept her up to carry her inside. He'd already lit the many candles perched in stands around the room, which offered a warmth she'd come to expect with Hades. At the foot of the bed, he set her on her feet again. He stood very close, his eyes like an ever-burning flame, his smile tilted higher on one side.

"May I divest you of your clothing, Lady Lexi? I wish to gaze upon your beautiful form unhindered."

Flames seemed to lick her body from the inside as Hades continued his poetic assault. Was all this adoration really in her future? She freaking hoped so.

After her nod of consent, Hades worked deftly to untie the tassels of her blouse. If she'd known she'd be escaping to the underworld today, she might have worn something more practical. But he reached her cleavage with no problem, pressing his lips there, and the ache building between her legs turned into delicious torture.

His hands slid down her body and under her shirt, and he caressed her skin like she was more valuable than any of the artifacts in his palace. This went on for several minutes, and when she thought her body couldn't handle the unrelenting rush of goose bumps, he grabbed a handful of fabric and lifted it over her head, casually tossing the shirt onto a nearby chair.

Again, Hades took his time tracing the outline of her bra, running a finger along the seam while holding his lower lip captive between his teeth. When he finally made it to the clasp, his breath left him in a low hiss as the bra fell to the floor. Lexi reveled in his teasing possession, dropping her head back as he bowed to her chest. A moment later, he took a nipple into his mouth, warming her even deeper, and she dragged her fingers through his hair as his tongue circled and flicked.

He was smiling when he broke away, his nimble fingers already working on her jeans. The zipper lowered, then he eased his hand down to cup her mound over her panties. Heat flooded from his palm, and she cried out softly. His fingers were so close, pressing gently, taunting her with the promise of more.

Her jeans left her hips, pooling at her ankles, and she stepped out of them, leaving her in a thin cover of lace. Hades backed up to take in the view. His eyes roamed her body with intent, one brow lifted in a sinful quirk. But she knew he was no villain. A villain wouldn't be able to melt her heart with a single look.

"I think I'll leave the lace on for now," he said. "All right, Lexi. It's your turn."

He held up his arms in surrender, and Lexi's heart pounded even harder. She'd never taken a man's clothes off before. But Hades's playful smile made her less nervous, and she slipped her hands under his shirt to explore the contours of his chest. She'd already sensed the power idling underneath, but it felt even stronger now.

Buoyed by adrenaline and a tidal wave of desire, she rolled up his shirt and jerked it over his head. Then she followed her instincts and stepped into his chest, pressing her breasts against him. The blood in her veins rushed southward, keeping her fueled as she pulled him in for a kiss. Tongues, lips, and hands all groped for purchase as the seduction notched up a level. With his hard-on grinding against her belly, her climax was already close enough to touch.

Almost greedily, Lexi lowered his zipper and slipped her hand inside. His pants dropped easily to the floor, granting her full access, and she traced his thickness through his briefs, imagining the strength behind it. She'd felt that strength before and was eager for more. When she started to remove the barrier, Hades caught her gently by the wrist.

"I want to savor this a little longer."

He tugged her onto the mattress, and she tried to relax against the headboard, which was made of polished tree branches, intertwining in a tangle of knots and limbs. It had not been built for comfort or promoting intimacy, but she couldn't help grinning at the thought of him forgetting this fact in his haste to take her to bed.

Hades crawled across her body, snugging his hardness against her center, and she was back in the race. She hooked her legs around his waist, maneuvering him toward her finish line. She was so close. Too close.

"I need this," she declared, more to herself than him, but Hades's breath hitched.

"You have it, Lexi. You deserve it."

Without further ado, he yanked off her panties. Apparently, he'd hit his wall of restraint because his briefs were the next to go.

Lexi bit her lip as she glanced down at him. So much had been hidden in the darkness of the limo.

"Do you want the reins? Or should I lead?" he asked as he fondled her. Of course, this didn't help her think.

What *did* she want? Was it too soon to know? If someone had forever, how would they want to kick things off? Life was a journey of one according to her father the hypocrite, and she needed to get a fucking move on.

Shifting her weight to the right, she rolled Hades onto his back, and he relinquished full control. When she had him pinned beneath her, she smiled like a fool. "That was fun."

"Indeed, it was." He offered her a deeper glimpse behind his eyes, and she thought she saw vulnerability there. "I'm afraid you have me at a loss, again. But your choices matter to me. There should be contraception under the pillow, should you require it."

She felt around beneath the pillows stacked two deep until she found the edges of a plastic wrapper.

"I assure you, they're fresh," he said as Lexi studied the silver packaging. She'd never seen one up close.

"We'll worry about it next time."

She threw the condom on the floor, having already done the math and deciding they were safe enough for eternity. If she had to endure one more distraction, she was going to scream, and Hades seemed happy to oblige. He stood at the ready as she lowered herself onto him. The fit was snug and perfect. Just like the first time.

Lexi felt like a horny schoolgirl cornering a boy in the locker room. Not that she'd ever done that. But now she had a god in her bed, filling her, plush and powerful, and she brought her mouth to his neck, tasting the salt on his skin and wishing she wasn't so close to losing it.

A strong gust of air suddenly swirled around them, forcing the curtains open like sails and whipping her hair into her face. She even felt a hum of energy building, as if a lightning strike was coming next. Who had invited the elements? Was it another wonder of the underworld?

In her wildest fantasies Lexi hadn't imagined it being this good. She arched her spine, rocking into his pelvis and taking him as far as her body would allow. A long moan escaped Hades's lips, something unrestrained and otherworldly, and he snuck his fingers between her legs.

Damn.

She gyrated into him like a horse bucking against its ties. If she truly had forever, then there was no reason to hold back now. She released the imaginary reins as she crossed the finish line, and Hades held on to her hips like a sailor battling a hurricane. The rush was fantastic, and she savored every moment of it. It felt like decadence, that thing the gods all sought. She could see herself falling victim.

When the sensations ebbed and the wind died down, Lexi realized she had shut her eyes. As she blinked, the room swam back into view, and she found Hades staring at her, his face awash with emotion. She was pretty sure he hadn't crossed the line yet, but he didn't seem one bit concerned. He slowly withdrew as the throb between her legs retreated. Then he took her hand and wrapped it around him.

"I'm all yours."

So *that* was his game. Despite her indifference toward their unprotected romp in the hay, he was making his own call. The only way to interpret that and not lose the mood was to consider him a gentleman.

The wind continued to keep them company, only now it came in the form of a sultry breeze, the air still tingling with electricity. She took him in hand and stroked from front to aft, the moisture collecting between her fingers as she watched him lose himself. Within a few moments, he was throwing his head back, lifting his ass off the bed, making a beautiful mess of the fresh linens.

Then they collapsed together in a heap of exhausted satisfaction. He pulled her into him and rested his brow on her forehead. She felt invincible and exposed at the same time. Maybe that was the euphoria of sex everyone talked about. Or could love have played a role?

Hades lifted his head lazily, introducing her to the smile of a contented god. "To hell with commanding the elements, I think you just came into your power."

She grinned. "You are my source, *mon ami*."

With her body humming and the air buzzing, Lexi felt like a goddess for the first time. She had a place among her peers, perhaps beside the ruler of the underworld. Something about it felt like fate, like everything that had come before had been guiding her to make this choice. Hades had given her the fuel she needed. No doubt, it would take her further than she'd ever been. And Lexi was sure she would need a lot of it to get her through eternity.

Acknowledgments

For the longest time, I didn't know what I wanted to be when I grew up. Two marriages and four kids later, I figured it out while obsessing over a popular fantasy series that must not be named. These stories inspired me to write a few of my own, and I eventually shared them on Wattpad. This is where I met my people—a huge, diverse group of storytellers and the readers who love them.

So, my most heartfelt acknowledgment goes out to my Wattpad readers. You laughed and gasped and fumed at the shit my characters did. You asked for second and third installments, and all of your comments encouraged me to keep on writing. Thank you for helping me believe in myself.

To the amazing group of Wattpad writers who I've had the privilege of connecting with (you know who you are), you rhapsodize each other as fiercely as a superfan with a backstage pass.

I've also been blessed with incredibly supportive family and friends. Hugs to my daughters, who share hilarious memes that keep me motivated. To my mom, who always reminds me that she's proud of me. And thank you, Trisha, for never letting me forget my worth.

Acknowledgments

About the Author

Morgan Rider is a romance author and a writing mentor. Her most popular work, a trilogy highlighting the escapades of the modern Greek gods, has seen over 43 million reads, which includes her debut novel, *A Goddess Unraveled.* Morgan grew up feral under the glitzy Las Vegas lights and now lives in mostly sunny Florida, where she still orders her drinks with extra sugar on the rim.

Can't wait for book two in the Olympus Rising series?

Read on for a sample of

A Queen Undone

by Morgan Rider

One

The imposing iron gates swung closed behind him as he took the enchanted path leading home. The number of arriving souls had been steady, with only a handful needing to be rounded up as they tried to escape into the darkness.

Hades had had enough of Thanatos's brittle wit and discomfiting methods for one day, having long ago given up on softening the god of death's abrasive manners. He slipped his hands into his robe, contentment sweeping over him as the foliage adopted the colors of autumn.

For nearly two seasons, Hades's heart had felt lighter than usual after a day's work. The weight of greeting hundreds, sometimes thousands, of souls didn't linger as long, dogging him until he laid his head down or drowned in too many glasses of scotch. Not to mention the monotony.

Now he had a sounder reason to hurry home than a silk-lined pillow or bottomless liquor cabinet, and this thought put a spring in his step as he left the path to follow the tree line north.

He kept his gaze on the western horizon, hoping to catch a glimpse of the source of his contentment, and when he saw her in the distance, riding bareback on one of his horses, he stilled for a moment, his chest feeling like it might open and release an explosion of blossoms.

Hades watched the young goddess, her hair waving like grains of wheat under a golden sky, commanding the horse as if she'd been born to do it. Even without a saddle, the auburn beauty rode with poise and confidence, wearing her self-assurance like a longsword, exercising her godly nature with ease.

Since joining Hades in the underworld, this particular goddess had demonstrated her intense spirit—testing his stamina and reminding him of his youth—and he gave daily thanks to Gaia for placing her in his care.

Her family had taken her departure rather poorly, but he'd expected as much. They had kept her too close, protected her from anyone or anything that might lead her away from the path they'd chosen for her. Ultimately, she'd chosen her own path, although under duress, and Hades refused to entertain the possibility that her conscience—or any guilt she felt—might one day become a burden to her.

There were marvels in the underworld that rivaled anything she could find in Olympus, and Hades had only begun to show her these wonders. His biggest challenge would be keeping her happy while fulfilling his duties as god of the underworld, a task he rarely received a reprieve from.

The underworld gods had been welcoming, as they should; Hecate with her motherly wisdom, Thanatos's grim humor. Of course, there was Melinoe, who often used her position to pop into the palace during mealtime. The goddess of nightmares always made sure conversations were awkward and exhausting. He was still waiting for her to reveal more of their private affairs and had to assume she'd been holding back solely to keep him on edge.

Still, like a seedling blessed by Demeter, Hades knew this bright young goddess, the focus of his waking thoughts and the subject of his dreams, was destined to flourish regardless of the conditions. He could already see her powers flowering under his domain. He simply needed to nurture her, a job he desperately hoped he was equipped to do.

Two

Lexi clung to Misty's harness as the horse sped toward home. While the beast was perfectly capable of flying, Lexi preferred to feel Misty's muscular hindquarters grinding against her buttocks and the sound of hooves pounding the dirt.

There was something erotic about riding bareback, although Lexi hadn't thought of it that way until she met Hades. Now she was living the life of a goddess and having regular sex with the god of the dead. Six months in, and the images she was able to conjure still sent chills up her spine.

Her fantasy life was a far cry from the life her family had imagined for her. They would have had her married off to a boastful, stuffed shirt wannabe from her parents' list of potential suitors. Or worse, an arrogant god who thought monogamy was some type of disease.

Of course, every fantasy had its version of stuffed shirts, and Hecate, goddess of sorcery and apothecary, held that position in the underworld. She was okay, in a mother-in-law sort of way, but she definitely had a different idea of how Lexi's time should be spent, like sitting through intensive lectures about the gods and requiring Lexi to practice her gifts until her fingers went numb.

Fortunately, Hecate had a sense of humor. She liked to pretend she didn't, but it was there, and it saved Lexi. Otherwise, she would have to find better places to hide from the matronly goddess.

Hecate also liked to use Lexi as her delivery girl. Today, Lexi was responsible for a bunch of fresh arugula, green onions, and cherry tomatoes for the palace nymphs. Fiona, who was a whiz in the kitchen, relied heavily on Hecate's gardening skills.

The other package Lexi carried held her monthly dose of wild yam powder, a medicinal she used as a contraceptive. She may have agreed to be Hades's lover, but she had no intention of getting knocked up. At least, not until she actually felt like a goddess. Besides, she had a long time to think about it, and she was having too much fun riding the waves of passion.

The palace bridge came into view, reminding Lexi that she would soon be with Hades again. It also reminded her of another bridge she had yet to cross. Persephone would arrive soon, and Lexi was worried as hell. The nymphs gushed about Persephone's kindness and grace, but Lexi couldn't decide if this made her feel better or worse. Would Persephone's goodness trump anything Lexi might bring to the table? Was Lexi destined to play backup for all of eternity? Sometimes she wondered if she was crazy-in-love or just plain crazy.

While most girls lost their virginity to their high school sweetheart or the boy next door, Lexi had celebrated her college graduation by climbing into the back of a limo and doing the deed with a near total stranger. Sure, she had made it with a god, but she couldn't exactly brag about it.

Now Lexi couldn't imagine her life without Hades. And his mate was about to arrive to burst their romantic bubble. She didn't want to see him in the arms of another woman, sharing a secret smile or a lusty kiss. Yet that was her reality. She was the mistress. The other woman. The meager demigod. But she still had a heart.

Misty snorted, distracting Lexi from her desperate thoughts, and she focused on the bridge and the figure waiting for her there. He wore a powder-blue shirt and heather-gray pants, his white robe slung over one arm. Even from a distance, Hades's elegant bearing gave him the appearance of royalty, and Lexi waved excitedly as she let the subject of mates and mistresses drop from her mind. For now, she was still his sole desire.

As soon as Misty arrived at the stone bridge, Hades hurried to Lexi's side, offering his arm as she dismounted. The rapid ticking of his pulse inside her hand made her own heart flutter as they smiled at each other like silly kids on the playground.

"Hello, my sweet," he said. "I have thought of you every moment since I left for the gates. You look stunning in that blouse."

Lexi glanced down at the silk shirt she wore. It was made from fabric Hades had purchased from a merchant in India. He said the vibrant colors made him think of spring. Blythe, one of the palace nymphs, had told Lexi that Persephone didn't like the fabric, so the nymphs stored it away until another purpose could be found. In a moment of weakness, or perhaps stupidity, Lexi let Blythe's bright eyes and bouncy enthusiasm convince her it was a fine idea to have a blouse made from the fabric.

"Blythe is amazing. She can sew, cook, sing harmony, play backgammon. So far, I haven't found a single thing she can't do."

Just then, the palace door opened, and Cerberus bounded

through it, plopping onto his hindquarters to wait for his master. Behind the oversized canine, the ever-cheerful Blythe smiled from the open doorway.

Lexi waved at Blythe, who broke into a bout of giggles then quickly disappeared behind the door, leaving Cerberus to his own affairs. Lexi didn't mind that the nymphs were never far away. She'd grown fond of each one and considered them to be better friends than she'd ever had at school.

Hades wove his arms around her waist, and he kissed her as he reached under the loose fabric of her blouse, trailing his fingers over her skin, causing a cascade of goose bumps.

"I think the nymphs are expecting us for dinner," she said. "If you keep that up, our soup will be cold by the time we eat it."

"I would rather eat you. What do you say to that?"

"I'd say you were a wicked god with an insatiable appetite. It's one of the things I love about you."

"Is that a yes?"

"Hades, we're on the bridge."

"Indulge me. I just want to see how this shirt looks as a dress." Hades began a slow descent to his knees, tugging Lexi's riding pants down to her feet. All further protests were squelched as he pressed his mouth over the fabric of her panties, blowing warmth against her skin.

She drew in a gasp. "We really shouldn't . . . Melinoe could be here any— Mmm . . . Oh, gods."

Lexi offered her weak pleas but allowed Hades to have his fun, and a rush of air circled them as her powers were triggered. Suddenly, he glanced up and schooled a grimace as he rose from the bridge.

"I'd take you right here if Melinoe weren't walking up the path."

"Oh, damn." Lexi stiffened as she turned toward the forest where a cloaked figure was emerging from the trees. "How did you know she was coming?"

"Let's just say I'm sensitive to her vibrations. While I was on my knees, I had an image of Cerberus ripping your head off."

"That's awful. Does she do that on purpose?"

Hades shrugged. "I assume it's a disturbing byproduct of her gifts, of which I have long been the unfortunate recipient."

"Well, I'm glad I'll never have to face her at the gates. Tormenting mortals in their dreams then confronting them when they die is a horrifying thought."

Hades brushed Lexi's flushed cheek with the back of his hand. "Even as a mortal, you would not encounter Melinoe at the gates. Your soul is too pure, almost too pure to be a god's. But we have time to work on defiling that."

Lexi fondled his backside as she brought her mouth to his ear. "If wanting you makes me impure, then you defile me every time you touch me."

Melinoe made the short journey across the field with effortless grace, as if her feet never touched the ground, and arrived at the bridge where Lexi and Hades waited to greet her. As usual, she had shrouded herself in black, giving off a sinister vibe, and Lexi wouldn't have been surprised if she kept a scythe hidden inside her clothing.

But Melinoe was no reaper. There was a raven-haired beauty beneath that gothic wardrobe. Her ivory face glowed against dark eyes heavily lined with kohl, and lips as crimson as blood, captivating even when she appeared as a phantom behind a veil. Yet, as far as Lexi could tell, beauty was the only trait Melinoe shared with her mother, Persephone. Her moodiness had surely come from Zeus, the father who refused to claim her.

"You two seem to be enjoying each other's company. Please, don't let me interrupt."

Melinoe's words held an acerbic tang as she stepped onto the bridge, her veil failing to hide a scowl as the air crackled with enough electricity to lift the hairs on Lexi's arms. The goddess of nightmares made no attempt to slow her pace, sweeping past them with a toss of her gloved hand, as if they were annoying apparitions, and Hades tsked at her retreating back. Even Cerberus offered a look of distaste from one of his heads.

Blythe, on the other hand, hurried outside to greet Melinoe with an animated wave. The nymphs, being perpetually happy, never seemed to notice Melinoe's gloomy personality. Or, at least, they never talked about it in front of the gods.

Inside the palace, Lexi handed off the garden supplies to Fiona, then Hades walked her to the dining room. With Thanksgiving a few days away, the table had been staged to impress. Lexi knew this was for her benefit. The nymphs were constantly trying to make her feel at home, and she loved them for it.

They had set out a wicker cornucopia spilling over with oranges, apples, and pomegranates. Maple leaves decorated the plates, and the wineglasses were trimmed in silver.

On both ends of the table, candelabras stood like gnarled trees, the wrought iron limbs stretching their bony fingers around black candles. They were macabre but beautiful, and Lexi assumed they'd been put out to impress Melinoe and her morbid tastes. Then Lexi blanched when she noticed the tablecloth. It featured centaurs and minotaurs wielding spears as they chased each other around the bottom hem—another choice presumably made for Melinoe's benefit. But she didn't seem impressed as she reached, single-mindedly, for a carafe of wine and floated into her chair.

"I take it there's been no word from the bearded wonder about your request to spend this feasting day with your family?" Melinoe said, gesturing at the table.

Lexi knew she was referring to Thanksgiving, and she knew the 'bearded wonder' was Zeus, although Melinoe used a different nickname for him every time the omnipotent god's name came up.

"We should hear back any moment," Hades offered smoothly. He had been a lot more confident about the outcome of their request than Lexi, especially after Zeus had been threatening every form of torture imaginable since the moment Lexi arrived in the underworld.

"The council meeting is tomorrow," Melinoe said, allowing the wine to slowly fill her glass as if she was running an experiment. "Do you really think his cronies would challenge him? He's done worse things than ask another god to break the rules on his behalf."

Hades relaxed into his heavily upholstered high-back chair as Blythe ladled soup into his bowl. "This is Mnemosyne we're talking about. A Titan, not a god. And she's Lexi's mother. I'm not worried."

It turned out that Zeus's rage-fueled request that Mnemosyne erase Lexi's memories in order to subdue and bind her to the mortal realm had come back to bite him like a dog scorned. All Lexi and Hades had to do was threaten to expose his egregious actions to the Council of the Gods, which Mnemosyne was all too happy to corroborate and present at tomorrow's council meeting.

"It sounds like you've worked your magic once again, Hades." Melinoe lifted her veil just high enough to sip from her glass. "Then I suppose you two have already packed for your visit to the land of the mortals. Who's invited? I might have to join you if Ares is planning to attend."

"It's not that kind of visit, Melinoe," Hades told her. "Thanksgiving is a family bonding holiday celebrated in a specific region. I doubt Ares would find an interest in it. Although, I am certain Z will be there. So, if you want to see a fight . . ."

Lexi reached over and tapped Hades's arm playfully, and Melinoe rolled her eyes.

"I have no interest in family gatherings," Melinoe offered. "If anything of importance happens, I'll just have Kade fill me in." She turned her dark eyes on Lexi, who knew exactly which of Hades's offspring she was talking about. Kade was the son Hades shared with Melinoe.

Lexi had not been introduced to any of Hades's offspring yet, but she knew Melinoe had given birth to two of them, a boy and a girl. The girl, Kylie, hated her mother and had escaped to Olympus to get away from her. The boy, Kade, was a typical cocky god who left the underworld to find more goddesses to screw.

"Kade will be at my parent's house for Thanksgiving? When were you planning to tell me this, Hades?" Lexi attempted to look more inquisitive than accusatory. She knew Hades didn't like sharing his long and polygamous history with her.

"Today?" Hades's golden eyes sparkled as he blinked them at her. The rogue.

Melinoe abandoned her wine to chuckle. "I'm sorry if I spoiled the surprise. Hades thought it would be best to introduce you to our delinquent son in a setting you're more familiar with. On your own turf, so to speak. He's quite thoughtful that way."

Lexi had been trying not to feel like the third wheel whenever she was the last to know about things. It was bound to happen. She knew it would take more than a few months to find her place among the gods.

She bobbed her head as she turned her attention to a bowl of pureed acorn squash. As the room filled with weighty silence, Lexi felt a paw plop across her shoe. Cerberus had taken his place at her feet, and the breath from all three heads warmed her legs as he waited for a handout.

She reached for the basket of bread and broke off three pieces, lifting the tablecloth to look at a trio of begging faces. "This is going to cost you one extra lap around the west tower." She tossed down the bread, watching three mouths scramble for their prize, and when she looked up, Hades was grinning at her.

"I see the nymphs have been preparing for Persephone's arrival." Melinoe gestured to a long strand of thick paper snowflakes swooping across the crown molding. Garlands of holly with bright red berries dangled vertically every few feet. "Are you anxious to meet the queen of the palace, Lexi?"

The veil may have obscured Melinoe's face, but Lexi knew the smirk was there. It wasn't simply that Melinoe had a jealous streak and had been chilly to Lexi since day one. It was no secret that Melinoe hated her mother, and it came down to one sore subject.

Despite Persephone's apparent kindness and grace, she had never forced Melinoe's paternity on Zeus, and that wound had been festering for centuries. But that wasn't Lexi's problem, and regardless of Melinoe's agenda, Lexi refused to let herself be antagonized by the bitter goddess.

"Who wouldn't be anxious to meet her?" Lexi said. "I've been reading stories about the gods my entire life, and I love the tale of Persephone and Hades. Not many people can say they've met their favorite storybook characters."

The scowl that replaced Melinoe's smirk said plenty, and she looked down at her soup, although she made no move to eat it.

"Don't tell me you're not the least bit concerned that you'll be tossed aside like roadkill when she arrives?"

"Melinoe . . ." Hades's voice rumbled like an ocean storm. Distant but still powerful.

"It's okay, Hades," said Lexi. "Of course, I'm concerned. I'm not an emotionless zombie. I'll tackle the situation with my eyes on the horizon and my head in the game, like I do everything else."

Lexi spooned soup into her mouth, keeping her gaze lifted to watch Melinoe. Why did she always wear that damned veil? It was unnerving. Did she do it to be mysterious? Maybe she used it as protection, the way some people used sunglasses or beards. What was she protecting?

Lexi had noticed that Hades held himself a little stiffer when Melinoe was around, and one eye always seemed to be on her, observing in silence. Still, there was something about Melinoe that Hades found attractive. They had made babies together. Or maybe the loneliness had simply gotten to him.

"Who's ready for stuffed peppers?" Fiona scurried into the dining room, balancing a full tray on her palm. She was followed by Blythe, who shared a sympathetic smile with Lexi as she picked up the empty soup bowls. Lexi wondered if the nymphs had timed their entrance to interrupt the thorny conversation. They were incredibly perceptive.

Melinoe managed to finish off two carafes of wine during dinner, changing the subject to the Acheron River, where a group of young satyrs had been seen bathing outside their territory. Lexi knew the Acheron River was also called the River of Pain, and it made her wonder what kind of karma the satyrs were bringing on themselves by bathing in it.

When the enchanted sky began to darken, and the mournful

cries of the underworld creatures echoed out of the forest, Melinoe left, promising to return after Persephone finished her winter visit and making it sound a lot like a threat.

True to his nature, Hades remained polite until Melinoe stepped off the bridge, at which point he grabbed Lexi's hand, a full carafe of wine, and led her up six flights of stairs to the dome room, the highest point in the palace. It was a favorite hideout of his when he needed to brood about something. She'd been invited a number of times to view the sky from the velvet chaise—or take part in more lustful activities.

"I hope you have a good reason . . . for dragging me all the way up here . . . after that heavy meal," Lexi said between breaths. "I might decorate the marble floor in orange and green."

Hades smiled as he filled her glass with wine. "I always have a good reason for bringing you up here, oh enchanting one. I'd like to finish what we started on the bridge before we were so rudely interrupted."